1

WHEN I swung out of the village street onto the main highway, there was a truck behind me. It was one of those big semi jobs and it was really rolling. The speed limit was forty-five on that stretch of road, running through one corner of the village, but at that time in the morning it wasn't reasonable to expect that anyone would pay attention to a posted speed.

I wasn't too concerned with the truck. I'd be stopping a mile or so up the road at Johnny's Motor Court to pick up Alf Peterson, who would be waiting for me, with his fishing tackle ready. And I had other things to think of, too – principally the phone and wondering who I had talked with on the phone. There had been three voices and it all was very strange, but I had the feeling that it may have been one voice, changed most wonderfully to make three voices, and that I would know that basic voice if I could only pin it down. And there had been Gerald Sherwood, sitting in his study, with two walls lined by books, telling me about the blueprints that had formed, unbidden, in his brain. There had been Stiffy Grant, pleading that I not let them use the bomb. And there had been, as well, the fifteen hundred dollars.

Just up the road was the Sherwood residence, set atop its hill, with the house almost blotted out, in the early dawn, by the bulking blackness of the great oak trees that grew all around the house. Staring at the hill, I forgot about the phone and Gerald Sherwood in his book-lined study with his head crammed full of blueprints, and thought instead of Nancy and how I'd met her once again, after all those years since high school. And I recalled those days when we had walked hand in hand, with a pride and happiness that could not come again, that can come but once when the world is young and the first, fierce love of youth is fresh and wonderful.

The road ahead was clear and wide; the four lanes continued for another twenty miles or so before they dwindled down to two. There was no one on the road except myself and the truck, which was coming up behind me and coming fairly fast. Watching the headlights in my rear vision mirror, I knew that in just a little while it would be swinging out to pass me.

I wasn't driving fast and there was a lot of room for the truck to pass me, and there was not a thing to hit – and then I did hit something.

It was like running into a strong elastic band. There was no thump or crash. The car began slowing down as if I had put on the brakes. There was nothing I could see and for a moment I thought that something must have happened to the car – that the motor had gone haywire or the brakes had locked, or something of the sort. I took my foot off the accelerator and the car came to a halt, then started to slide back, faster and faster, for all the world as if I'd run into that rubber band and now it was snapping back. I flipped the drive to neutral because I could smell the rubber as the tyres screeched on the road, and as soon as I flipped it over, the car snapped back so fast that I was thrown against the wheel.

Behind me the horn of the truck blared wildly and tyres howled on the pavement as the driver swung his rig to miss me. The truck made a swishing sound as it went rushing past and beneath the swishing, I could hear the rubber of the tyres sucking at the roadbed, and the whole thing rumbled as if it might be angry at me for causing it this trouble. And as it went rushing past, my car came to a halt, over on the shoulder of the road.

Then the truck hit whatever I had hit. I could hear it when it struck. It made a little plop. For a single instant, I thought the truck might break through whatever the barrier might be, for it was heavy and had been going fast and for a second or so there was no sign that it was slowing down. Then it began to slow and I could see the wheels of that big job skidding and humping, so that they seemed to be skipping on the pavement, still moving forward doggedly, but still not getting through.

'What's the matter, Brad?' he asked.

'I don't know,' I told him. 'There is something happening down on the road.'

'An accident?' he asked.

'No, not an accident. I tell you I don't know. There's something across the road. You can't see it, but it's there. You run into it and it stops you cold. It's like a wall, but you can't touch or feel it.'

'Come on in,' said Bill, 'You could do with a cup of coffee. It's time for breakfast anyhow. The wife is getting up.'

Somewhere in the house a woman screamed. If I live to be a hundred, I'll not forget what that scream was like.

The woman screamed again, but this time the scream was muffled, as if she might be screaming with her mouth pressed against a pillow, or a wall.

I blundered out of the kitchen into the dining-room and I hit it again, that same resistant wall that I'd walked into down on the road. I could sense it right in front of me, although I no longer touched it. And whereas before, out in the open, on the road, it had been no more than a wonder too big to comprehend, here beneath this roof, inside this family home, it became an alien blasphemy that set one's teeth on edge.

'My babies!' screamed the woman. 'I can't reach my babies!'

*Also by Clifford D. Simak
and in Magnum Books*

WAY STATION

CEMETERY WORLD

TIME IS THE SIMPLEST THING

TIME AND AGAIN

A CHOICE OF GODS

SO BRIGHT THE VISION

SHAKESPEARE'S PLANET

Clifford D. Simak

All Flesh Is Grass

MAGNUM BOOKS
Methuen Paperbacks Ltd

A Magnum Book

ALL FLESH IS GRASS
ISBN 0 417 02170 4

First published in Great Britain 1965
by Victor Gollancz Ltd
Pan edition published 1968
Magnum edition published 1979

Copyright © 1965 by Clifford D. Simak

Magnum Books are published
by Methuen Paperbacks Ltd
11 New Fetter Lane, London EC4P 4EE

Made and printed in Great Britain
by Cox & Wyman Ltd
London, Reading and Fakenham

It moved ahead for a hundred feet or so beyond the point where I had stopped. And there the rig came to a halt and began skidding back. It slid smoothly for a moment, with the tyres squealing on the pavement, then it began to jackknife. The rear end buckled around and came sideways down the road, heading straight for me.

I had been sitting calmly in the car, not dazed, not even too much puzzled. It all had happened so fast that there had not been time to work up much puzzlement. Something strange had happened, certainly, but I think I had the feeling that in just a little while I'd get it figured out and it would all come right again.

So I had stayed sitting in the car, absorbed in watching what would happen to the truck. But when it came sliding back down the road, jackknifing as it slid, I slapped the handle of the door and shoved it with my shoulder and rolled out of the seat. I hit the pavement and scrambled to my feet and ran.

Behind me the tyres of the truck were screaming and then there was a crash of metal, and when I heard the crash, I jumped out on the grassy shoulder of the road and had a look behind me. The rear end of the truck had slammed into my car and shoved it in the ditch and now was slowly, almost majestically, toppling into the ditch itself, right atop my car.

'Hey, there!' I shouted. It did no good, of course, and I knew it wouldn't. The words were just jerked out of me.

The cab of the truck had remained upon the road, but it was canted with one wheel off the ground. The driver was crawling from the cab.

It was a quiet and peaceful morning. Over in the west some heat lightning was skipping about the dark horizon. There was that freshness in the air that you never get except on a summer morning before the sun gets up and the heat closes down on you. To my right, over in the village, the street lights were still burning, hanging still and bright, unstirred by any breeze. It was too nice a morning, I thought, for anything to happen.

There were no cars on the road. There were just the two

of us, the trucker and myself, and his truck in the ditch, squashing down my car. He came down the road toward me.

He came up to me and stopped, peering at me, his arms hanging at his side. 'What the hell is going on?' he asked. 'What did we run into?'

'I don't know,' I said.

'I'm sorry about your car,' he told me. 'I'll report it to the company. They'll take care of it.'

He stood, not moving, acting as if he might never move again. 'Just like running into nothing,' he declared. 'There's nothing there.'

Then slow anger flared in him.

'By God,' he said, 'I'm going to find out!'

He turned abruptly and went stalking up the highway, heading toward whatever we had hit. I followed along behind him. He was grunting like an angry hog.

He went straight up the middle of the road and he hit the barrier, but by this time he was roaring mad and he wasn't going to let it stop him, so he kept ploughing into it and he got a good deal farther than I had expected that he would. But finally it stopped him and he stood there for a moment, with his body braced ridiculously against a nothingness, leaning into it, and with his legs driving like well-oiled pistons in an attempt to drive himself ahead. In the stillness of the morning I could hear his shoes chuffing on the pavement.

Then the barrier let him have it. It snapped him back. It was as if a sudden wind had struck him and was blowing him down the road, tumbling as he rolled. He finally ended up jammed half underneath the front end of the cab.

I ran over and grabbed him by the ankles and pulled him out and stood him on his feet. He was bleeding a little from where he'd rubbed along the pavement and his clothes were torn and dirty. But he wasn't angry any more; he was just plain scared. He was looking down the road as if he'd seen a ghost and he still was shaking.

'But there's nothing there,' he said.

'There'll be other cars,' I said, 'and you are across the road.

Hadn't we ought to put out some flares or flags or something?'

That seemed to snap him out of it.

'Flags,' he said.

He climbed into the cab and got out some flags.

I walked down the road with him while he set them out.

He put the last one down and squatted down beside it. He took out a handkerchief and began dabbing at his face.

'Where can I get a phone?' he asked. 'We'll have to get some help.'

'Someone has to figure out a way to clear the barrier off the road,' I said. 'In a little while there'll be a lot of traffic. It'll be piled up for miles.'

He dabbed at his face some more. There was a lot of dust and grease. And a little blood.

'A phone?' he asked.

'Oh, any place,' I told him. 'Just go up to any house. They'll let you use a phone.'

And here we were, I thought, talking about this thing as if it were an ordinary road block, as if it were a fallen tree or a washed-out culvert.

'Say, what's the name of this place, anyhow? I got to tell them where I am calling from.'

'Millville,' I told him.

'You live here?'

I nodded.

He got up and tucked the handkerchief back into his pocket.

'Well,' he said, 'I'll go and find that phone.'

He wanted me to offer to go with him, but I had something else to do. I had to walk around the road block and get up to Johnny's Motor Court and explain to Alf what had happened to delay me.

I stood in the road and watched him plod along.

Then I turned around and went up the road in the opposite direction, walking toward that something which would stop a car. I reached it and it stopped me, not abruptly, nor roughly, but gently, as if it didn't intend to let me through under any circumstances, but was being polite and reasonable about it.

I put out my hand and I couldn't feel a thing. I tried rubbing my hand back and forth, as you would to feel a surface, but there was no surface, there was not a thing to rub; there was absolutely nothing, just that gentle pressure pushing you away from whatever might be there.

I looked up and down the road and there was still no traffic, but in a little while, I knew, there would be. Perhaps, I told myself, I should set out some flags in the east-bound traffic lane to convey at least some warning that there was something wrong. It would take no more than a minute or two to set up the flags when I went around the end of the barrier to get to Johnny's Motor Court.

I went back to the cab and found two flags and climbed down the shoulder of the road and clambered up the hillside, making a big sweep to get around the barrier – and even as I made the sweep I ran into the barrier again. I backed away from it and started to walk alongside it, climbing up the hill. It was hard to do. If the barrier had been a solid thing, I would have had no trouble, but since it was invisible, I kept bumping into it. That was the way I traced it, bumping into it, then sheering off, then bumping into it again.

I thought that the barrier would end almost any time, or that it might get thinner. A couple of times I tried pushing through it, but it still was as stiff and strong as ever. There was an awful thought growing in my mind. And the higher up the hill I climbed, the more persistent grew the thought. It was about this time that I dropped the flags.

Below me I heard the sound of skidding tyres and swung around to look. A car on the east-bound lane had slammed into the barrier, and in sliding back, had skidded broadside across both lanes. Another car had been travelling behind the first and was trying to slow down. But either its brakes were bad or its speed had been too high, for it couldn't stop. As I watched, its driver swung it out, with the wheels upon the shoulder, skinning past the broadside car. Then he slapped into the barrier, but his speed had been reduced, and he didn't go far in. Slowly the barrier pushed back the car and it slid into the other car and finally came to rest.

The driver had gotten out of the first car and was walking around his car to reach the second car. I saw his head tilt up and it was clear he saw me. He waved his arms at me and shouted, but I was too far away to make out what he said.

The truck and my car, lying crushed beneath it, still were alone on the west-bound lanes. It was curious, I told myself, that no one else had come along.

There was a house atop the hill and for some reason I didn't recognize it. It had to be a house of someone that I knew, for I'd lived all my life in Millville except for a year at college and I knew everyone. I don't know how to explain it, but for a moment I was all mixed up. Nothing looked familiar and I stood confused, trying to get my bearings and figure where I was.

The east was brightening and in another thirty minutes the sun would be poking up. In the west a great angry cloud bank loomed, and at its base I could see the rapier flickering of the lightning that was riding with the storm.

I stood and stared down at the village and it all came clear to me exactly where I was. The house up on the hill was Bill Donovan's. Bill was the village garbage man.

I followed along the barrier, heading for the house and for a moment I wondered just where the house might be in relation to the barrier. More than likely, I told myself, it stood just inside of it.

I came to a fence and climbed it and crossed the littered yard to the rickety back stairs. I climbed them gingerly to gain the stoop and looked for a bell. There wasn't any bell. I lifted a fist and pounded on the door, then waited. I heard someone stirring around inside, then the door came open and Bill stared out at me. He was an unkempt bear of a man and his bushy hair stood all on end and he looked at me from beneath a pair of belligerent eyebrows. He had pulled his trousers over his pyjamas, but he hadn't taken the time to zip up the fly and a swatch of purple pyjama cloth stuck out. His feet were bare and his toes curled up a bit against the cold of the kitchen floor.

'What's the matter, Brad?' he asked.

'I don't know,' I told him. 'There is something happening down on the road.'

'An accident?' he asked.

'No, not an accident. I tell you I don't know. There's something across the road. You can't see it, but it's there. You run into it and it stops you cold. It's like a wall, but you can't touch or feel it.'

'Come on in,' said Bill. 'You could do with a cup of coffee. I'll put on the pot. It's time for breakfast anyhow. The wife is getting up.'

He reached behind him and snapped on the kitchen light, then stood to one side so that I could enter.

Bill walked over to the sink. He picked a glass off the counter top and turned on the water, then stood waiting.

'Have to let it run a while until it gets cold,' he told me.

He filled the glass and held it out to me. 'Want a drink?' he asked.

'No, thanks,' I told him.

He put the glass to his mouth and drank in great slobbering gulps.

Somewhere in the house a woman screamed. If I live to be a hundred, I'll not forget what that scream was like.

Donovan dropped the glass on the floor and it broke, spraying jagged glass and water.

'Liz!' he cried. 'Liz, what's wrong?'

He charged out of the room and I stood there, frozen, looking at the blood on the floor, where Donovan's bare feet had been gashed by the broken glass.

The woman screamed again, but this time the scream was muffled, as if she might be screaming with her mouth pressed against a pillow or a wall.

I blundered out of the kitchen into the dining-room, stumbling on something in my path – a toy, a stool, I don't know what it was – and lunging halfway across the room to try to catch my balance, afraid of falling and hitting my head against a chair or table.

And I hit it again, that same resistant wall that I'd walked into down on the road. I braced myself against it and pushed, getting upright on my feet, standing in the dimness of the dining-room with the horror of that wall rasping at my soul.

I could sense it right in front of me, although I no longer touched it. And whereas before, out in the open, on the road, it had been no more than a wonder too big to comprehend, here beneath this roof, inside this family home, it became an alien blasphemy that set one's teeth on edge.

'My babies!' screamed the woman. 'I can't reach my babies!'

Now I began to get my bearings in the curtained room. I saw the table and the buffet and the door that led into the bedroom hallway.

Donovan was coming through the doorway. He was half leading, half carrying the woman.

'I tried to get to them,' she cried. 'There's something there – something that stopped me. I can't get to my babies!'

He let her down on the floor and propped her against the wall and knelt gently beside her. He looked up at me and there was a baffled, angry terror in his eyes.

'It's the barrier,' I told him. 'The one down on the road. It runs straight through the house.'

'I don't see no barrier,' he said.

'Damn it, man, you don't see it. It just is there, is all.'

'What can we do?' he asked.

'The children are OK,' I assured him, hoping I was right. 'They're just on the other side of the barrier. We can't get to them and they can't get to us, but everything's all right.'

'I just got up to look in on them,' the woman said. 'I just got up to look at them and there was something in the hall . . .'

'How many?' I asked.

'Two,' said Donovan. 'One is six, the other eight.'

'Is there someone you can phone? Someone outside the village. They could come and take them in and take care of them until we get this thing figured out. There must be an end to this wall somewhere. I was looking for it . . .'

'She's got a sister,' said Donovan, 'up the road a ways. Four or five miles.'

'Maybe you should call her.'

And as I said it, another thought hit me straight between the eyes. The phone might not be working. The barrier might have cut the phone lines.

'You be all right, Liz?' he asked.

She nodded dumbly, still sitting on the floor, not trying to get up.

'I'll go call Myrt,' he said.

I followed him into the kitchen and stood beside him as he lifted the receiver of the wall phone, holding my breath in a fierce hope that the phone would work. And for once my hoping must have done some good, for when the receiver came off the hook I could hear the faint buzz of an operating line.

Out in the dining-room, Mrs Donovan was sobbing very quietly.

Donovan dialled, his big, blunt, grease-grimed fingers seemingly awkward and unfamiliar at the task. He finally got it done.

He waited with the receiver at his ear. I could hear the signal ringing in the quietness of the kitchen.

'That you, Myrt?' said Donovan. 'Yeah, this is Bill. We run into a little trouble. I wonder could you and Jake come over. . . . No, Myrt, just something wrong. I can't explain it to you. Could you come over and pick up the kids? You'll have to come the front way; you can't get in the back. . . . Yeah, Myrt, I know it sounds crazy. There's some sort of wall. Liz and me, we're in the back part of the house and we can't get up to the front. The kids are in the front. . . . No, Myrt, I don't know what it is. But you do like I say. Them kids are up there all alone and we can't get to them. . . . Yes, Myrt, right through the house. Tell Jake to bring along an axe. This thing runs right straight through the house. The front door is locked and Jake will have to chop it down. Or bust a window, if that's easier. . . . Sure, sure, I know what I'm saying. You just go ahead and do it. Anything to get them kids. I'm not crazy. Something's wrong, I tell you. Something's gone way wrong. You do what I say, Myrt. . . . Don't mind about the door. Just chop the damn thing down. You just get the kids any way you can and keep them safe for us.'

He hung up the receiver and turned from the phone. He used his forearm to wipe the sweat off his face.

'Damn woman,' he said. 'She just stood there and argued. She's a flighty bitch.'

He looked at me. 'Now, what do we do next?'

'Trace the barrier,' I said. 'See where it goes. See if we can get around it. If we can find a way around it, we can get your kids.'

'I'll go with you.'

I gestured toward the dining-room. 'And leave her here alone?'

'No,' he said. 'No, I can't do that. You go ahead. Myrt and Jake, they'll come and get the kids. Some of the neighbours will take Liz in. I'll try to catch up with you. Thing like this, you might need some help.'

'Thanks,' I said.

Outside the house, the paleness of the dawn was beginning to flow across the land. Everything was painted that ghostly brightness, not quite white, not quite any other colour either, that marks the beginning of an August day.

On the road below, a couple of dozen cars were jammed up in front of the barrier on the east-bound lane and there were groups of people standing around. I could hear one loud voice that kept booming out in excited talk – one of those aggressive loudmouths you find in any kind of crowd. Someone had built a small campfire out on the boulevard between the lanes – God knows why, the morning was surely warm enough and the day would be a scorcher.

And now I remembered that I had meant to get hold of Alf and tell him that I wasn't coming. I could have used the phone in the Donovan kitchen, but I'd forgotten all about it. I stood undecided, debating whether to go back in again and ask to

15

use the phone. That had been the main reason, I realized, that I'd stopped at Donovan's.

There was this pile of cars on the east-bound lane and only the truck and my battered car on the west-bound lane and that must mean, I told myself, that the west-bound lane was closed, as well, somewhere to the east. And could that mean, I wondered, that the village was enclosed, was encircled by the wall?

I decided against going back to make the phone call, and moved on around the house. I picked up the wall again and began to follow it. I was getting the hang of it by now. It was like feeling this thing alongside me, and following the feeling, keeping just a ways away from it, bumping into it only now and then.

The wall roughly skirted the edge of the village, with a few outlying houses on the other side of it. I followed along it and I crossed some paths and a couple of bob-tailed, dead-end streets, and finally came to the secondary road that ran in from Coon Valley, ten miles or so away.

The road slanted on a gentle grade in its approach into the village and on the slant, just on the other side of the wall, stood an older model car, somewhat the worse for wear. Its motor was still running and the door on the driver's side was open, but there was no one in it and no one was around. It looked as if the driver, once he'd struck the barrier, might have fled in panic.

As I stood looking at the car, the brakes began to slip and the car inched forward, slowly at first, then faster, and finally the brakes gave out entirely and the car plunged down the hill, through the barrier wall, and crashed into a tree. It slowly toppled over on its side and a thin trickle of smoke began to seep from underneath the hood.

But I didn't pay much attention to the car, for there was something more important. I broke into a run, heading up the road.

The car had passed the barrier and had gone down the road to crash and that meant there was no barrier. I had reached the end of it!

I ran up the road, exultant and relieved, for I'd been fighting down the feeling, and having a hard time to fight it down entirely, that the barrier might run all around the village. And in the midst of all my exultation and relief, I hit the wall again. I hit it fairly hard, for I was running hard, sure that it wasn't there, but in a terrible hurry to make sure it wasn't there. I went into it for three running strides before it tossed me back. I hit the roadbed flat on my back and my head banged upon the pavement. There were a million stars.

I rolled over and got on my hands and knees and stayed there for a moment, like a gutted hound, with my head hanging limp between my shoulders, and I shook it now and then to shake the stars away.

I heard the crackle and the roar of flames and that jerked me to my feet. I still was fairly wobbly, but wobbly or not, I got away from there. The car was burning briskly and at any moment the flames would reach the gas tank and the car would go sky high.

But the explosion, when it came, was not too spectacular – just an angry, muffled whuff and a great gout of flame flaring up into the sky. But it was loud enough to bring some people out to see what was going on. Doc Fabian and lawyer Nichols were running up the road, and behind them came a bunch of yelling kids and a pack of barking dogs.

I didn't wait for them although I had half a mind to, for I had a lot to tell and here was an audience. But there was something else that stopped me from turning back – I had to go on tracking down the barrier and try to find its end, if it had an end.

My head had begun to clear and all the stars were gone and I could think a little better.

There was one thing that stood out plain and clear: a car could go through the barrier when there was no one in it, but when it was occupied, the barrier stopped it dead. A man could not go through the barrier, but he could pick up a phone and talk to anyone he wanted. And I remembered that I had heard the voices of the men shouting in the road, had heard them very clearly even when they were on the other side.

I picked up some sticks and stones and tossed them at the barrier. They went sailing through as if nothing had been there.

There was only one thing that the barrier would stop and that single thing was life. And why in the world should there be a barrier to shut out, or shut in, life?

The village was beginning to stir to life.

I watched Floyd Caldwell come out on his back porch, dressed in his undershirt and a pair of pants with the suspenders hanging. Except for old Doc Fabian, Floyd was the only man in Millville who ever wore suspenders. But while old Doc wore sedate and narrow black ones, Floyd wore a pair that was broad and red. Floyd was the barber and he took a lot of kidding about his red suspenders, but Floyd didn't mind. He was the village smart guy and he worked at it all the time and it probably was all right, for it brought him a lot of trade from out in the farming country. People who might just as well have gone to Coon Valley for their haircuts came, instead, to Millville to listen to Floyd's jokes and to see him clown.

Floyd stood out on the back porch and stretched his arms and yawned. Then he took a close look at the weather and he scratched his ribs. Down the street a woman called the family dog and in a little while I heard the flat snap of a screen door shutting and I knew the dog was in.

It was strange, I thought, that there'd been no alarm. Perhaps it was because few people as yet knew about the barrier. Perhaps the few who had found out about it were still a little numb. Perhaps most of them couldn't quite believe it. Maybe they were afraid, as I was, to make too much fuss about it until they knew something more about it.

But it couldn't last for long – this morning calm. Before too long, Millville would be seething.

Now, as I followed it, the barrier cut through the back yard of one of the older houses in the village. In its day it had been a place of elegance, but years of poverty and neglect had left it tumbledown.

An old lady was coming down the steps from the shaky back porch, balancing her frail body with a steadying cane. Her hair was thin and white and even with no breeze to stir the air, ragged ends of it floated like a fuzzy halo all around her head.

She started down the path to the little garden, but when she saw me she stopped and peered at me, with her head tilted just a little in a bird-like fashion. Her pale blue eyes glittered at me through the thickness of her glasses.

'Brad Carter, isn't it?' she asked.

'Yes, Mrs Tyler,' I said. 'How are you this morning?'

'Oh, just tolerable,' she told me. 'I'm never more than that. I thought that it was you, but my eyes have failed me and I never can be sure.'

'It's a nice morning, Mrs Tyler. This is good weather we are having.'

'Yes,' she said, 'it is. I was looking for Tupper. He seems to have wandered off again. You haven't seen him, have you?'

I shook my head. It had been ten years since anyone had seen Tupper Tyler.

'He is such a restless boy,' she said. 'Always wandering off. I declare, I don't know what to do with him.'

'Don't you worry,' I told her. 'He'll show up again.'

'Yes,' she said, 'I suppose he will. He always does, you know.' She prodded with her cane at the bed of purple flowers that grew along the walk. 'They're very good this year,' she said. 'The best I've ever seen them. I got them from your father twenty years ago. Mr Tyler and your father were such good friends. You remember that, of course.'

'Yes,' I said. 'I remember very well.'

'And your mother? Tell me how she is. We used to see a good deal of one another.'

'You forget, Mrs Tyler,' I told her, gently. 'Mother died almost two years ago.'

'Oh, so she did,' she said. 'It's true, I am forgetful. Old age does it to one. No one should grow old.'

'I must be getting on,' I said. 'It was good to see you.'

'It was kind of you to call,' she said. 'If you have the time, you might step in and we could have some tea. It is so seldom now that anyone ever comes for tea. I suppose it's because the times have changed. No one, any more, has the time for tea.'

'I'm sorry that I can't,' I said. 'I just stopped by for a moment.'

'Well,' she said, 'it was very nice of you. If you happen to see Tupper would you mind, I wonder, to tell him to come home.'

'Of course I will,' I promised.

I was glad to get away from her. She was nice enough, of course, but just a little mad. In all the years since Tupper's disappearance, she had gone on looking for him, and always as if he'd just stepped out the door, always very calm and confident in the thought that he'd be coming home in just a little while. Quite reasonable about it and very, very sweet, no more than mildly worried about the idiot son who had vanished without trace.

Tupper, I recalled, had been something of a pest. He'd been a pest with everyone, of course, but especially with me. He loved flowers and he'd hung around the greenhouse that my father had, and my father, who was constitutionally unable to be unkind to anyone, had put up with him and his continual jabber. Tupper had attached himself to me and no matter what I did or said, he'd tag along behind me. The fact that he was a good ten years older than I was made no difference at all; in his own mind Tupper never had outgrown childhood. In the back of my mind I still could hear his jaunty voice, mindlessly happy over anything at all, cooing over flowers or asking endless, senseless questions. I had hated him, of course, but there was really nothing one could pin a good hate on. Tupper was just something that one had to tolerate. But I knew that I never would forget that jaunty, happy voice, or his drooling as he talked, or the habit that he had of counting on his fingers – God knows why he did it – as if he were in continual fear that he might have lost one of them in the last few minutes.

The sun had come up by now and the world was flooded with a brilliant light, and I was becoming more certain by the minute that the village was encircled and cut off, that some-one or something, for no apparent reason, had dropped a cage around us. Looking back along the way that I had come, I could see that I'd been travelling on the inside of a curve. Looking ahead, the curve wasn't difficult to plot.

And why should it be us, I wondered. Why a little town like ours? A town that was no different from ten thousand other towns.

Although, I told myself, that might not be entirely true. It was exactly what I would have said and perhaps everybody else. Everyone, that is, except for Nancy Sherwood – Nancy, who only the night before had told me her strange theory that this town of ours was something very special. And could she be right, I wondered? Was our little town of Millville somehow set apart from all other little towns?

Just ahead was my home street and my calculations told me that it was located just inside the encircling barricade.

There was, I told myself, no sense in going farther. It would be a waste of time. I did not need to complete the circle to convince myself that we were hemmed in.

I cut across the backyard of the Presbyterian parsonage and there, just across the street, was my house, set within its wilderness of flowers and shrubs, with the abandoned green-house standing in the back and the old garden around it, a field of purple flowers, those same purple flowers that Mrs Tyler had poked at with her cane and said were doing well this season.

I heard the steady squeaking as I reached the street and I knew that some kids had sneaked into the yard and were play-ing in the old lawn swing that stood beside the porch.

I hurried up the street, a little wrathful at the squeaking. I had told those kids, time and time again, to leave that swing alone. It was old and rickety and one of these days one of the uprights or something else would break, and one of the kids might be badly hurt. I could have taken it down, of course, but I was reluctant to, for it was Mother's swing. She had spent many hours out in the yard, swinging gently and sedately, looking at the flowers.

The yard was closed in by the old-time lilac hedge and I couldn't see the swing until I reached the gate.

I hurried for the gate and jerked it open savagely and took two quick steps through it, then stopped in my tracks.

There were no kids in the swing. There was a man, and except for a battered hat of straw set squarely atop his head, he was as naked as a jaybird.

He saw me and grinned a foolish grin. 'Hi, there,' he said, with jaunty happiness. And even as he said it, he began a counting of his fingers, drooling as he counted.

And at the sight of him, at the sound of that remembered but long forgotten voice, my mind went thudding back to the afternoon before.

2

ED ADLER had come that afternoon to take out the phone and he had been embarrassed. 'I'm sorry, Brad,' he said. 'I don't want to do this, but I guess I have to. I have an order from Tom Preston.'

Ed was a friend of mine. We had been good pals in high school and good friends ever since. Tom Preston had been in school with us, of course, but he'd been no friend of mine or of anybody else's. He'd been a snotty kid and he had grown up into a snotty man.

That was the way it went, I thought. The heels always were the ones who seemed to get ahead. Tom Preston was the manager of the telephone office and Ed Adler worked for him as a phone installer and a trouble shooter, and I was a realtor and insurance agent who was going out of business. Not because I wanted to, but because I had to, because I was delinquent in my office phone bill and way behind in rent.

Tom Preston was successful and I was a business failure and Ed Adler was earning a living for his family, but not getting anywhere. And the rest of them, I wondered. The rest of the high school gang – how were they getting on? And I couldn't answer, for I didn't know. They all had drifted off. There wasn't much in a little town like Millville to keep a man around. I probably wouldn't have stayed myself if it hadn't been for Mother. I'd come home from school after Dad had died and had helped out with the greenhouse until Mother had joined Dad. And by that time I had been so long in Millville that it was hard to leave.

'Ed,' I had asked, 'do you ever hear from any of the fellows?'

'No, I don't,' said Ed. 'I don't know where any of them are.'

I said: 'There was Skinny Austin and Charley Thompson, and Marty Hall and Alf – I can't remember Alf's last name.'

'Peterson,' said Ed.

'Yes, that's it,' I said. 'It's a funny thing I should forget his name. Old Alf and me had a lot of fun together.'

Ed got the cord unfastened and stood up, with the phone dangling from his hand.

'What are you going to do now?' he asked me.

'Lock the door, I guess,' I said. 'It's not just the phone. It's everything. I'm behind in rent as well. Dan Willoughby, down at the bank, is very sad about it.'

'You could run the business from the house.'

'Ed,' I told him shortly, 'there isn't any business. I just never had a business. I couldn't make a start. I lost money from the first.'

I got up and put on my hat and walked out of the place. The street was almost empty. There were a few cars at the kerb and a dog was smelling of a lamp post and old Stiffy Grant was propped up in front of the Happy Hollow tavern, hoping that someone might come along and offer him a drink.

I was feeling pretty low. Small thing as it had been, the phone had spelled the end. It was the thing that finally signified for me what a failure I had been. You can go along for months and kid yourself that everything's all right and will work out in the end, but always something comes up that you can't kid away. Ed Adler coming to disconnect and take away the phone had been that final thing I couldn't kid away.

I stood there on the sidewalk, looking down the street, and I felt hatred for the town – not for the people in it, but for the town itself, for the impersonal geographic concept of one particular place.

The town lay dusty and arrogant and smug beyond all telling and it sneered at me and I knew that I had been mistaken in not leaving it when I'd had the chance. I had tried to live with it for very love of it, but I'd been blind to try. I had known what all my friends had known, the ones who'd gone away, but I had closed my mind to that sure and certain knowledge: there was nothing left in Millville to make one stay around. It was an old town and it was dying, as old things always die. It was being strangled by the swift and easy roads that took customers to better shopping areas; it was dying with the decline of marginal agriculture, dying along with the little vacant hillside farms that no longer would support a family. It was a place of genteel poverty and it had its share of musty quaintness, but it was dying just the same, albeit in the polite scent of lavender and impeccable good manners.

I turned down the street, away from the dusty business section and made my way down to the little river that flowed close against the east edge of the town. There I found the ancient footpath underneath the trees and walked along, listening in the summer silence to the gurgle of the water as it flowed between the grassy banks and along the gravel bars. And as I walked the lost and half-forgotten years came crowding in upon me. There, just ahead, was the village swimming hole, and below it the stretch of shallows where I'd netted suckers in the spring.

Around the river's bend was the place we had held our picnics. We had built a fire to roast the wieners and to toast the marshmallows and we had sat and watched the evening steal in among the trees and across the meadows. After a time the

24

moon would rise, making the place a magic place, painted by the lattice of shadow and of moonlight. Then we talked in whispers and we willed that time should move at a slower pace so we might hold the magic longer. But for all our willing, it had never come to pass, for time, even then, was something that could not be slowed or stopped.

There had been Nancy and myself and Ed Adler and Priscilla Gordon, and at times Alf Peterson had come with us as well, but as I remembered it he had seldom brought the same girl twice.

I stood for a moment in the path and tried to bring it back, the glow of moonlight and the glimmer of the dying fire, the soft girl voices and the soft girl-flesh, the engulfing tenderness of that youthful miracle, the tingle and excitement and the thankfulness. I sought the enchanted darkness and the golden happiness, or at least the ghosts of them; all that I could find was the intellectual knowledge of them, that they once had been and were not any more.

So I stood, with the edge worn off a tarnished memory, and a business failure. I think I faced it squarely then; the first time that I'd faced it. What would I do next?

Perhaps, I thought, I should have stayed in the greenhouse business, but it was a foolish thought and a piece of wishfulness, for after Dad had died it had been, in every way, a losing proposition. When he had been alive, we had done all right, but then there'd been the three of us to work, and Dad had been the kind of man who had an understanding with all growing things. They grew and flourished under his care and he seemed to know exactly what to do to keep them green and healthy. Somehow or other, I didn't have the knack. With me the plants were poor and puny at the best, and there were always pests and parasites and all sorts of plant diseases.

Suddenly, as I stood there, the river and the path and trees became ancient, alien things. As if I were a stranger in this place, as if I had wandered into an area of time and space where I had no business being. And more terrifying than if it had been a place I'd never seen before because I knew in a chill, far corner of my mind that here was a place that held a part of me.

I turned around and started up the path and back of me was a fear and panic that made me want to run. But I didn't run. I went even slower than I ordinarily would have, for this was a victory that I needed and was determined I would have – any sort of little futile victory, like walking very slowly when there was the urge to run.

Back on the street again, away from the deep shadow of the trees, the warmth and brilliance of the sunlight set things right again. Not entirely right, perhaps, but as they had been before. The street was the same as ever. There were a few more cars and the dog had disappeared and Stiffy Grant had changed his loafing place. Instead of propping up the Happy Hollow tavern, he was propping up my office.

Or at least what had been my office. For now I knew that there was no point in waiting. I might as well go in right now and clean out my desk and lock the door behind me and take the key down to the bank. Daniel Willoughby would be fairly frosty, but I was beyond all caring about Daniel Willoughby. Sure, I owed him rent that I couldn't pay and he probably would resent it, but there were a lot of other people in the village who owed Daniel Willoughby without much prospect of paying. That was the way he'd worked it and that was the way he had it and that was why he resented everyone. I'd rather be like myself, I thought, than like Dan Willoughby, who walked the streets each day, chewed by contempt and hatred of everyone he met.

Under other circumstances I would have been glad to have stopped and talked a while with Stiffy Grant. He might be the village bum, but he was a friend of mine. He was always ready to go fishing and he knew all the likely places and his talk was far more interesting than you might imagine. But right now I didn't care to talk with anyone.

'Hi, there, Brad,' said Stiffy, as I came up to him. 'You wouldn't happen, would you, to have a dollar on you?'

It had been a long time since Stiffy had put the bite on me

and I was surprised that he should do it now. For whatever else Stiffy Grant might be, he was a gentleman and most considerate. He never tapped anyone for money unless they could afford it. Stiffy had a ready genius for knowing exactly when and how he could safely make a touch.

I dipped into my pocket and there was a small wad of bills and a little silver. I hauled out the little wad and peeled off a bill for him.

'Thank you, Brad,' he said. 'I ain't had a drink all day.'

He tucked the dollar into the pocket of a patched and flapping vest and hobbled swiftly up the street, heading for the tavern.

I opened the office door and stepped inside and as I shut the door behind me, the phone began to ring.

I stood there, like a fool, rooted to the floor, staring at the phone.

It kept on ringing, so I went and answered it.

'Mr Bradshaw Carter?' asked the sweetest voice I have ever heard.

'This is he,' I said. 'What can I do for you?'

I knew that it was no one in the village, for they would have called me Brad. And, besides, there was no one I knew who had that kind of voice. It had the persuasive purr of a TV glamour girl selling soap or beauty aids, and it had, as well, that clear, bright timbre one would expect when a fairy princess spoke.

'You, perhaps, are the Mr Bradshaw Carter whose father ran a greenhouse?'

'Yes, that's right,' I said.

'You, yourself, no longer run the greenhouse?'

'No,' I said, 'I don't.'

And then the voice changed. Up till now it had been sweet and very feminine, but now it was male and businesslike. As if one person had been talking, then had gotten up and gone and an entirely different person had picked up the phone. And yet, for some crazy reason, I had the distinct impression that there had been no change of person, but just a change of voice.

27

'We understand,' this new voice said, 'that you might be free to do some work for us.'

'Why, yes, I would,' I said. 'But what is going on? Why did your voice change? Who am I talking with?'

And it was a silly thing to ask, for no matter what my impression might have been, no human voice could have changed so completely and abruptly. It had to be two persons.

But the question wasn't answered.

'We have hopes,' the voice said, 'that you can represent us. You have been highly recommended.'

'In what capacity?' I asked.

'Diplomatically,' said the voice. 'I think that is the proper term.'

'But I'm no diplomat. I have no . . .'

'You mistake us, Mr Carter. You do not understand. Perhaps I should explain a little. We have contact with many of your people. They serve us in many ways. For example, we have a group of readers . . .'

'Readers?'

'That is what I said. Ones who read to us. They read many different things, you see. Things of many interests. The *Encyclopaedia Britannica* and the Oxford dictionary and many different textbooks. Literature and history. Philosophy and economics. And it's all so interesting.'

'But you could read these things yourself. There is no need of readers. All you need to do is to get some books . . .'

The voice sighed resignedly. 'You do not understand. You are springing at conclusions.'

'All right, then,' I said, 'I do not understand. We'll let it go at that. What do you want of me? Remembering that I'm a lousy reader.'

'We want you to represent us. We would like first to talk with you, so that you may give us your appraisal of the situation, and from there we can . . .'

There was more of it, but I didn't hear it. For now, suddenly, I knew what had seemed so wrong. I had been looking at it all the while, of course, but it was not until this moment

28

that a full realization of it touched my consciousness. There had been too many other things – the phone when there should have been no phone, the sudden change of voices, the crazy trend of the conversation. My mind had been too busy to grasp the many things in their entirety.

But now the wrongness of the phone punched through to me and what the voice might be saying became a fuzzy sound. For this was not the phone that had been on the desk an hour before. This phone had no dial and it had no cord connected to the wall outlet.

'What's going on?' I shouted. 'Who am I talking to? Where are you calling from?'

And there was yet another voice, neither feminine nor male, neither businesslike nor sweet, but an empty voice that was somehow jocular, but without a trace of character in the fibre of it.

'Mr Carter,' said the empty voice, 'you need not be alarmed. We take care of our own. We have much gratitude. Believe us, Mr Carter, we are very grateful to you.'

'Grateful for what?' I shouted.

'Go see Gerald Sherwood,' said the emptiness. 'We will speak to him of you.'

'Look here,' I yelled, 'I don't know what's going on, but . . .'

'Just talk to Gerald Sherwood,' said the voice.

Then the phone went dead. Dead, completely dead. There was no humming on the wire. There was just an emptiness.

'Hello, there,' I shouted. 'Hello, whoever you may be.'

But there was no answer.

I took the receiver from my ear and stood with it in my hand, trying to reach back into my memory for something that I knew was there. That final voice – I should know that voice. I had heard it somewhere. But my memory failed me.

I put the receiver back on the cradle and picked up the phone. It was, to all appearance, an ordinary phone, except that it had no dial and was entirely unconnected. I looked for a trademark or a manufacturer's designation and there was no such thing.

Ed Adler had come to take out the phone. He had disconnected it and had been standing, with it dangling from his hand, when I'd gone out for my walk.

When I had returned and heard the ringing of the phone and seen it on the desk, the thing that had run through my mind (illogical, but the only ready explanation), had been that for some reason Ed had reconnected the phone and had not taken it. Perhaps because of his friendship for me; willing, perhaps, to disregard an order so that I could keep the phone. Or, perhaps, that Tom Preston might have reconsidered and decided to give me a little extra time. Or even that some unknown benefactor had come forward to pay the bill and save the phone for me.

But I knew now that it had been none of these things. For this phone was not the phone that Ed had disconnected.

I reached out and took the receiver from the cradle and put it to my ear.

The businesslike voice spoke to me. It didn't say hello, it did not ask who called. It said: 'It is clear, Mr Carter, that you are suspicious of us. We can understand quite well your confusion and your lack of confidence in us. We do not blame you for it, but feeling as you do, there is no use of further conversation. Talk first to Mr Sherwood and then come back and talk with us.'

The line went dead again. This time I didn't shout to try to bring the voice back. I knew it was no use. I put the receiver back on the cradle and shoved the phone away.

See Gerald Sherwood, the voice had said, and then come back and talk. And what in the world could Gerald Sherwood have to do with it?

I considered Gerald Sherwood and he seemed a most unlikely person to be mixed up in any business such as this.

He was Nancy Sherwood's father and an industrialist of sorts who was a native of the village and lived in the old ancestral home on top of the hill at the village edge. Unlike the rest of us, he was not entirely of the village. He owned and ran a factory at Elmore, a city of some thirty or forty thousand about fifty miles away. It was not his factory, really; it had been his father's factory, and at one time it had been engaged in making farm machinery. But some years ago the bottom had fallen out of the farm machinery business and Sherwood had changed over to the manufacturing of a wide variety of gadgets. Just what kind of gadgets, I had no idea, for I had paid but small attention to the Sherwood family, except for a time, in the closing days of high school, when I had held a somewhat more than casual interest in Gerald Sherwood's daughter.

He was a solid and substantial citizen and he was well accepted. But because he, and his father before him, had not made their living in the village, because the Sherwood family had always been well-off, if not exactly rich, while the rest of us were poor, they had always been considered just a step this side of strangers. Their interests were not entirely the interests of the village; they were not tied as tightly to the community as the rest of us. So they stood apart, perhaps not so much that they wanted to as that we forced them to.

So what was I to do? Drive out to Sherwood's place and play the village fool? Go barging in and ask him what he knew of a screwy telephone?

I looked at my watch and it was only four o'clock. Even if I decided to go out and talk with Sherwood, I couldn't do it until early evening. More than likely, I told myself, he didn't return from Elmore until six o'clock or so.

I pulled out the desk drawer and began taking out my stuff. Then I put it back again and closed the drawer. I'd have to keep the office until sometime tonight because I'd have to come to it to talk with the person (or the persons?) on that nightmare phone. After it was dark, if I wanted to, I could walk out with the phone and take it home with me. But I couldn't walk the streets in broad daylight with a phone tucked beneath my arm.

I went out and closed the door behind me and started down the street. I didn't know what to do and stood at the first street corner for a moment to make up my mind. I could go home, of course, but I shrank from doing it. It seemed a bit too much like hunting out a hole to hide in. I could go down to the village hall and there might be someone there to talk with. Although there was a chance, as well, that Hiram Martin, the village constable, would be the only one around. Hiram would want me to play a game of checkers with him and I wasn't in the mood for playing any checkers. Hiram was a rotten loser, too, and you had to let him win to keep him from getting nasty. Hiram and I had never got along too well together. He had been a bully on the schoolground and he and I had fought a dozen times a year. He always licked me, but he never made me say that I was licked, and he never liked me. You had to let Hiram lick you once or twice a year and then admit that you were licked and he'd let you be his friend. And there was a chance, as well, that Higman Morris would be there, and on a day like this, I couldn't stomach Higgy. Higgy was the mayor, a pillar of the church, a member of the school board, a director of the bank, and a big stuffed shirt. Even on my better days, Higgy was a chore; I ducked him when I could.

Or I could go up to the *Tribune* office and spend an hour or so with the editor, Joe Evans, who wouldn't be too busy, because the paper had been put out this morning. But Joe would be full of county politics and the proposal to build a swimming pool and a lot of other things of lively public interest and somehow or other I couldn't stir up too much interest in any one of them.

I would go down to the Happy Hollow tavern, I decided, and take one of the booths in back and nurse a beer or two while I killed some time and tried to do some thinking. My finances didn't run to drinking, but a beer or two wouldn't make me much worse off than I was already, and there is, at times, an awful lot of comfort in a glass of beer. It was too early for many people to be in the place and I could be alone. Stiffy Grant, more than likely would be there, spending the dollar that I had given him. But Stiffy was a gentleman and a most perceptive person. If he saw I wanted to be by myself, he wouldn't bother me.

The tavern was dark and cool and I had to feel my way along, after coming in from the brilliance of the street. I reached the back booth and saw that it was empty, so I sat down in it. There were some people in one of the booths up front, but that was all there were.

Mae Hutton came from behind the bar.

'Hello, Brad,' she said. 'We don't see much of you.'

'You holding down the place for Charley?' I asked her.

Charley was her father and the owner of the tavern.

'He's catching a nap,' she said. 'It's not too busy this time of day. I can handle it.'

'How about a beer?' I asked.

'Sure thing. Large or small?'

'Make it large,' I told her.

She brought the beer and went back behind the bar. The place was quiet and restful – not elegant, and perhaps a little dirty, but restful. Up front the brightness of the street made a splash of light, but it faded out before it got too far, as if it were soaked up by the quiet dusk that lurked within the building.

A man got up from the booth just ahead of me. I had not seen him as I came in. Probably he'd been sitting in the corner, against the wall. He held a half-filled glass and he turned and stared at me. Then he took a step or two and stood beside my booth. I looked up and I didn't recognize him. My eyes had not as yet become adjusted to the place.

'Brad Carter?' he asked. 'Could you be Brad Carter?'

'Yes, I could,' I said.

He put his glass down on the table and sat down across from me. And as he did, those fox-like features fell into shape for me and I knew who he was.

'Alf Peterson!' I said, surprised. 'Ed Adler and I were talking about you just an hour or so ago.'

He thrust his hand across the table and I grabbed it, glad to see him, glad for some strange reason for this man out of the past. His handclasp was firm and strong and I knew he was glad to see me, too.

'Good Lord,' I said, 'how long has it been?'

'Six years,' he told me. 'Maybe more than that.'

We sat there, looking at one another, in that awkward pause that falls between old friends after years of not seeing one another, neither one quite sure of what should be said, searching for some safe and common ground to begin a conversation.

'Back for a visit?' I inquired.

'Yeah,' he said. 'Vacation.'

'You should have looked me up at once.'

'Just got in three or four hours ago.'

It was strange, I thought, that he should have come back to Millville, for there was no one for him here. His folks had moved away, somewhere east, several years ago. They'd not been Millville people. They'd been in the village for only four or five years, while his father worked as an engineer on a highway project.

'You're going to stay with me,' I said. 'There's a lot of room. I am all alone.'

'I'm at a motel west of town. Johnny's Motor Court, they call it.'

'You should have come straight to my place.'

'I would have,' he said, 'but I didn't know. I didn't know that you were in town. Even if you were, I thought you might be married. I didn't want to just come barging in.'

I shook my head. 'None of those things,' I said.

We each had a drink of beer.

He put down his glass. 'How are things going, Brad?'

My mouth got set to tell a lie, and then I stopped. What the hell, I thought. This man across from me was old Alf Peterson, one of my best friends. There was no point in telling him a lie. There was no pride involved. He was too good a friend for pride to be involved.

'Not so good,' I told him.

'I'm sorry, Brad.'

'I made a big mistake,' I said. 'I should have gotten out of here. There's nothing here in Millville, not for anyone.'

'You used to want to be an artist. You used to fool around

with drawing and there were those pictures that you painted.'

I made a motion to sweep it all away.

'Don't tell me,' said Alf Peterson, 'that you didn't even try. You were planning to go on to school that year we graduated.'

'I did,' I said. 'I got in a year of it. An art school in Chicago. Then Dad passed away and Mother needed me. And there wasn't any money. I've often wondered how Dad got enough together to send me that one year.'

'And your mother? You said you are alone.'

'She died two years ago.'

He nodded. 'And you still run the greenhouse.'

I shook my head. 'I couldn't make a go of it. There wasn't much to go on. I've been selling insurance and trying to handle real estate. But it's no good, Alf. Tomorrow morning I'll close up the office.'

'What then?' he asked.

'I don't know. I haven't thought about it.'

Alf signalled to Mae to bring another round of beers.

'You don't feel,' he said, 'there's anything to stay for.'

I shook my head. 'There's the house, of course. I would hate to sell it. If I left, I'd just lock it up. But there's no place I want to go, Alf, that's the hell of it. I don't know if I can quite explain. I've stayed here a year or two too long; I have Millville in my blood.'

Alf nodded. 'I think I understand. It got into my blood as well. That's why I came back. And now I wonder if I should have. Of course I'm glad to see you, and maybe some other people, but even so I have a feeling that I should not have come. The place seems sort of empty. Sucked dry, if you follow me. It's the same as it always was, I guess, but it has that empty feeling.'

Mae brought the beers and took the empty glasses.

'I have an idea,' Alf said, 'if you care to listen.'

'Sure,' I said. 'Why not?'

'I'll be going back,' he said, 'in another day or so. Why don't you come with me? I'm working with a crazy sort of project. There would be room for you. I know the supervisor pretty well and I could speak to him.'

'Doing what?' I asked. 'Maybe it would be something that I couldn't do.'

'I don't know,' said Alf, 'if I can explain it very logically. It's a research project – a thinking project. You sit in a booth and think.'

'Think?'

'Yeah. It sounds crazy, doesn't it? But it's not the way it sounds. You sit down in a booth and you get a card that has a question or a problem printed on it. Then you think about that problem and you're supposed to think out loud, sort of talking to yourself, sometimes arguing with yourself. You're self-conscious to start with, but you get over that. The booth is soundproofed and no one can see or hear you. I suppose there is a recorder of some sort to take down what you say, but if there is, it's not in sight.'

'And they pay you for this?'

'Rather well,' said Alf. 'A man can get along.'

'But what is it for?' I asked.

'We don't know,' said Alf. 'Not that we haven't asked. But that's the one condition of the job – that you don't know what it's all about. It's an experiment of some sort, I'd guess. I imagine that it's financed by a university or some research outfit. We are told that if we knew what was going on it might influence the way we are thinking. A man might unconsciously pattern his thinking to fit the purpose of the research.'

'And the results?' I asked.

'We aren't told results. Each thinker must have a certain kind of pattern and if you knew that pattern it might influence you. You might try to conform to your own personal pattern, to be consistent, or perhaps there'd be a tendency to break out of it. If you don't know the results, you can't guess at the pattern and there is then no danger.'

A truck went by in the street outside and its rumble was loud in the quietness of the tavern. And after it went past, there was a fly buzzing on the ceiling. The people up in front apparently had left – at least, they weren't talking any more. I looked around for Stiffy Grant and he wasn't there. I recalled now that I had not seen him and that was funny, for I'd just given him the dollar.

'Where is this place?' I asked.

'Mississippi. Greenbriar, Mississippi. It's just a little place. Come to think of it, it's a lot like Millville. Just a little village, quiet and dusty and hot. My God, how hot it is. But the project centre is air conditioned. It isn't bad in there.'

'A little town,' I said. 'Funny that there'd be a place like that in a little town.'

'Camouflage,' said Alf. 'They want to keep it quiet. We're asked not to talk about it. And how could you hide it better than in a little place like that? No one would ever think there'd be a project of that sort in a stuck-off village.'

'But you were a stranger . . .'

'Sure, and that's how I got the job. They didn't want too many local people. All of them would have a tendency to think pretty much alike. They were glad to get someone from out of town. There are quite a lot of out-of-towners in the project.'

'And before that?'

'Before that? Oh, yes, I see. Before that there was everything. I floated, bummed around. Never stayed too long in any spot. A job for a few weeks here, then a job for a few weeks a little farther on. I guess you could say I drifted. Worked on a concrete gang for a while, washed dishes for a while when the cash ran out and there was nothing else to do. Was a gardener on a big estate down in Louisville for a month or two. Picked tomatoes for a while, but you can starve at that sort of work, so I moved on. Did a lot of things. But I've been down in Greenbriar for eleven months.'

'The job can't last forever. After a while they'll have all the data they need.'

He nodded. 'I know. I'll hate to have it end. It's the best work I ever found. How about it, Brad? Will you go back with me?'

37

'I'll have to think about it,' I told him. 'Can't you stay a little longer than that day or two?'

'I suppose I could,' said Alf. 'I've got two weeks' vacation.'

'Like to do some fishing?'

'Nothing I'd like better.'

'What do you say we leave tomorrow morning? Go up north for a week or so? It should be cool up there. I have a tent and a camping outfit. We'll try to find a place where we can get some wall-eyes.'

'That sounds fine to me.'

'We can use my car,' I said.

'I'll buy the gas,' said Alf.

'The shape I'm in,' I said, 'I'll let you.'

3

IF IT had not been for its pillared front and the gleaming white rail of the widow walk atop its roof, the house would have been plain and stark. There had been a time, I recalled, when I had thought of it as the most beautiful house in the entire world. But it had been six or seven years since I had been at the Sherwood house.

I parked the car and got out and stood for a moment, looking at the house. It was not fully dark as yet and the four great pillars gleamed softly in the fading light of day. There were no lights in the front part of the house, but I could see that they had been turned on somewhere in the back.

I went up the shallow steps and across the porch. I found the bell and rang.

Footsteps came down the hall, a hurrying woman's footsteps. More than likely, I thought, it was Mrs Flaherty. She had been housekeeper for the family since that time Mrs Sherwood had left the house, never to return.

But it wasn't Mrs Flaherty.

The door came open and she stood there, more mature than I remembered her, more poised, more beautiful than ever.

'Nancy!' I exclaimed. 'Why, you must be Nancy!'

It was not what I would have said if I'd had time to think about it.

'Yes,' she said, 'I'm Nancy. Why be so surprised?'

'Because I thought you weren't here. When did you get home?'

'Just yesterday,' she said.

And, I thought, she doesn't know me. She knows that she should know me. She's trying to remember.

'Brad,' she said, proving I was wrong, 'it's silly just to stand there. Why don't you come in.'

I stepped inside and she closed the door and we were facing one another in the dimness of the hall.

She reached out and laid her fingers on the lapel of my coat. 'It's been a long time, Brad,' she said. 'How is everything with you?'

'Fine,' I said. 'Just fine.'

'There are not many left, I hear. Not many of the gang.'

I shook my head. 'You sound as if you're glad to be back home.'

She laughed, just a flutter of a laugh. 'Why, of course I am,' she said. And the laugh was the same as ever, that little burst of spontaneous merriment that had been a part of her.

Someone stepped out into the hall.

'Nancy,' a voice called, 'is that the Carter boy?'

'Why,' Nancy said to me, 'I didn't know that you wanted to see Father.'

'It won't take long,' I told her. 'Will I see you later?'

'Yes, of course,' she said. 'We have a lot to talk about.'

'Nancy!'

'Yes, Father.'

'I'm coming,' I said.

I strode down the hall toward the figure there. He opened a door and turned on the lights in the room beyond.

I stepped in and he closed the door.

He was a big man with great broad shoulders and an aristocratic head, with a smart trim moustache.

'Mr Sherwood,' I told him, angrily, 'I am not the Carter boy. I am Bradshaw Carter. To my friends, I'm Brad.'

It was an unreasonable anger, and probably uncalled for. But he had burned me up, out there in the hall.

'I'm sorry, Brad,' he said. 'It's so hard to remember that you all are grown up – the kids that Nancy used to run around with.'

He stepped from the door and went across the room to a desk that stood against one wall. He opened a drawer and took out a bulky envelope and laid it on the desk top.

'That's for you,' he said.

'For me?'

'Yes, I thought you knew.'

I shook my head and there was something in the room that was very close to fear. It was a sombre room, two walls filled with books, and on the third heavily draped windows flanking a marble fireplace.

'Well,' he said, 'it's yours. Why don't you take it?'

I walked to the desk and picked up the envelope. It was unsealed and I flipped up the flap. Inside was a thick sheaf of currency.

'Fifteen hundred dollars,' said Gerald Sherwood. 'I presume that is the right amount.'

'I don't know anything,' I told him, 'about fifteen hundred dollars. I was simply told by phone that I should talk with you.'

He puckered up his face and looked at me intently, almost as if he might not believe me.

'On a phone like that,' I told him, pointing to the second phone that stood on the desk.

He nodded tiredly. 'Yes,' he said, 'and how long have you had the phone?'

'Just this afternoon. Ed Adler came and took out my other phone, the regular phone, because I couldn't pay for it. I went for a walk, to sort of think things over, and when I came back this other phone was ringing.'

He waved a hand. 'Take the envelope,' he said. 'Put it in your pocket. It is not my money. It belongs to you.'

I laid the envelope back on top the desk. I needed fifteen hundred dollars. I needed any kind of money, no matter where it came from. But I couldn't take that envelope. I don't know why I couldn't.

'All right,' he said, 'sit down.'

A chair stood angled in front of the desk and I sat down in it.

He lifted the lid of a box on the desk. 'A cigar?' he asked.

'I don't smoke,' I told him.

'A drink, perhaps?'

'Yes. I would like a drink.'

'Bourbon?'

'Bourbon would be fine.'

He went to a cellaret that stood in a corner and put ice into two glasses.

'How do you drink it, Brad?'

'Just ice, if you don't mind.'

He chuckled. 'It's the only civilized way to drink the stuff,' he said.

I sat, looking at the rows of books that ran from floor to ceiling. Many of them were in sets and, from the looks of them, in expensive bindings.

It must be wonderful, I thought, to be, not exactly rich, but to have enough so you didn't have to worry when there was some little thing you wanted, not to have to wonder if it would be all right if you spent the money for it. To be able to live in a house like this, to line the walls with books and have rich draperies and to have more than just one bottle of booze and a place to keep it other than a kitchen shelf.

He handed me the glass of whisky and walked around the desk. He sat down in the chair behind it. Raising his glass, he took a couple of thirsty gulps, then set the glass down on the desk top.

'Brad,' he asked, 'how much do you know?'

'Not a thing,' I said. 'Only what I told you. I talked with someone on the phone. They offered me a job.'

'And you took the job?'

'No,' I said, 'I didn't, but I may. I could use a job. But what they – whoever it was – had to say didn't make much sense.'

'They?'

'Well, either there were three of them – or one who used three different voices. Strange as it may sound to you, it seemed to me as if it were one person who used different voices.'

He picked up the glass and gulped at it again. He held it up to the light and saw in what seemed to be astonishment that it was nearly empty. He hoisted himself out of the chair and went to get the bottle. He slopped liquor in his glass and held the bottle out to me.

'I haven't started yet,' I told him.

He put the bottle on the desk and sat down again.

'OK,' he said, 'you've come and talked with me. It's all right to take the job. Pick up your money and get out of here. More than likely Nancy's out there waiting. Take her to a show or something.'

'And that's all?' I asked.

'That is all,' he said.

'You changed your mind,' I told him.

'Changed my mind?'

'You were about to tell me something. Then you decided not to.'

He looked at me levelly and hard. 'I suppose you're right,' he said. 'It really makes no difference.'

'It does to me,' I told him. 'Because I can see you're scared.'

I thought he might get sore. Most men do when you tell them they are scared.

He didn't. He just sat there, his face unchanging.

Then he said: 'Start on that drink, for Christ's sake. You make me nervous, just roosting there and hanging onto it.'

I had forgotten all about the drink. I had a slug.

'Probably,' he said, 'you are thinking a lot of things that aren't true. You more than likely think that I'm mixed up in some dirty kind of business. I wonder, would you believe me if I told you I don't really know what kind of business I'm mixed up in.'

'I think I would,' I said. 'That is, if you say so.'

'I've had a lot of trouble in life,' he said, 'but that's not unusual. Most people do have a lot of trouble, one way or the other. Mine came in a bunch. Trouble has a way of doing that.'

I nodded, agreeing with him.

'First,' he said, 'my wife left me. You probably know all about that. There must have been a lot of talk about it.'

'It was before my time,' I said. 'I was pretty young.'

'Yes, I suppose it was. Say this much for the two of us, we were civilized about it. There wasn't any shouting and no nastiness in court. That was something neither of us wanted. And, then, on top of that I was facing business failure. The bottom went out of the farm machinery business and I feared that I might have to shut down the plant. There were a lot of other small farm machinery firms that simply locked their doors. After fifty or sixty or more years as going, profitable concerns, they were forced out of business.'

He paused, as if he wanted me to say something. There wasn't anything to say.

He took another drink, then began to talk again. 'I'm a fairly stupid man in a lot of ways. I can handle a business. I can keep it going if there's any chance to keep it going and I can wring a profit from it. I suppose that you could say I'm rather astute when it comes to business matters. But that's the end of it. In the course of my lifetime I have never really had a big idea or a new idea.'

He leaned forward, clasping his hands together and putting them on the desk.

'I've thought about it a lot,' he said, 'this thing that happened to me. I've tried to see some reason in it and there is no reason. It's a thing that should not have happened, not to a man like me. There I was, on the verge of failure, and not

43

a thing that I could do about it. The problem was quite simple, really. For a number of good economic reasons, less farm machinery was being sold. Some of the big concerns, with big sales departments and good advertising budgets, could ride out a thing like that. They had some elbow room to plan, there were steps that they could take to lessen the effects of the situation. But a small concern like mine didn't have the room or the capital reserve. My firm, and others, faced disaster. And in my case, you understand, I didn't have a chance. I had run the business according to old and established practices and time-tested rules, the same sort of good, sound business practices that had been followed by my grandfather and my father. And these practices said that when your sales dwindled down to nothing you were finished. There were other men who might have been able to figure out a way to meet the situation, but not me. I was a good businessman, but I had no imagination. I had no ideas. And then, suddenly, I began to get ideas. But they were not my own ideas. It was as if the ideas of some other person were being transplanted to my brain.

'You understand,' he said, 'that an idea sometimes comes to you in the matter of a second. It just pops from nowhere. It has no apparent point of origin. Try as you may, you cannot trace it back to anything you did or heard or read. Somehow, I suppose, if you dug deep enough, you'd find its genesis, but there are few of us who are trained to do that sort of digging. But the point is that most ideas are no more than a germ, a tiny starting point. An idea may be good and valid, but it will take some nursing. It has to be developed. You must think about it and turn it around and around and look at it from every angle and weigh it and consider it before you can mould it into something useful.

'But this wasn't the way with these ideas that I got. They sprang forth full and round and completely developed. I didn't have to do any thinking about them. They just popped into my mind and I didn't need to do another thing about them. There they were, all ready for one's use. I'd wake up in the morning and I'd have a new idea, a new mass of knowledge in my brain. I'd go for a walk and come back with another. They came in bunches, as if someone had sown a crop of them inside my brain and they had lain there for a while and then begun to sprout.'

'The gadgets?' I said.

He looked at me curiously. 'Yes, the gadgets. What do you know about them?'

'Nothing,' I told him. 'I just knew that when the bottom fell out of the farm machinery business you started making gadgets. I don't know what kind of gadgets.'

He didn't tell me what kind of gadgets. He went on talking about those strange ideas. 'I didn't realize at first what was happening. Then, as the ideas came piling in on me, I knew there was something strange about it. I knew that it was unlikely that I'd think of any one of them, let alone the many that I had. More than likely I'd never have thought of them at all, for I have no imagination and I am not inventive. I tried to tell myself that it was just barely possible I might have thought of two or three of them, but even that would have been most unlikely. But of more than two or three of them I knew I was not capable. I was forced, finally, to admit that I had been the recipient of some sort of outside help.'

'What kind of outside help?'

'I don't know,' he said. 'Even now I don't.'

'But it didn't stop you from using these ideas.'

'I am a practical man,' he said. 'Intensely practical. I suppose some people might even say hard-headed. But consider this: the business was gone. Not my business, mind you, but the family business, the business my grandfather had started and my father had handed on to me. It wasn't my business; it was a business I held in trust. There is a great distinction. You could see a business you had built yourself go gurgling down the drain and still stand the blow of it, telling yourself that you had been successful once and you could start over and be successful once again. But it's different with a family business. In the first place, there is the shame. And in the second place, you can't be sure that you can recoup. You were no success to start with. Success had been handed to you and you'd merely carried on. You never could be sure that you could start over and build the business back. In fact, you're so conditioned that you're pretty sure you couldn't.'

He quit speaking and in the silence I could hear the ticking of a clock, faint and far off, but I couldn't see the clock and I resisted the temptation to turn my head to see if I could find it. For I had the feeling that if I turned my head, if I stirred at all, I'd break something that lay within the room. As if I stood in a crowded china shop, where all the pieces were precarious and tilted, fearing to move, for if one piece were dislodged, all of them would come crashing down.

'What would you have done?' asked Sherwood.

'I'd have used anything I had,' I said.

'That's what I did,' said Sherwood. 'I was desperate. There was the business, this house, Nancy, the family name – all of it at stake. I took all of those ideas and I wrote them down and I called in my engineers and draughtsmen and production people and we got to work. I got the credit for it all, of course. There was nothing I could do about it. I couldn't tell them I wasn't the one who'd dreamed up all those things. And you know, strange as it may sound, that's the hardest part of all. That I have to go on taking credit for all those things I didn't do.'

'So that is that,' I said. 'The family business saved and everything is fine. If I were you, I wouldn't let a guilt complex bother me too much.'

'But it didn't stop,' he said. 'If it had, I'd have forgotten it. If there'd just been this single spurt of help to save the company, it might have been all right. But it kept right on. As if there might be two of me – the real, apparent Gerald Sherwood, the one sitting at this desk, and another one who did the thinking for me. The ideas kept on coming and some of them made a lot of sense and some made no sense at all. Some of them, I tell you, were out of this world, literally out of this world. They had no point of reference, they didn't seem to square with any situation. And while one could sense that they

46

had potential, while there was a feeling of great importance in the very texture of them, they were entirely useless.

'And it was not only the ideas; it was knowledge also. Bits and bursts of knowledge. Knowledge about things in which I had no interest, things I had never thought of. Knowledge about certain things I'm certain no man knows about. As if someone took a handful of fragmented knowledge, a sort of grab-bag, junk-heap pile of knowledge and dumped it in my brain.'

He reached out for the bottle and filled his glass. He gestured at me with the bottle neck and I held out my glass. He filled it to the brim.

'Drink up,' he said. 'You got me started and now you hear me out. Tomorrow morning I'll ask myself why I told you all of this. But tonight it seems all right.'

'If you don't want to tell me. If it seems that I am prying . . .'

He waved a hand at me. 'All right,' he said, 'if you don't want to hear it. Pick up your fifteen hundred.'

I shook my head. 'Not yet. Not until I know how come you're giving it to me.'

'It's not my money. I'm just acting as an agent.'

'For this other man? For this other you?'

He nodded. 'That's right,' he said. 'I wonder how you guessed.'

I gestured at the phone without a dial.

He grimaced. 'I've never used the thing,' he said. 'Until you told me about the one you found waiting in your office, I never knew anyone who had. I make them by the hundreds . . .'

'You make them!'

'Yes, of course I do. Not for myself. For this second self. Although,' he said, leaning across the desk and lowering his voice to a confidential tone, 'I'm beginning to suspect it's not a second self.'

'What do you think it is?'

He leaned slowly back in the chair. 'Damned if I know,' he said. 'There was a time I thought about it and wondered at it and worried over it, but there was no way of knowing. I just don't bother any more. I tell myself there may be others like me. Maybe I am not alone – at least, it's good to think so.'

'But the phone?' I asked.

'I designed the thing,' he said. 'Or perhaps this other person, if it is a person, did. I found it in my mind and I put it down on paper. And I did this, mind you, without knowing what it was or what it was supposed to do. I knew it was a phone of some sort, naturally. But I couldn't, for the life of me, see how it could work. And neither could any of the others who put it into production at the plant. By all the rules of reason, the damn thing shouldn't work.'

'But you said there were a lot of other things that seemed to have no purpose.'

'A lot of them,' he said, 'but with them I never drew a blueprint, I never tried to make them. But the phone, if that is what you want to call it, was a different proposition. I knew that I should make them and how many might be needed and what to do with them.'

'What did you do with them?'

'I shipped them to an outfit in New Jersey.'

It was utterly insane.

'Let me get this straight,' I pleaded. 'You found the blueprints in your head and you knew you should make these phones and that you should send them to some place in New Jersey. And you did it without question?'

'Oh, certainly with question. I felt somewhat like a fool. But consider this: this second self, this auxiliary brain, this contact with something else had never let me down. It had saved my business, it had provided good advice, it had never failed me. You can't turn your back on something that has played good fairy to you.'

'I think I see,' I said.

'Of course you do,' he told me. 'A gambler rides his luck. An investor plays his hunches. And neither luck nor hunch are as solid and consistent as this thing I have.'

He reached out and picked up the dialless phone and looked

48

at it, then set it down again. 'I brought this one home,' he said, 'and put it on the desk. All these years I've waited for a call, but it never came.'

'With you,' I told him, 'there is no need of any phone.'

'You think that's it?' he asked.

'I'm sure of it.'

'I suppose it is,' he said. 'At times it's confusing.'

'This Jersey firm?' I asked. 'You corresponded with them?'

He shook his head. 'Not a line. I just shipped the phones.'

'There was no acknowledgement?'

'No acknowledgement,' he said. 'No payment. I expected none. When you do business with yourself . . .'

'Yourself! You mean this second self runs that New Jersey firm?'

'I don't know,' he said. 'Christ, I don't know anything. I've lived with it all these years and I tried to understand, but I never understood.'

And now his face was haunted and I felt sorry for him.

He must have noticed that I felt sorry for him. He laughed and said. 'Don't let me get you down. I can take it. I can take anything. You must not forget that I've been well paid. Tell me about yourself. You're in real estate.'

I nodded. 'And insurance.'

'And you couldn't pay your phone bill.'

'Don't waste sympathy on me,' I said. 'I'll get along somehow.'

'Funny thing about the kids,' he said. 'Not many of them stay here. Not much to keep them here, I guess.'

'Not very much,' I said.

'Nancy is just home from Europe,' he told me. 'I'm glad to have her home. It got lonesome here with no one. I haven't seen much of her lately. College and then a fling at social work and then the trip to Europe. But she tells me now that she plans to stay a while. She wants to do some writing.'

'She should be good at it,' I said. 'She got good marks in composition when we were in high school.'

'She has the writing bug,' he said. 'Had half a dozen things published in, I guess you call them little magazines. The ones that come out quarterly and pay you nothing for your work except half a dozen copies. I'd never heard of them before. I read the articles she wrote, but I have no eye for writing. I don't know if it's good or bad. Although I suppose it has to have a certain competence to have been accepted. But if writing keeps her here with me, I'll be satisfied.'

I got out of my chair. 'I'd better go,' I said. 'Maybe I have stayed longer than I should.'

He shook his head. 'No, I was glad to talk with you. And don't forget the money. This other self, this whatever-you-may-call-it told me to give it to you. I gather that it's in the nature of a retainer of some sort.'

'But this is double talk,' I told him, almost angrily. 'The money comes from you.'

'Not at all,' he said. 'It comes from a special fund that was started many years ago. It didn't seem quite right that I should reap all benefit from all of these ideas which were not really mine. So I began paying ten per cent profits into a special fund . . .'

'Suggested, more than likely, by this second self.'

'Yes,' he said. 'I think you are right, although it was so long ago that I cannot truly say. But in any case, I set up the fund and through the years have paid out varying amounts at the direction of whoever it may be that shares my mind with me.'

I stared at him, and it was rude of me, I know. But no man, I told myself, could sit as calmly as Sherwood sat and talk about an unknown personality that shared his mind with him. Even after all the years, it still would not be possible.

'The fund,' said Sherwood, quietly, 'is quite a tidy sum, even with the amounts I've paid out of it. It seems that since this fellow came to live with me, everything I've touched has simply turned to money.'

'You take a chance,' I said, 'telling this to me.'

'You mean that you could tell it around about me?'

I nodded. 'Not that I would,' I said.

'I don't think you will,' he said. 'You'd get laughed at for your trouble. No one would believe you.'

'I don't suppose they would.'

'Brad,' he said, almost kindly, 'don't be a complete damn fool. Pick up that envelope and put it in your pocket. Come back some other time and talk with me – any time you want. I have a hunch there may be a lot of things we'll want to talk about.'

I reached out my hand and picked up the money. I stuffed it in my pocket.

'Thank you, sir,' I said.

'Don't mention it,' he told me. He raised a hand. 'Be seeing you,' he said.

4

I WENT slowly down the hall and there was no sign of Nancy, nor was she on the porch, where I had half expected to find her waiting for me. She had said yes, that I would see her later, that we had a lot to talk about, and I had thought, of course, that she meant tonight. But she might not have meant tonight. She might have meant some other time than this. Or she might have waited and then grown tired of waiting. After all, I had spent a long time with her father.

The moon had risen in a cloudless sky and there was not a breath of breeze. The great oaks stood like graven monuments and the summer night was filled with the glittering of moonbeams. I walked down the stairs and stood for a moment at their foot and it seemed for all the world that I was standing in a circle of enchantment. For this, I thought, could not be the old, familiar earth, this place of ghostly, brooding oaken sentinels, this air so drenched with moonlight, this breathless, waiting silence hanging over all, and the faint, other-world perfume that hung above the soft blackness of the ground.

Then the enchantment faded and the glitter went away and I was back once more in the world I knew.

There was a chill in the summer air. Perhaps a chill of disappointment, the chill of being booted out of fairyland, the chill of knowing there was another place I could not hope to stay. I felt the solid concrete of the walk underneath my feet and I could see that the shadowed oaks were only oaks and not graven monuments.

I shook myself, like a dog coming out of water, and my wits came back together and I went on down the walk. As I neared the car, I fumbled in my pocket for my keys, walking around on the driver's side and opening the door.

I was halfway in the seat before I saw her sitting there, next to the other door.

'I thought,' she said, 'that you were never coming. What did you and Father find to talk so long about?'

'A number of things,' I told her. 'None of them important.'

'Do you see him often?'

'No,' I said. 'Not often.' Somehow I didn't want to tell her this was the first time I had ever talked with him.

I groped in the dark and found the lock and slid in the key.

'A drive,' I said. 'Perhaps some place for a drink.'

'No, please,' she said. 'I'd rather sit and talk.'

I settled back into the seat.

'It's nice tonight,' she said. 'So quiet. There are so few places that are really quiet.'

'There's a place of enchantment,' I told her, 'just outside your porch. I walked into it, but it didn't last. The air was full of moonbeams and there was a faint perfume . . .'

'That was the flowers,' she said.

'What flowers?'

'There's a bed of them in the curve of the walk. All of them those lovely flowers that your father found out in the woods somewhere.'

'So you have them too,' I said. 'I guess everyone in the village has a bed of them.'

'Your father,' she said, 'was one of the nicest men I ever

52

knew. When I was a little girl he always gave me flowers. I'd go walking past and he'd pick a flower or two for me.'

Yes, I thought, I suppose he could be called a nice man. Nice and strong and strange, and yet, despite his strength and strangeness, a very gentle man. He had known the ways of flowers and of all other plants. His tomato plants, I remembered, had grown big and stout and of a dark, deep green, and in the spring everyone had come to get tomato plants from him.

And there had been that day he'd gone down Dark Hollow way to deliver some tomato plants and cabbage and a box full of perennials to the widow Hicklin and had come back with half a dozen strange, purple-blossomed wild flowers, which he had dug up along the road and brought home, their roots wrapped carefully in a piece of burlap.

He had never seen such flowers before and neither, it turned out, had anybody else. He had planted them in a special bed and had tended them with care and the flowers had responded gratefully underneath his hands. So that today there were few flower beds in the village that did not have some of those purple flowers, my father's special flowers.

'Those flowers of his,' asked Nancy. 'Did he ever find what kind of flowers they were?'

'No,' I said, 'he didn't.'

'He could have sent one of them to the university or someplace. Someone could have told him exactly what he'd found.'

'He talked of it off and on. But he never got around to really doing it. He always kept so busy. There were so many things to do. The greenhouse business keeps you on the run.'

'You didn't like it, Brad?'

'I didn't really mind it. I'd grown up with it and I could handle it. But I didn't have the knack. Stuff wouldn't grow for me.'

She stretched, touching the roof with balled fists.

'It's good to be back,' she said. 'I think I'll stay a while. I think Father needs to have someone around.'

'He said you planned to write.'

'He told you that?'

'Yes,' I said. 'he did. He didn't act as if he shouldn't.'

'Oh, I don't suppose it makes any difference. But it's a thing that you don't talk about – not until you're well along on it. There are so many things that can go wrong with writing. I don't want to be one of those pseudo-literary people who are always writing something they never finish, or talking about writing something that they never start.'

'And when you write,' I asked, 'what will you write about?'

'About right here,' she said. 'About this town of ours.'

'Millville?'

'Why, yes, of course,' she said. 'About the village and its people.'

'But,' I protested, 'there is nothing here to write about.'

She laughed and reached out and touched my arm. 'There's so much to write about,' she said. 'So many famous people. And such characters.'

'Famous people?' I said, astonished.

'There are,' she said, 'Belle Simpson Knowles, the famous novelist, and Ben Jackson, the great criminal lawyer, and John M. Hartford, who heads the department of history at . . .'

'But those are the ones who left,' I said. 'There was nothing here for them. They went out and made names for themselves and most of them never set foot in Millville again, not even for a visit.'

'But,' she said, 'they got their start here. They had the capacity for what they did before they ever left this village. You stopped me before I finished out the list. There are a lot of others. Millville, small and stupid as it is, has produced more great men and women than any other village of its size.'

'You're sure of that?' I asked, wanting to laugh at her earnestness, but not quite daring to.

'I would have to check,' she said, 'but there have been a lot of them.'

'And the characters,' I said. 'I guess you're right. Millville has its share of characters. There are Stiffy Grant and Floyd Caldwell and Mayor Higgy . . .'

'They aren't really characters,' said Nancy. 'Not the way you think of them. I shouldn't have called them characters to start with. They're individualists. They've grown up in a free and easy atmosphere. They've not been forced to conform to a group of rigid concepts and so they've been themselves. Perhaps the only truly unfettered human beings who still exist to-day can be found in little villages like this.'

In all my life I'd never heard anything like this. Nobody had ever told me that Higgy Morris was an individualist. He wasn't. He was just a big stuffed shirt. And Hiram Martin was no individualist. Not in my book, he wasn't. He was just a schoolyard bully who had grown up into a stupid cop.

'Don't you think so?' Nancy asked.

'I don't know,' I said. 'I have never thought about it.'

And I thought – for God's sake, her education's showing, her years in an eastern college, her fling at social work in the New York welfare centre, her year-long tour of Europe. She was too sure and confident, too full of theory and of knowledge. Millville was her home no longer. She had lost the feel and sense of it, for you do not sit off to one side and analyse the place that you call your home. She still might call this village home, but it was not her home. And had it ever been, I wondered? Could any girl (or boy) call a bone-poor village home when they lived in the one big house the village boasted, when their father drove a Cadillac, and there was a cook and maid and gardener to care for house and yard? She had not come home; rather she had come back to a village that would serve her as a social research area. She would sit up here on her hilltop and subject the village to inspection and analysis and she'd strip us bare and hold us up, flayed and writhing, for the information and amusement of the kind of people who read her kind of book.

'I have a feeling,' she said, 'that there is something here that the world could use, something of which there is not a great deal in the world. Some sort of catalyst that sparks creative effort, some kind of inner hunger that serves to trigger greatness.'

'That inner hunger,' I said. 'There are families in town who can tell you all you want to know about that inner hunger.'

And I wasn't kidding. There were Millville families that at times went just a little hungry; not starving, naturally, but never having quite enough to eat and almost never the right kind of things to eat. I could have named her three of them right off, without even thinking.

'Brad,' she said, 'you don't like the idea of the book.'

'I don't mind,' I said. 'I have no right to mind. But when you write it, please, write it as one of us, not as someone who stands off and is a bit amused. Have a bit of sympathy. Try to feel a little like these people you write about. That shouldn't be too hard; you've lived here long enough.'

She laughed, but it was not one of her merry laughs. 'I have a terrible feeling that I may never write it. I'll start it and I'll write away at it, but I'll keep going back and changing it, because the people I am writing of will change, or I'll see them differently as time goes on, and I'll never get it written. So you see, there's no need to worry.'

More than likely she was right, I thought. You had to have a hunger, a different kind of hunger, to finish up a book. And I rather doubted that she was as hungry as she thought.

'I hope you do,' I said. 'I mean I hope you get it written. And I know it will be good. It can't help but be.'

I was trying to make up for my nastiness and I think that she knew I was. But she let it pass.

It had been childish and provincial, I told myself, to have acted as I had. What difference did it make? What possible difference could it make for me, who had stood on the street that very afternoon and felt a hatred for the geographic concept that was called the town of Millville?

This was Nancy Sherwood. This was the girl with whom I had walked hand in hand when the world had been much younger. This was the girl I had thought of this very afternoon as I'd walked along the river, fleeing from myself.

What was wrong, I asked myself.

And: 'Brad, what is wrong?' she asked.

56

'I don't know,' I said. 'Is there something wrong?'

'Don't be defensive. You know there's something wrong. Something wrong with us.'

'I suppose you're right,' I told her. 'It's not the way it should be. It's not the way I had thought it would be, if you came home again.'

I wanted to reach out for her, to take her in my arms – but I knew, even as I wanted it, that it was not the Nancy Sherwood who was sitting here beside me, but that other girl of long ago I wanted in my arms.

We sat in silence for a moment, then she said, 'Let's try again some other time. Let's forget about all this. Some evening I'll dress up my prettiest and we'll go out for dinner and some drinks.'

I turned and put out my hand, but she had opened the door and was halfway out of the car.

'Good night, Brad,' she said, and went running up the walk.

I sat and listened to her running, up the walk and across the porch. I heard the front door close and I kept on sitting there, with the echo of her running still sounding in my brain.

5

I TOLD myself that I was going home. I told myself that I would not go near the office or the phone that was waiting on the desk until I'd had some time to think. For even if I went and picked up the phone and one of the voices answered, what would I have to tell them? The best that I could do would be to say that I had seen Gerald Sherwood and had the money, but that I'd have to know more about what the situation was before I took their job. And that wasn't good enough, I told myself; that would be talking off the cuff and it would gain me nothing.

And then I remembered that early in the morning I'd be

going fishing with Alf Peterson and I told myself, entirely without logic, that in the morning there'd be no time to go down to the office.

I don't suppose it would have made any difference if I'd had that fishing date or not. I don't suppose it would have made any difference, no matter what I told myself. For even as I swore that I was going home, I knew, without much question, that I'd wind up at the office.

Main Street was quiet. Most of the stores were closed and only a few cars were parked along the kerb. A bunch of farm boys, in for a round of beers, were standing in front of the Happy Hollow tavern.

I parked the car in front of the office and got out. Inside I didn't even bother to turn on the light. Some light was shining through the window from a street light at the intersection and the office wasn't dark.

I strode across the office to the desk, with my hand already reaching out to pick up the phone – and there wasn't any phone.

I stopped beside the desk and stared at the top of it, not believing. I bent over and, with the flat of my hand, swept back and forth across the desk, as if I imagined that the phone had somehow become invisible and while I couldn't see it I could locate it by the sense of touch. But it wasn't that, exactly. It was simply, I guess, that I could not believe my eyes.

I straightened up from feeling along the desk top and stood rigid in the room, while an icy-footed little creature prowled up and down my spine. Finally I turned my head, slowly, carefully, looking at the corners of the office, half expecting to find some dark shadow crouching there and waiting. But there wasn't anything. Nothing had been changed. The place was exactly as I had left it, except there wasn't any phone.

Turning on the light, I searched the office. I looked in all the corners, I looked beneath the desk, I ransacked the desk drawers and went through the filing cabinet.

There wasn't any phone.

For the first time, I felt the touch of panic. Someone, I

thought, had found the phone. Someone had managed to break in, to unlock the door somehow, and had stolen it. Although, when I thought of it, that didn't make much sense. There was nothing about the phone that would have attracted anyone's attention. Of course it had no dial and it was not connected, but looking through the window, that would not have been apparent.

More than likely, I told myself, whoever had put it on the desk had come back and taken it. Perhaps it meant that the ones who had talked to me had reconsidered and had decided I was not the man they wanted. They had taken back the phone and, with it, the offer of the job.

And if that were the case, there was only one thing I could do – forget about the job and take back the fifteen hundred. Although that, I knew, would be rather hard to do. I needed that fifteen hundred so bad I could taste it.

Back in the car, I sat for a moment before starting the motor, wondering what I should do next. And there didn't seem to be anything to do, so I started the engine and drove slowly up the street.

Tomorrow morning, I told myself, I'd pick up Alf Peterson and we'd have our week of fishing. It would be good, I thought, to have old Alf to talk with. We'd have a lot to talk about – his crazy job down in Mississippi and my adventure with the phone.

And maybe, when he left, I'd be going with him. It would be good, I thought, to get away from Millville.

I pulled the car into the driveway and left it standing there. Before I went to bed, I'd want to get the camping and the fishing gear together and packed into the car against an early start, come morning. The garage was small and it would be easier to do the packing with the car standing in the driveway.

I got out and stood beside the car. The house was a hunched shadow in the moonlight and past one corner of it I could see the moonlit glitter of an unbroken pane or two in the sagging greenhouse. I could just see the tip of the elm tree, the seedling elm that stood at one corner of the greenhouse. I remembered the day I had been about to pull the seedling out, when it was no more that a sprout, and how my dad had stopped me, telling me that a tree had as much right to live as anybody else. That's exactly what he'd said – as much as anybody else. He'd been a wonderful man, I thought; he believed, deep inside his heart, that flowers and trees were people.

And once again I smelled the faint perfume of the purple flowers that grew in profusion all about the greenhouse – the same perfume I'd smelled at the foot of the Sherwood porch. But this time there was no circle of enchantment.

I walked around the house and as I approached the kitchen door I saw there was a light inside. More than likely, I thought, I had forgotten it, although I could not remember that I had turned it on.

The door was open, too, and I could remember shutting it and pushing on it with my hand to make sure the latch had caught before I'd gone out to the car.

Perhaps, I thought, there was someone in there waiting for me, or someone had been here and left and the place was looted, although there was, God knows, little enough to loot. It could be kids, I thought – some of these mixed-up kids would do anything for kicks.

I went through the door fast and then came to a sudden halt in the middle of the kitchen. There was someone there, all right; there was someone waiting.

Stiffy Grant sat in a kitchen chair and he was doubled over, with his arms wrapped about his middle, and rocking slowly, from side to side, as if he were in pain.

'Stiffy!' I shouted, and Stiffy moaned at me.

Drunk again, I thought. Stiffer than a goat and sick, although how in the world he could have gotten drunk on the dollar I had given him was more than I could figure. Maybe, I thought, he had made another touch or two, waiting to start drinking until he had cash enough to really hang one on.

'Stiffy,' I said sharply, 'what the hell's the matter?'

I was plenty sore at him. He could get plastered as often as he liked and it was all right with me, but he had no right to come busting in on me.

Stiffy moaned again, then he fell out of the chair and sprawled untidily on the floor. Something that clattered and jangled flew out of the pocket of his ragged jacket and skidded across the worn-out linoleum.

I got down on my knees and tugged and hauled at him and got him straightened out. I turned him over on his back. His face was splotched and puffy and his breath was jerky, but there was no smell of liquor. I bent close over him in an effort to make certain, and there was no smell of booze.

'Brad?' he mumbled. 'Is that you, Brad?'

'Yes,' I told him. 'You can take it easy now. I'll take care of you.'

'It's getting close,' he whispered. 'The time is coming close.'

'What is getting close?'

But he couldn't answer. He had a wheezing fit. He worked his jaws, but no words came out. They tried to come, but he choked and strangled on them.

I left him and ran into the living-room and turned on the light beside the telephone. I pawed, all fumble-fingered, through the directory, to find Doc Fabian's number. I found it and dialled and waited while the phone rang on and on. I hoped to God that Doc was home and not out on a call somewhere. For when Doc was gone, you couldn't count on Mrs Fabian answering. She was all crippled up with arthritis and half the time couldn't get around. Doc always tried to have someone there to watch after her and to take the calls when he went out, but there were times when he couldn't get anyone to stay. Old Mrs Fabian was hard to get along with and no one liked to stay.

When Doc answered, I felt a great surge of relief.

'Doc,' I said. 'Stiffy Grant is here at my place and there's something wrong with him.'

'Drunk, perhaps,' said Doc.

'No, he isn't drunk. I came home and found him sitting in the kitchen. He's all twisted up and babbling.'

'Babbling about what?'

'I don't know,' I said. 'Just babbling – when he can talk, that is.'

'All right,' said Doc. 'I'll be right over.'

That's one thing about Doc. You can count on him. At any time of day or night, in any kind of weather.

I went back to the kitchen. Stiffy had rolled over on his side and was clutching at his belly and breathing hard. I left him where he was. Doc would be here soon and there wasn't much that I could do for Stiffy except to try to make him comfortable, and maybe, I told myself, he might be more comfortable lying on his side than turned over on his back.

I picked up the object that had fallen out of Stiffy's coat. It was a key ring, with half a dozen keys. I couldn't imagine what need Stiffy might have for half a dozen keys. More than likely he just carried them around for some smug feeling of importance they might give to him.

I put them on the counter top and went back and squatted down alongside Stiffy. 'I called Doc,' I told him. 'He'll be here right away.'

He seemed to hear me. He wheezed and sputtered for a while, then he said in a broken whisper: 'I can't help no more. You are all alone.' It didn't go as smooth as that. His words were broken up.

'What are you talking about?' I asked him, as gently as I could. 'Tell me what it is.'

'The bomb,' he said. 'The bomb. They'll want to use the bomb. You must stop them, boy.'

I had told Doc that he was babbling and now I knew I had been right.

I headed for the front door to see if Doc might be in sight and when I got there he was coming up the walk.

Doc went ahead of me into the kitchen and stood for a moment, looking down at Stiffy. Then he set down his bag and hunkered down and rolled Stiffy on his back.

'How are you, Stiffy?' he demanded.

Stiffy didn't answer.

'He's out cold,' said Doc.

'He talked to me just before you came in.'

'Say anything?'

I shook my head. 'Just nonsense.'

Doc hauled a stethoscope out of his pocket and listened to Stiffy's chest. He rolled Stiffy's eyelids back and beamed a light into his eyes. Then he got slowly to his feet.

'What's the matter with him?' I asked.

'He's in shock,' said Doc. 'I don't know what's the matter. We'd better get him into the hospital over at Elmore and have a decent look at him.'

He turned wearily and headed for the living-room.

'You got a phone in here?' he asked.

'Over in the corner. Right beside the light.'

'I'll call Hiram,' he said. 'He'll drive us into Elmore. We'll put Stiffy in the back seat and I'll ride along and keep an eye on him.'

He turned in the doorway. 'You got a couple of blankets you could let us have?'

'I think I can find some.'

He nodded at Stiffy. 'We ought to keep him warm.'

I went to get the blankets. When I came back with them, Doc was in the kitchen. Between the two of us, we got Stiffy all wrapped up. He was limp as a kitten and his face was streaked with perspiration.

'Damn wonder,' said Doc, 'how he keeps alive, living the way he does, in that shack stuck out beside the swamp. He drinks anything and everything he can get his hands on and he pays no attention to his food. Eats any kind of slop he can throw together easy. And I doubt he's had an honest bath in the last ten years. It does beat hell,' he said with sudden anger, 'how little care some people ever think to give their bodies.'

'Where did he come from?' I asked. 'I always figured he wasn't a native of this place. But he's been here as long as I remember.'

'Drifted in,' said Doc, 'some thirty years ago, maybe more than that. A fairly young man then. Did some odd jobs here and there and just sort of settled down. No one paid attention to him. They figured, I guess, that he had drifted in and would drift out again. But then, all at once, he seemed to have become a fixture in the village. I would imagine that he just liked the place and decided to stay on. Or maybe lacked the gumption to move on.'

We sat in silence for a while.

'Why do you suppose he came barging in on you?' asked Doc.

'I wouldn't know,' I said. 'We always got along. We'd go fishing now and then. Maybe he was just walking past when he started to get sick.'

'Maybe so,' said Doc.

The doorbell rang and I went and let Hiram Martin in. Hiram was a big man. His face was mean and he kept the constable's badge pinned to his coat lapel so polished that it shone.

'Where is he?' he asked.

'Out in the kitchen,' I said. 'Doc is sitting with him.'

It was very plain that Hiram did not take to being drafted into the job of driving Stiffy in to Elmore.

He strode into the kitchen and stood looking down at the swathed figure on the floor.

'Drunk?' he asked.

'No,' said Doc. 'He's sick.'

'Well, OK,' said Hiram, 'the car is out in front and I left the engine running. Let's heave him in and be on our way.'

The three of us carried Stiffy out to the car and propped him in the back seat.

I stood on the walk and watched the car go down the street and I wondered how Stiffy would feel about it when he woke up and found that he was in a hospital. I rather imagined that he might not care for it.

I felt bad about Doc. He wasn't a young man any longer and more than likely he'd had a busy day, and yet he took it for granted that he should ride with Stiffy.

Once in the house again, I went into the kitchen and got

out the coffee and went to the sink to fill the coffee pot, and there, lying on the counter top, was the bunch of keys I had picked up off the floor. I picked them up again and had a closer look at them. There were two of them that looked like padlock keys and there was a car key and what looked like a key to a safety deposit box and two others that might have been any kind of keys. I shuffled them around, scarcely seeing them, wondering about that car key and that other one which might have been for a safety box. Stiffy didn't have a car and it was a good, safe bet that he had nothing for which he'd ever need a safety deposit box.

The time is getting close, he'd told me, and they'll want to use the bomb. I had told Doc that it was babbling, but now, remembering back, I was not so sure it was. He had wheezed out the words and he'd worked to get them out. They had been conscious words, words he had managed with some difficulty. They were words that he had meant to say and had laboured to get said. They had not been the easy flow of words that one mouths when babbling. But they had not been enough. He had not had the strength or time. The few words that he'd managed made no particular sense.

There was a place where I might be able to get some further information that might piece out the words, but I shrank from going there. Stiffy Grant had been a friend of mine for many years, ever since that day he'd gone fishing with a boy of ten and had sat beside him on the river bank all the afternoon, spinning wondrous tales. As I recalled it, standing in the kitchen, we had caught some fish, but the fish were not important. What had been important then, what was still important, was that a grown man had the sort of understanding to treat a ten-year-old as an equal human being. On that day, in those few hours of an afternoon, I had grown a lot. While we sat on that river bank I had been as big as he was, and that was the first time such a thing had ever happened to me.

There was something that I had to do and yet I shrank from doing it – and still, I told myself, Stiffy might not mind. He had tried to tell me something and he had failed because he didn't have the strength. Certainly he would understand that if I used these keys to get into his shack, that I had not done it in a spirit of maliciousness, or of idle curiosity, but to try to attain that knowledge he had tried to share with me.

No one had ever been in Stiffy's shack. He had built it through the years, out at the edge of town, beside a swamp in the corner of Jack Dickson's pasture, and he had built it out of lumber he had picked up and out of flattened tin cans and all manner of odd junk he had run across. At first it had been little more than a lean-to, a shelter from the wind and rain. But bit by bit, year by year, he had added to it until it was a structure of wondrous shape and angles, but it was a home.

I made up my mind and gave the keys a final toss and caught them and put them in my pocket. Then I went out of the house and got into the car.

6

A THIN FOG of ghostly white lay just above the surface of the swamp and curled about the foot of the tiny knoll on which Stiffy's shack was set. Across the stretch of whiteness loomed a shadowed mass, the dark shape of a wooded island that rose out of the marsh.

I stopped the car and got out of it and as I did, my nostrils caught the rank odour of the swamp, the scent of old and musty things, the smell of rotting vegetation, and ochre-coloured water. It was not particularly offensive and yet there was about it an uncleanliness that set one's skin to crawling. Perhaps, I told myself, a man got used to it. More than likely Stiffy had lived with it so long that he never noticed it.

I glanced back toward the village and through the darkness of the nightmare trees I could catch an occasional glimpse of a swaying street lamp. No one, I was certain, could have seen me come here. I'd switched off the headlights before I turned off the highway and had crawled along the twisting cart track that led in to the shack with no more than a sickly moonlight to help me on my way.

Like a thief in the night, I thought. And that, of course, was what I was – except I had no intent of stealing.

I walked up the path that led to the crazy door fashioned out of uneven slabs of salvaged lumber, closed by a metal hasp guarded by a heavy padlock. I tried one of the padlock keys and it fitted and the lock snicked back. I pushed on the door and it creaked open.

I pulled the flashlight I had taken from the glove compartment of the car out of my pocket and thumbed its switch. The fan of light thrust out, spearing through the doorway. There was a table and three chairs, a stove against one wall, a bed against another.

The room was clean. There was a wooden floor, covered by scraps of linoleum carefully patched together. The linoleum was so thoroughly scrubbed that it fairly shone. The walls had been plastered and then neatly papered with scraps of wall-paper, and with a complete and cynical disregard for any colour scheme.

I moved farther into the room, swinging the light slowly back and forth. At first it had been the big things I had seen – the stove, the table and the chairs, the bed. But now I began to become aware of the other things and the little things.

And one of these smaller things, which I should have seen at once, but hadn't, was the telephone that stood on the table.

I shone the light on it and spent long seconds making sure of what I'd known to start with – for it was apparent at a glance that the phone was without a dial and had no connection cord. And it would have done no good if it had had a cord, for no telephone line had ever been run to this shack beside the swamp.

Three of them, I thought – three of them I knew of. The one that had been in my office and another in Gerald Sherwood's study and now this one in the shack of the village bum.

Although, I told myself, not quite so much a bum as the

67

village might believe. Not the dirty slob most people thought he was. For the floor was scrubbed and the walls were papered and everything was neat.

Me and Gerald Sherwood and Stiffy Grant – what kind of common bond could there be among us? And how many of these dialless phones could there be in Millville; for how many others of us did that unknown bond exist?

I moved the light and it crept across the bed with its patterned quilt – not rumpled, not messed up, and very neatly made. Across the bed and to another table that stood beyond the bed. Underneath the table were two cartons. One of them was plain, without any lettering, and the other was a whisky case with the name of an excellent brand of Scotch writ large across its face.

I walked over to the table and pulled the whisky case out from underneath it. And in it was the last thing in the world I had expected. It was not an emptied carton packed with personal belongings, not a box of junk, but a case of whisky.

Unbelieving, I lifted out a bottle and another and another, all of them still sealed. I put them back in the case again and lowered myself carefully to the floor, squatting on my heels. I felt the laughter deep inside of me, trying to break out – and yet it was, when one came to think of it, not a laughing matter.

This very afternoon Stiffy had touched me for a dollar because, he'd said, he'd not had a drink all day. And all the time there had been this case of whisky, pushed underneath the table.

Were all the outward aspects of the village bum no more than camouflage? The broken, dirty nails; the rumpled, thread-bare clothing; the unshaven face and the unwashed neck; the begging of money for a drink; the seeking of dirty little piddling jobs to earn the price of food – was this all a sham?

And if it were a masquerade, what purpose could it serve?

I pushed the case back underneath the table and pulled out the other carton. And this one wasn't whisky and neither was it junk. It was telephones.

68

I hunkered, staring at them, and it now was crystal clear how that telephone had gotten on my desk. Stiffy had put it there and then had waited for me, propped against the building. Perhaps he had seen me coming down the street as he came out of the office and had done the one thing that would seem entirely natural to explain his waiting there. Or it might equally well have been just plain bravado. And all the time he has been laughing at me deep inside himself.

But that must be wrong, I told myself. Stiffy never would have laughed at me. We were old and trusted friends and he'd never laugh at me, he would never do anything to fool me. This was a serious business, too serious for any laughing to be done.

If Stiffy had put the phone there, had he also been the one who had come back and taken it? Could that have been the reason he had come to my place – to explain to me why the phone was gone?

Thinking of it, it didn't seem too likely.

But if it had not been Stiffy, then there was someone else involved.

There was no need to lift out the phones, for I knew exactly what I'd find. But I did lift them out and I wasn't wrong. They had no dials and no connection cords.

I got to my feet and for a moment stood uncertain, staring at the phone standing on the table, then, making up my mind, strode to the table and lifted the receiver.

'Hello,' said the voice of the businessman. 'What have you to report?'

'This isn't Stiffy,' I said. 'Stiffy is in a hospital. He was taken sick.'

There was a moment's hesitation, then the voice said, 'Oh, yes, it's Mr Bradshaw Carter, isn't it. So nice that you could call.'

'I found the phones,' I said. 'Here in Stiffy's shack. And the phone in my office has somehow disappeared. And I saw Gerald Sherwood. I think perhaps, my friend, it's time that you explained.'

'Of course,' the voice said. 'You, I suppose, have decided that you will represent us.'

'Now,' I said, 'just a minute, there. Not until I know about it. Not until I've had a chance to give it some consideration.'

'I tell you what,' the voice said, 'you consider it and then you call us back. What was this you were saying about Stiffy being taken somewhere?'

'A hospital,' I said. 'He was taken sick.'

'But he should have called us,' the voice said, aghast. 'We would have fixed him up. He knew good and well . . .'

'He maybe didn't have the time. I found him . . .'

'Where was this place you say that he was taken?'

'Elmore. To the hospital at . . .'

'Elmore. Of course. We know where Elmore is.'

'And Greenbriar, too, perhaps.' I hadn't meant to say it; I hadn't even thought it. It just popped into my mind, a sudden, unconscious linking of what was happening here and the project that Alf had talked to me about.

'Greenbriar? Why, certainly. Down in Mississippi. A town very much like Millville. And you will let us know? When you have decided, you will let us know?'

'I'll let you know,' I promised.

'And thank you very much, sir. We shall be looking forward to your association with us.'

And then the line went dead.

Greenbriar, I thought. It was not only Millville. It might be the entire world. What the hell, I wondered, could be going on?

I'd talk to Alf about it. I'd go home and phone him now. Or I could drive out and see him. He'd probably be in bed, but I would get him up. I'd take along a bottle and we'd have a drink or two.

I picked up the phone and tucked it underneath my arm and went outside. I closed the door behind me. I snapped the padlock shut and then went to the car. I opened the back door and put the telephone on the floor and covered it with a rain-coat that was folded on the seat. It was a silly thing to do, but

I felt a little better with the phone tucked away and hidden.

I got behind the wheel and sat for a moment, thinking. Perhaps, I told myself, it would be better if I didn't rush into things too fast. I would see Alf tomorrow and we'd have a lot of time to talk, an entire week to talk if we needed it. And that way I'd have some time to try to think the situation out.

It was late and I had to pack the camping stuff and the fishing tackle in the car and I should try to get some sleep.

Be sensible, I told myself. Take a little time. Try to think it out.

It was good advice. Good for someone else. Good even for myself at another time and under other circumstances. I should not have taken it, however. I should have gone out to Johnny's Motor Court and pounded on Alf's door. Perhaps then things would have worked out differently. But you can't be sure. You never can be sure.

But, anyhow, I did go home and I did pack the camping stuff and the fishing gear into the car and had a few hours of sleep (I wonder now how I ever got to sleep), then was routed out by the alarm clock early in the morning.

And before I could pick up Alf I hit the barrier.

7

'HI, THERE,' said the naked scarecrow, with jaunty happiness. He counted on his fingers and slobbered as he counted.

And there was no mistaking him. He came clear through the years. The same placid, vacant face, with its frog-like mouth and its misty eyes. It had been ten years since I had seen him last, since anyone had seen him, and yet he seemed only slightly older than he had been then. His hair was long, hanging down his back, but he had no whiskers. He had a heavy growth of fuzz, but he'd never sprouted whiskers. He was entirely naked except for the outrageous hat. And he was the same old Tupper. He hadn't changed a bit. I'd have known him anywhere.

He quit his finger-counting and sucked in his slobber. He reached up and took off his hat and held it out so that I could see it better.

'Made it myself,' he told me, with a wealth of pride.

'It's very fine,' I said.

He could have waited, I told myself. No matter where he'd come from, he could have waited for a while. Millville had enough trouble at this particular moment without having to contend once again with the likes of Tupper Tyler.

'Your papa,' Tupper said. 'Where is your papa, Brad? There is something I have to tell him.'

And that voice, I thought. How could I ever have mistaken it? And how could I ever have forgotten that Tupper was, of all things, an accomplished mimic? He could be any bird he wanted and he could be a dog or cat and the kids used to gather round him, making fun of him, while he put on a mimic show of a dog-and-cat fight or of two neighbours quarrelling.

'Your papa!' Tupper said.

'We'd better get inside,' I told him. 'I'll get some clothes and you climb into them. You can't go on running around naked.'

He nodded vaguely. 'Flowers,' he said. 'Lots of pretty flowers.'

He spread his arms wide to show me how many flowers there were. 'Acres and acres,' he said. 'There is no end to them. They just keep on forever. Every last one purple. And they are so pretty and they smell so sweet and they are so good to me.'

His chin was covered with a dampness from his talking and he wiped it with a claw-like hand. He wiped his hand upon a thigh.

I got him by the elbow and got him turned around, headed for the house.

'But your papa,' he protested. 'I want to tell your papa all about the flowers.'

'Later on,' I said.

I got him on the porch and thrust him through the door and followed after him. I felt easier. Tupper was no decent sight for the streets of Millville. And I had had, for a while, about all that I could stand. Old Stiffy Grant laid out in my kitchen just the night before and now along comes Tupper, without a stitch upon him. Eccentrics were all right, and in a little town you get a lot of them, but there came a time when they ran a little thin.

I still held tightly to his elbow and marched him to the bedroom.

'You stand right there,' I told him.

He stood right there, not moving, gaping at the room with his vacant stare.

I found a shirt and a pair of trousers. I got out a pair of shoes and, after looking at his feet, put them back again. They were, I knew, way too small. Tupper's feet were all spraddled out and flattened. He'd probably been going without shoes for years.

I held out the trousers and the shirt.

'You get into these,' I said. 'And once you have them on, stay here. Don't stir out of this room.'

He didn't answer and he didn't take the clothes. He'd fallen once again to counting his fingers.

And now, for the first time, I had a chance to wonder where he'd been. How could a man drop out of sight, without a trace, stay lost for ten years, and then pop up again, out of that same thin air into which he had disappeared?

It had been my first year in high school that Tupper had turned up missing and I remembered it most vividly because for a week all of the boys had been released from school to join the hunt for him. We had combed miles of fields and woodlands, walking slowly in line an arm's length from one another, and finally we had been looking for a body rather than a man. The state police had dragged the river and several nearby ponds. The sheriff and a posse of townspeople had worked carefully through the swamp below Stiffy's shack,

73

prodding with long poles. They had found innumerable logs and a couple of wash boilers that someone had thrown away and on the farther edge of the swamp an anciently dead dog. But no one had found Tupper.

'Here,' I told him, 'take these clothes and get into them.'

Tupper finished with his fingers and politely wiped his chin.

'I must be getting back,' he said. 'The flowers can't wait too long.'

He reached out a hand and took the clothes from me.

'My other ones wore out,' he said. 'They just dropped off of me.'

'I saw your mother just half an hour ago,' I said. 'She was looking for you.'

It was a risky thing to say, for Tupper was the kind of jerk that you handled with kid gloves. But I took the calculated risk and said it, for I thought that maybe it would jolt some sense into him.

'Oh,' he said lightly, 'she's always hunting for me. She thinks I ain't big enough to look out for myself.'

As if he'd never been away. As if ten years hadn't passed. As if he'd stepped out of his mother's house no more than an hour ago. As if time had no meaning for him – and perhaps it hadn't.

'Put on the clothes,' I told him. 'I'll be right back.'

I went out into the living-room and picked up the phone. I dialled Doc Fabian's number. The busy signal blurped at me.

I put the receiver back and tried to think of someone else to call. I could call Hiram Martin. Perhaps he was the one to call. But I hesitated. Doc was the man to handle this; he knew how to handle people. All that Hiram knew was how to push them around.

I dialled Doc once more and still got the busy signal.

I slammed down the receiver and hurried toward the bedroom. I couldn't leave Tupper alone too long. God knows what he might do.

But I already had waited too long. I never should have left him.

74

The bedroom was empty. The window was open and the screen was broken out and there was no Tupper.

I rushed across the room and leaned out of the window and there was no sign of him.

Blind panic hit me straight between the eyes. I don't know why it did. Certainly, at that moment, Tupper's escaping from the bedroom was not all that important. But it seemed to be important and I knew, without knowing why, that I must run him down and bring him back, that I must not let him out of my sight again.

Without thinking, I stepped back from the window and took a running jump, diving through the opening. I landed on one shoulder and rolled, then jumped up to my feet.

Tupper was not in sight, but now I saw where he had gone. His dewy tracks led across the grass, back around the house and down to the old greenhouse. He had waded out into the patch of purple flowers that covered the old abandoned area where once my father and, later, I myself had tended rows of flowers and other plants. He had waded out some twenty feet or so into the mass of flowers. His trail was clearly shown, for the plants had been brushed over and had not had time to straighten yet, and they were a darker hue where the dew had been knocked off them.

The trail went twenty feet and stopped. All about it and ahead of it the purple flowers stood straight, silvered by the tiny dewdrops.

There was no other trail. Tupper had not backed out along the trail and then gone another way. There was just the single trail that headed straight into the patch of purple flowers and ended. As if the man might have taken wing and flown away, or dropped straight into the ground.

But no matter where he was, I thought, no matter what kind of tricks he played, he couldn't leave the village. For the village was closed in by some sort of barrier that ran all the way around it.

A wailing sound exploded and filled the universe, a shrieking, terrible sound that reverberated and beat against itself. It came so suddenly that it made me jump and stiffen. The sound seemed to fill the world and to clog the sky and it didn't stop, but kept on and on.

Almost at once I knew what it was, but my body still stayed tense for long seconds and my mind was curdled with a nameless fear. For there had been too much happening in too short a time and this metallic yammering had been the trigger that had slammed it all together and made the world almost unendurable.

Gradually I relaxed and started for the house.

And still the sound kept on, the frantic, full-throated wailing of the siren down at the village hall.

8

BY THE TIME I got up to the house there were people running in the street – a wild-eyed, frantic running with a sense of panic in it, all of them heading toward that screeching maelstrom of sound, as if the siren were the monstrous tootling of a latter-day Pied Piper and they were the rats which must not be left behind.

There was old Pappy Andrews, hobbling along, cracking his cane on the surface of the street with unaccustomed vigour and the wind blowing his long chin whiskers up into his face. There was Grandma Jones, who had her sunbonnet socked upon her head, but had forgotten to tie the strings, which floated and bobbed across her shoulders as she stumped along with grim determination. She was the only woman in all of Millville (perhaps in all the world) who still owned a sunbonnet and she took a malicious pride in wearing it, as if the very fact of appearing with it upon her head was a somehow commendable flaunting of her fuddy-duddyness. And after her came Pastor Silas Middleton, with a prissy look of distaste fastened on his face, but going just the same. An old jalopy clattered past with that crazy Johnson kid crouched behind the wheel and a bunch of his hoodlum pals yelling and cat-calling, glad of any kind of excitement and willing to contribute to it. And a lot of others, including a slew of kids and dogs.

I opened the gate and stepped into the street. But I didn't run like all the rest of them, for I knew what it was all about and I was all weighed down with a lot of things that no one knew as yet. Especially about Tupper Tyler and what Tupper might have had to do with what was happening. For insane as it might sound, I had a sneaky sort of hunch that Tupper had somehow had a hand in it and had made a mess of things.

I tried to think, but the things I wanted to think about were too big to get into mind and there were no mental handholds on them for my mind to grab a-hold of. So I didn't hear the car when it came sneaking up beside me. The first thing I heard was the click of the door as it was coming open.

I swung around and Nancy Sherwood was there behind the wheel.

'Come on, Brad,' she yelled, to make herself heard above the siren noise.

I jumped in and closed the door and the car slid up the street. It was a big and powerful thing. The top was down and if felt funny to be riding in a car that didn't have a top.

The siren stopped. One moment the world had been filled to bursting with its brazen howling and then the howling stopped and for a little moment there was the feeble keening as the siren died. Then the silence came, and in the weight and mass of silence a little blot of howling still stayed within one's mind, as if the howling had not gone, but had merely moved away.

One felt naked in the coldness of the silence and there was the absurd feeling that in the noise there had been purpose and direction. And that now, with the howling gone, there was no purpose or direction.

'This is a nice car you have,' I said, not knowing what to say, but knowing that I should say something.

'Father gave it to me,' she said, 'on my last birthday.'

It moved along and you couldn't hear the motor. All you could hear was the faint rumble of the wheels turning on the roadbed.

'Brad,' she asked, 'what's going on? Someone told me that your car was wrecked and there was no sign of you. What has your car to do with the siren blowing? And there were a lot of cars down on the road . . .'

I told her. 'There's a fence of some sort built around the town.'

'Who would build a fence?'

'It's not that kind of fence. You can't see this fence.'

We had gotten close to Main Street and there were more people. They were walking on the sidewalk and walking on the lawns and walking in the road. Nancy slowed the car to crawling.

'You said there was a fence.'

'There is a fence. An empty car can get through it, but it will stop a man. I have a hunch it will stop all life. It's the kind of fence you'd expect in fairyland.'

'Brad,' she said, 'you know there is no fairyland.'

'An hour ago I knew,' I said. 'I don't know any more.'

We came out on Main Street and a big crowd was standing out in front of the village hall and more coming all the time. George Walker, the butcher at the Red Owl store, was running down the street, with his white apron tucked up into his belt and his white cap set askew upon his head. Norma Shepard, the receptionist at Doc Fabian's office, was standing on a box out on the sidewalk so that she could see what was going on, and Butch Ormsby, the owner of the service station just across the street from the hall, was standing at the kerb, wiping and wiping at his greasy hands with a ball of waste, as if he knew he would never get them clean, but was bound to keep on trying.

Nancy pulled the car up into the approach to the filling station and shut off the motor.

A man came across the concrete apron and stopped beside

78

the car. He leaned down and rested his folded arms on the top part of the door.

'How are things going, pal?' he asked.

I looked at him for a moment, not remembering him at first, then suddenly remembering. He must have seen that I remembered him.

'Yeah,' he said, 'the guy who smacked your car.'

He straightened and reached out his hand. 'Name is Gabriel Thomas,' he said. 'You just call me Gabe. We never got around to trading names down there.'

I shook his hand and told him who I was, then introduced Nancy.

'Mr Thomas,' Nancy said, 'I heard about the accident. Brad won't talk about it.'

'Well,' said Gabe, 'it was a strange thing, miss. There was nothing there and you ran into it and it stopped you as if it had been a wall of stone. And even when it was stopping you, you could see right through it.'

'Did you phone your company?' I asked.

'Yeah. Sure I phoned them. But no one will believe me. They think I'm drunk. They think I am so drunk I wouldn't dare to drive and I'm holing up somewhere. They think I dreamed up this crazy story as a cover-up.'

'Did they say so, Mr Thomas?'

'No, miss,' he said, 'but I know how them jokers think. And the thing that hurts me is that they ever should have thought it. I ain't a drinking man. And I got a good record. Why, I won driving awards, three years in a row.'

He said to me, 'I don't know what to do. I can't get out of here. There's no way to get out. That barrier is all around the town. I live five hundred miles from here and my wife is all alone. Six kids and the youngest one a baby. I don't know what she'll do. She's used to it, of course, with me off on the road. But never for longer than three or four days, the time it takes for me to make a run. What if I can't get back for two or three weeks, maybe two or three months? What will she do then? There won't be any money coming in and there are the house payments to be made and them six kids to feed.'

'Maybe you won't be here for long,' I said, doing my best to make him feel a little better. 'Maybe someone can get it figured out and do something about it. Maybe it will simply go away. And even if it doesn't, I imagine that your company will keep your salary going. After all, it's not your . . .'

He made an insulting, disgusted noise. 'Not that bunch,' he said. 'Not that gang of chisellers.'

'It's too soon to start worrying,' I told him. 'We don't know what has happened and until we do . . .'

'I guess you're right,' he said. 'Of course, I'm not the only one. I been talking to a lot of people and I'm not the only one. I was talking to a guy down in front of the barber shop just a while ago and his wife is in the hospital over at – what's the name of that town?'

'Elmore,' Nancy said.

'Yes, that was it. She's in the hospital at Elmore and he is out of his mind, afraid he can't go to visit her. Kept saying over and over that maybe it would be all right in a little while, that he could get out of town. Sounds like she may be pretty bad off and he goes over every day. She'll be expecting him, he says, and maybe she won't understand why he doesn't come. Talked as if a good part of the time she's not in her right mind. And there was this other fellow. His family is off on a vacation, out to Yellowstone, and he was expecting them to get home today. Says they'll be all tired out from travelling and now they can't reach their home after they have travelled all those miles to get back into it again. Was expecting them home early in the afternoon. He's planning to go out on the road and wait for them at the edge of the barrier. Not that it will do any good, meeting them out there, but he said it was the only thing he could do. And then there are a lot of people who work out of town and now they can't get to their jobs, and there was someone telling me about a girl here in town who was going to marry a fellow from a place called Coon Valley and they were going to get married tomorrow and now, of course, they can't.'

'You must have talked to a lot of people,' I said.

'Hush,' said Nancy.

Across the street Mayor Higgy Morris was standing on the top step of the flight of stairs that led up to the village hall and he was waving his arms to get the people quiet.

'Fellow citizens,' yelled Higgy in that phony political voice that makes you sick at heart. 'Fellow citizens, if you'll just be quiet.'

Someone yelled, 'You tell 'em Higgy!' There was a wave of laughter, but it was a nervous laugh.

'Friends,' said Higgy, 'we may be in a lot of trouble. You probably have heard about it. I don't know what you heard, for there are a lot of stories. I don't know, myself, everything that's happened.

'I'm sorry for having to use the siren to call you all together, but it seemed the quickest way.'

'Ah, hell,' yelled someone. 'Get on with it, Higgy.'

No one laughed this time.

'Well, all right,' said Higgy. 'I'll get on with it. I don't know quite how to say this, but we've been cut off. There is some sort of fence around us that won't let anybody in or anybody out. Don't ask me what it is or how it got there. I have no idea. I don't think, right now, that anybody knows. There may be nothing for us to get disturbed about. It may be only temporary; it may go away.

'What I do want to say is that we should stay calm. We're all in this together and we got to work together to get out of it. Right now we haven't got anything to be afraid of. We are only cut off in the sense that we can't go anywhere. But we are still in touch with the outside world. Our telephones are working and so are the gas and electric lines. We have plenty of food to last for ten days, maybe more than that. And if we should run short, we can get more food. Trucks loaded with it, or with anything we need, can be brought up to the barrier and the driver can get out, then the truck can be pulled or pushed through the barrier. It doesn't stop things that are not alive.'

81

'Just a minute, mayor,' someone shouted.

'Yes,' the mayor said, looking around to see who had dared to interrupt him.

'Was that you, Len?' he asked.

'Yes, it was,' said the man.

I could see now that it was Len Streeter, our high school science teacher.

'What did you want?' asked Higgy.

'I suppose you're basing that last statement of yours – about only non-living matter getting through the barrier – on the car that was parked on the Coon Valley road.'

'Why, yes,' said Higgy, condescendingly, 'that is exactly what I was basing the statement on. What do you know about it?'

'Nothing,' Len Streeter told him. 'Nothing about the car itself. But I presume you do intend to go about the investigation of this phenomenon within well restricted bounds of logic.'

'That's right,' said Higgy, sanctimoniously. 'That's exactly what we intend to do.'

And you could tell by the way he said it he had no idea of what Streeter had said or what he was driving at.

'In that case,' said Streeter. 'I might caution you against accepting facts at their first face value. Such as presuming that because there was no human in the car, there was nothing living in it.'

'Well, there wasn't,' Higgy argued. 'The man who had been driving it had left and gone away somewhere.'

'Humans,' said Streeter, patiently, 'aren't the only forms of life. We can't be certain there was no life in that car. In fact, we can be pretty sure there was life of some sort in it. There probably was a fly or two shut up inside of it. There might have been a grasshopper sitting on the hood. It was absolutely certain that the car had in it and about it and upon it many different kinds of micro-organisms. And a micro-organism is a form of life, just the same as we are.'

Higgy stood up on the steps and he was somewhat flustered. He didn't know whether Streeter was making a fool of him or not. Probably never in his life had he heard of such a thing as a micro-organism.

'You know, Higgy,' said a voice I recognized as Doc Fabian's, 'our young friend is right. Of course there would be micro-organisms. Some of the rest of us should have thought of it at once.'

'Well, all right, then,' said Higgy. 'If you say so, Doc. Let's say that Len is right. It don't make any difference, does it?'

'At the moment, no,' said Doc.

'The only point I wanted to make,' said Streeter, 'is that life can't be the entire answer. If we are going to study the situation, we should get a right start at it. We shouldn't begin with a lot of misconceptions.'

'I got a question, mayor,' said someone else. I tried to see who it was, but couldn't.

'Go ahead,' said Higgy, cordially, happy that someone was about to break up this Streeter business.

'Well, it's like this,' said the man. 'I've been working on the highway job south of town. And now I can't get to it and maybe they'll hold the job for me for a day or two, but it isn't reasonable to expect the contractor to hold it very long. He's got a contract he has to meet – a time limit, you know, and he pays a penalty for every day he's late. So he's got to have men to do the job. He can't hold no job open for more than a day or two.'

'I know all that,' said Higgy.

'I ain't the only one,' said the man. 'There are a lot of other fellows who work out of town. I don't know about the rest of them, but I got to have my pay. I ain't got any backlog I can fall back on. What's going to happen to us if we can't get to our jobs and there isn't any pay cheque and no money in the bank?'

'I was coming to that,' said Higgy. 'I know exactly what your situation is. And the situations of a lot of other men.

83

There isn't enough work in a little town like this for everyone who lives here, so a great many of our residents have work outside of town. And I know a lot of you haven't too much money and that you need your pay cheques. We hope this thing clears up soon enough that you can go back and your jobs will still be there.

'But let me tell you this. Let me make a promise. If it doesn't clear up, there aren't any of you going to go hungry. There aren't any of you who are going to be turned out of your homes because you can't make your payments or can't manage to scrape the rent together. There won't nothing happen to you. A lot of people are going to be without jobs because of what has happened, but you'll be taken care of, every one of you. I am going to name a committee that will talk with the merchants and the bank and we'll arrange for a line of credit that will see you through. Anyone who needs a loan or credit can be sure of getting it.'

Higgy looked down at Daniel Willoughby, who was standing a step or two below him.

'Ain't that right, Dan?' he demanded.

'Yes,' said the banker. 'Yes. Sure, it's quite all right. We'll do everything we can.'

But he didn't like it. You could see he didn't. It hurt him to say it was all right. Daniel liked security, good security, for each dollar he put out.

'It's too early yet,' said Higgy, 'to know what has happened to us. By tonight maybe we'll know a whole lot more about it. The main thing is to keep calm and not start going off half-cocked.

'I can't pretend to know what is going to happen. If this barrier stays in place, there'll be some difficulties. But as it stands right now, it's not entirely bad. Up until an hour or so ago, we were just a little village that wasn't too well known. There wasn't, I suppose, much reason that we should have been well known. But now we're getting publicity over the entire world. We're in the newspapers and on the radio and TV. I'd like Joe Evans to come up here and tell you all about it.'

He looked around and spotted Joe in the crowd.

'You folks,' he said, 'make way, won't you, so Joe can come up here.'

The editor climbed the steps and turned around to face the crowd.

'There isn't much to tell so far,' he said. 'I've had calls from most of the wire services and from several newspapers. They all wanted to know what was going on. I told them what I could, but it wasn't much. One of the TV stations over in Elmore is sending a mobile camera unit. The phone was still ringing when I left the house and I suppose there are calls coming into the office, too.

'I think we can expect that the news media will pay a lot of attention to the situation here and there's no question in my mind that the state and federal governments will take a hand in it, and if I understand it rightly, more than likely the scientific community will have a considerable interest, as well.'

The man who had the highway job spoke up again. 'Joe, you think them science fellows can get it figured out?'

'I don't know,' said Joe.

Hiram Martin had pushed his way through the crowd and was crossing the street. He had a purposeful look about him and I wondered what he could be up to.

Someone else was asking a question, but the sight of Hiram had distracted me and I lost the gist of it.

'Brad,' said someone at my elbow.

I looked around.

Hiram was standing there. The trucker, I saw, had left.

'Yes,' I said. 'What is it?'

'If you got the time,' said Hiram. 'I'd like to talk with you.'

'Go ahead,' I said. 'I have the time.'

He jerked his head toward the village hall.

'All right,' I said.

I opened the door and got out.

'I'll wait for you,' said Nancy.

85

Hiram moved off around the crowd, flanking it, heading for the side door of the hall. I followed close behind him.

But I didn't like it.

9

HIRAM'S OFFICE was a little cubbyhole just off the stall where the fire engine and ladder rig were housed. There was barely room in it for two chairs and a desk. On the wall above the desk hung a large and garish calendar with a naked woman on it.

And on the desk stood one of the dialless telephones.

Hiram gestured at it. 'What is that?' he asked.

'It's a telephone,' I said. 'Since when did you get so important that you have two phones?'

'Take another look,' he said.

'It's still a telephone,' I said.

'A closer look,' he told me.

'It's a crazy looking thing. It hasn't any dial.'

'Anything else?'

'No, I guess not. It just doesn't have a dial.'

'And,' said Hiram, 'it has no connection cord.'

'I hadn't noticed that.'

'That's funny,' Hiram said.

'Why funny?' I demanded. 'What the hell is going on? You didn't get me in here just to show me a phone.'

'It's funny,' Hiram said, 'because it was in your office.'

'It couldn't be. Ed Adler came in yesterday and took out my phone. For non-payment of my bill.'

'Sit down, Brad,' he said.

I sat down and he sat down facing me. His face was still pleasant enough, but there was that odd glitter in his eyes – the glitter that in the olden days I'd seen too often in his eyes when he'd cornered me and knew he had me cornered and was about to force me to fight him, in the course of which endeavour he would beat the living Jesus out of me.

'You never saw this phone?' he asked.

I shook my head. 'When I left the office yesterday I had no telephone. Not this one or any other.'

'That's strange,' he said.

'As strange to me as to you,' I told him. 'I don't know what you're getting at. Suppose you try to tell me.'

I knew the lying in the long run would not get me anywhere, but for the moment it was buying me some time. I was pretty sure that right now he couldn't tie me to the telephone.

'All right,' he said, 'I'll tell you. Tom Preston was the man who saw it. He'd sent Ed to take out your phone, and later in the afternoon he was walking past your office and he happened to look in and saw the phone standing on your desk. It made him pretty sore. You can see how it might have made him sore.'

'Yes,' I said. 'Knowing Tom, I presume he would be sore.'

'He'd sent Ed out to get that phone and the first thing he thought of was that you'd talked Ed out of taking it. Or maybe Ed had just sort of failed to drop around and get it. He knew you and Ed were friends.'

'I suppose he was so sore that he broke in and took it.'

'No,' said Hiram, 'he never did break in. He went down to the bank and talked Daniel Willoughby into giving him the key.'

'Without considering,' I said, 'that I was renting the office.'

'But you hadn't paid your rent for three solid months. If you ask me, I'd figure Daniel had the right.'

'In my book,' I told him, 'Tom and Daniel broke into my place and robbed me.'

'I told you. They didn't do any breaking. And Daniel had no part in it. Except giving Tom the extra key. Tom went back alone. Besides, you say you'd never seen this phone, that you never owned it.'

'That's beside the point. No matter what was in my office, he had no right to take it. Whether it was mine or not.

87

How do I know he didn't walk away with some other stuff?'

'You know damn well he didn't,' Hiram told me. 'You said you wanted to hear about this.'

'So go ahead and tell me.'

'Well, Tom got the key and got into your office and he saw right away that it was a different kind of phone. It didn't have a dial and it wasn't connected. So he turned around and started to walk out and before he reached the door, the phone rang.'

'It what?'

'It rang.'

'But it wasn't connected.'

'I know, but anyhow, it rang.'

'So he answered it,' I said, 'and there was Santa Claus.'

'He answered it,' said Hiram, 'and there was Tupper Tyler.'

'Tupper! But Tupper . . .'

'Yeah, I know,' said Hiram. 'Tupper disappeared. Ten years ago or so. But Tom said it was Tupper's voice. He said he couldn't be mistaken.'

'And what did Tupper tell him?'

'Tom said hello and Tupper asked him who he was and Tom told him who he was. Then Tupper said get off this phone, you're not authorized to use it. Then the phone went dead.'

'Look, Hiram, Tom was kidding you.'

'No, he wasn't. He thought someone was kidding him. He thought you and Ed had cooked it up. He thought it was a joke. He thought you were trying to get even with him.'

'But that's crazy,' I protested. 'Even if Ed and I had fixed up a gag like that, how could we have known that Tom would come busting in?'

'I know,' said Hiram.

'You mean you believe all this?'

'You bet I believe it. There's something wrong, something awfully wrong.'

But his tone of voice was defensive. I had him on the run. He had hauled me in to pin me to the wall and it hadn't worked that way and now he was just a little sheepish about the entire matter. But in a little while he'd start getting sore. He was that kind of jerk.

'When did Tom tell you all of this?'

'This morning.'

'Why not last night? If he thought it was so important . . .'

'But I told you. He didn't think it was important. He thought it was a joke. He thought it was you getting back at him. He didn't think it was important until all hell broke loose this morning. After he answered and heard Tupper's voice, he took the phone. He thought that might reverse the joke, you see. He thought you'd gone to a lot of work . . .'

'Yes, I see,' I said. 'But now he thinks that it was really Tupper calling and that the call actually was for me.'

'Well, yes, I'd say so. He took the phone home and a couple of times early that evening he picked up the receiver and the phone was alive, but no one answered. That business about the phone being alive puzzled him. It bothered him a lot. It wasn't tied into any line, you see.'

'And now the two of you want to make some sort of case against me.'

Hiram's face hardened. 'I know you're up to something,' he said. 'I know you went out to Stiffy's shack last night. After Doc and I had taken Stiffy in to Elmore.'

'Yes, I did,' I said. 'I found his keys where they had fallen out of his pocket. So I went out to his place to see if it was locked and everything was all right.'

'You sneaked in,' Hiram said. 'You turned off your lights to go up Stiffy's lane.'

'I didn't turn them off. The electrical circuit shorted. I got them fixed before I left the shack.'

It was pretty weak. But it was the best I could think of fast. Hiram didn't press the point.

'This morning,' he said, 'me and Tom went out to the shack.'

'So it was Tom who was spying on me.'

Hiram grunted. 'He was upset about the phone. He got suspicious of you.'

'And you broke into the shack. You must have. I locked it when I left.'

'Yeah,' said Hiram, 'we broke in. And we found more of them telephones. A whole box full of them.'

'You can quit looking at me like that,' I said. 'I saw no telephones. I didn't snoop around.'

I could see the two of them, Hiram and Tom, roaring out to the shack in full cry, convinced that there existed some sinister plot which they could not understand, but that whatever it might be, both Stiffy and myself were neck-deep in it.

And there was some sort of plot, I told myself, and Stiffy and myself were both entangled in it and I hoped that Stiffy knew what it was all about, for certainly I didn't. The little I knew only made it more confused. And Gerald Sherwood, unless he'd lied to me (and I was inclined to think he hadn't) knew little more about it than I did.

Suddenly I was thankful that Hiram did not know about the phone in Sherwood's study, or all those other phones which must be in the village, in the hands of those persons who had been employed as readers by whoever used the phones for communication.

Although, I told myself, there was little chance that Hiram would ever know about those phones, for the people who had them certainly would hide them most securely and would keep very mum about them once this business of the phones became public knowledge. And I was certain that within a few hours' time the story of the mystery phones would be known to everyone. Neither Hiram nor Tom Preston could keep their big mouths shut.

Who would these other people be, I wondered, the ones who had the phones – and all at once I knew. They would be the down-and-outers, the poor unfortunates, the widows who had been left without savings or insurance, the aged who had not been able to provide for their later years, the failures and the no-goods and the hard-of-luck.

For that was the way it had worked with Sherwood and myself. Sherwood had not been contacted (if that was the word for it) before he faced financial ruin and they (whoever they might be) had not been concerned with me until I was a business failure and willing to admit it. And the man who seemed to have had the most to do with all of it was the village bum.

'Well?' asked the constable.

'You want to know what I know about it?'

'Yes, I do,' said Hiram, 'and if you know what's good for you . . .'

'Hiram,' I told him, 'don't you ever threaten me. Don't you even look as though you meant to threaten me. Because if you do . . .'

Floyd Caldwell stuck his head inside the door.

'It's moving!' he yelled at us. 'The barrier is moving!'

Both Hiram and I jumped to our feet and headed for the door. Outside people were running and yelling and Grandma Jones was standing out in the middle of the street, jumping up and down, with the sunbonnet flapping on her head. With every jump she uttered little shrieks.

I saw Nancy in her car across the street and ran straight for it. She had the motor going and when she saw me, she moved the car out from the kerb, rolling slowly down the street. I put my hands on the back door and vaulted into the back, then clambered up in front. By the time I got there the car had reached the drugstore corner and was picking up some speed. There were a couple of other cars heading out toward the highway, but Nancy cut around them with a burst of speed.

'Do you know what happened?' she asked.

I shook my head. 'Just that the barrier is moving.'

We came to the stop sign that guarded the highway, but Nancy didn't even slow for it. There was no reason that she should, for there was no traffic on the highway. The highway was cut off.

She slewed the car out onto the broad slab of pavement

and there, up ahead of us, the eastbound lane was blocked by a mass of jam-packed cars. And there, as well, was Gabe's truck, its trailer lying in the ditch, with my car smashed underneath it, and its cab half canted in the air. Beyond the truck other cars were tangled in the westbound lane, cars which apparently had crossed the centre strip in an effort to get turned around, in the process getting caught in another minor traffic jam before the barrier had moved.

The barrier was no longer there. You couldn't see, of course, whether it was there or not, but up the road, a quarter mile or so, there was evidence of it.

Up there, a crowd of people was running wildly, fleeing from an invisible force that advanced upon them. And behind the fleeing people a long windrow of piled-up vegetation, including, in places, masses of uprooted trees, marked the edge of the moving barrier. It stretched as far as the eye could see, on either side of the road, and it seemed to have a life of its own, rolling and tossing and slowly creeping forward, the masses of trees tumbling awkwardly on their outstretched roots and branches.

The car rolled up to the traffic jam in the westbound lane and stopped. Nancy turned off the ignition. In the silence one could hear the faint rustling of that strange windrow that moved along the road, a small whisper of sound punctuated now and then by the cracking and the popping of the branches as the uprooted trees toppled in their unseemly tumbling.

I got out of the car and walked around it and started down the road, working my way through the tangle of the cars. As I came clear of them the road stretched out before me and up the road the people still were running – well, not running exactly, not the way they had been. They would run a ways and then stand in little groups and look behind them, at the writhing windrow, then would run a ways and stop to look again. Some of them didn't run at all, but just kept plodding up the road at a steady walk.

It was not only people. There was something else, a strange fluttering in the air, a darting of dark bodies, a cloud of insects and of birds, retreating before this inexorable force that moved like a wraith across the surface of the land.

The land was bare behind the barrier. There was nothing on it except two leafless ⊹trees. And they, I thought – they would be left behind. For they were lifeless things and for them the barrier had no meaning, for it was only life that the barrier rejected. Although, if Len Streeter had been right, then it was not all life, but a certain kind, or a certain size, or a certain condition of life.

But aside from the two dead trees, the ground lay bare. There was no grass upon it, not a single weed, not a bush or tree. All that was green was gone.

I stepped off the roadbed onto the shoulder and knelt down and ran my fingers along the barren ground. It was not only bare; it was ploughed and harrowed, as if some giant agricultural rig had gone over it and made it ready for new seed. The soil, I realized, had been loosened by the uprooting of its mat of vegetation. In all that ground, I knew, no single root existed, no fragment of a root, down to the finest rootlet. The land had been swept clean of everything that grew and all that once had grown here was now a part of that fantastic windrow that was being swept along before the barrier.

Above me a dull rumble of thunder rippled in the sky and rolled along the air. I glanced backward over my shoulder, and saw that the thunderstorm which had been threatening all morning now was close upon us, but it was a ragged storm, with wind-twisted clouds, broken and fragmented, fleeing through the upper emptiness.

'Nancy,' I said, but she did not answer.

I got quickly to my feet and swung around. She had been right behind me when I'd started through the traffic tangle, but now there was no sign of her.

I started back down the road to find her and as I did a blue sedan that was over on the opposite shoulder rolled off down the shoulder and swung out on the pavement – and there, behind the wheel, was Nancy. I knew then how I'd lost her. She had looked among the cars until she had found one that was not blocked by other cars and with the key still in the lock.

The car came up beside me, moving slowly, and I trotted along to match its speed. Through the half-open window came the sound of an excited commentator on the radio. I got the door open and jumped in and slammed the door behind me.

'. . . called out the national guard and had officially informed Washington. The first units will move out in another – no, here is word just now that they have already moved out . . .'

'That,' said Nancy, 'is us he's talking about.'

I reached out and twisted the dial. '. . . just came in. The barrier is moving! I repeat, the barrier is moving. There is no information how fast it's moving or how much distance it has covered. But it is moving outward from the village. The crowd that had gathered outside of it is fleeing wildly from it. And here is more – the barrier is moving no faster than a man may walk. It already has swept almost a mile . . .'

And that was wrong, I thought, for it was now less than half a mile from its starting point.

'. . . question, of course, is will it stop? How far will it move? Is there some way of stopping it? Can it keep on indefinitely; is there any end to it?'

'Brad,' Nancy said, 'do you think it will push everyone off the earth? Everyone but the people here in Millville?'

'I don't know,' I said, rather stupidly.

'And if it does, where will it push them? Where is there to go?'

'. . . London and Berlin,' blared the radio speaker. 'Apparently the Russian people have not as yet been told what is happening. There have been no official statements. Not from anywhere. Undoubtedly this is something about which the various governments may have some difficulty deciding if there should be a statement. It would seem, at first thought, that here is a situation which came about through no act of any man or any government. But there is some speculation that this may be a testing of some new kind of defence. Although it is difficult to imagine why, if it should be such, it be tested in a place like Millville. Ordinarily such tests would take place in a military area and be conducted in the greatest secrecy.'

The car had been moving slowly down the road all the time we'd been listening to the radio and now we were no more than a hundred feet or so behind the barrier. Ahead of us, on either side of the pavement, the great windrow of vegetation inched itself forward, while further up the road the people still retreated.

I twisted around in the seat and glanced through the rear window, back toward the traffic snarl. A crowd of people stood among the cars and out on the pavement just beyond the cars. The people from the village had finally arrived to watch the moving barrier.

'. . . sweeping everything before it,' screamed the radio.

I glanced around and we were almost at the barrier.

'Careful there,' I warned. 'Don't run into it.'

'I'll be careful,' said Nancy, just a bit too meekly.

'. . . like a wind,' the announcer said, 'blowing a long line of grass and trees and bushes steadily before it. Like a wind . . .'

And there was a wind, first a preliminary gust that raised spinning dust devils in the stripped and denuded soil behind the barrier, then a solid wall of wind that slewed the car around and howled against the metal and glass.

It was the thunderstorm, I thought, that had stalked the land since early morning. But there was no lightning and no thunder and when I craned my neck to look out the windshield at the sky, there still were no more than ragged clouds, the broken, fleeing tatters of a worn-out storm.

The wind had swung the car around and now it was skidding down the road, pushed by the roaring wind, and threatening to tip over. Nancy was fighting the wheel, trying to bring the car around, to point it into the direction of the wind.

'Brad!' she shouted.

But even as she shouted, the storm hit us with the hard, peppering sound of raindrops splashing on the car.

The car began to topple and this time I knew that it was

going over, that there was nothing in the world that could keep it from going over. But suddenly it slammed into something and swung upright once again and in one corner of my mind I knew that it had been shoved against the barrier by the wind and that it was being held there.

With one corner of my mind, for the greater part of it was filled with astonishment at the strangest raindrops I had ever seen.

They weren't raindrops, although they fell like raindrops, in drumming sheets that filled the inside of the car with the rolling sound of thunder.

'Hail,' Nancy shouted at me.

But it wasn't hail.

Little round, brown pellets hopped and pounded on the car's hood and danced like crazy buckshot across the hard flatness of the pavement.

'Seeds!' I shouted back. 'Those things out there are seeds!'

It was no regular storm. It was not the thunderstorm, for there was no thunder and the storm had lost its punch many miles away. It was a storm of seeds driven by a mighty wind that blew without regard to any earthly weather.

There was, I told myself, in a flash of logic that was not, on the face of it, very logical, no further need for the barrier to move. For it had ploughed the ground, had ploughed and harrowed it and prepared it for the seed, and then there'd been the sowing, and everything was over.

The wind stopped and the last seed fell and we sat in a numbing silence, with all the sound and fury gone out of the world. In the place of sound and fury there was a chilling strangeness, as if someone or something had changed all natural law around, so that seed fell from the sky like rain and a wind blew out of nowhere.

'Brad,' said Nancy, 'I think I'm beginning to get scared.'

She reached out a hand and put it on my arm. Her fingers tightened, hanging onto me.

'It makes me mad,' she said, 'I've never been scared, never in my life. Never scared like this.'

'It's all over now,' I said. 'The storm is ended and the barrier has stopped moving. Everything's all right.'

'It's not like that at all,' she told me. 'It's only just beginning.'

A man was running up the road toward us, but he was the only one in sight. All the other people who had been around the parked cars were no longer there. They had run for cover, back to the village, probably, when the blast of wind had come and the seeds had fallen.

The running man, I saw, was Ed Adler, and he was shouting something at us as he ran.

We got out of the car and walked around in front of it and stood there, waiting for him.

He came up to us, panting with his running.

'Brad,' he gasped, 'maybe you don't know this, but Hiram and Tom Preston are stirring up the people. They think you have something to do with what's happening. Some talk about a phone or something.'

'Why, that's crazy!' Nancy cried.

'Sure it is,' said Ed, 'but the village is on edge. It wouldn't take too much to get them thinking it. They're ready to think almost anything. They need an explanation; they'll grab at anything. They won't stop to think if it's right or wrong.'

I asked him: 'What do you have in mind?'

'You better hide out, Brad, until it all blows over. In another day or two . . .'

I shook my head. 'I have too many things to do.'

'But, Brad . . .'

'I didn't do it, Ed. I don't know what happened, but I didn't have a thing to do with it.'

'That don't make no difference.'

'Yes, it does,' I said.

'Hiram and Tom are saying they found these funny phones . . .'

Nancy started to say something, but I jumped in ahead of her and cut her off, so she didn't have a chance to say it.

'I know about those phones,' I said. 'Hiram told me all

about them. Ed, take my word for it. The phones are out of it. They are something else entirely.'

Out of the corner of my eye, I saw Nancy staring at me.

'Forget about the phones,' I said.

I hoped she'd understand and apparently she did, for she didn't say a thing about the phones. I wasn't actually sure that she'd intended to, for I had no idea if she knew about the phone in her father's study. But I couldn't take a chance.

'Brad,' warned Ed, 'you're walking into it.'

'I can't run away,' I told him. 'I can't run somewhere and hide. Not from anyone, especially not from a pair like Tom and Hiram.'

He looked me up and down.

'No, I guess you can't,' he said. 'Is there anything I can do?'

'Maybe,' I said. 'You can see that Nancy gets home safely. I've got a thing or two to do.'

I looked at Nancy. She nodded at me. 'It's all right, Brad, but the car's just down the road. I could drive you home.'

'I'd better take a short cut. If Ed is right, there's less chance of being seen.'

'I'll stay with her,' said Ed, 'until she's inside the house.'

Already, in two hour's time, I thought, it had come to this – to a state of mind where one questioned the safety of a girl alone upon the street.

10

NOW, FINALLY, I had to do a thing I had intended to do ever since this morning – a thing I probably should have done last night – get in touch with Alf. It was more important now than ever that I get in touch with him, for in the back of my mind was a growing conviction that there must be some connection between what was happening here in Millville and that strange research project down in Mississippi.

I reached a dead-end street and started walking down it. There was not a soul in sight. Everyone who could either walk or ride would be down in the business section.

I got to worrying that maybe I'd not be able to locate Alf, that he might have checked out of the motel when I failed to get there, or that he might be out gawping at the barrier with a lot of other people.

But there was no need to worry, for when I reached my house the phone was ringing and Alf was on the line.

'I've been trying for an hour to get you,' he said. 'I wondered how you were.'

'You know what happened, Alf?'

He told me that he did. 'Some of it,' he said.

'Minutes earlier,' I said, 'and I would have been with you instead of penned up in the village. I must have hit the barrier when it first appeared.'

I went ahead and told him what had happened after I had hit the barrier. Then I told him about the phones.

'They told me they had a lot of readers. People who read books to them.'

'A way of getting information.'

'I gathered that was it.'

'Brad,' he said, 'I've got a terrible hunch.'

'So have I,' I said.

'Do you think this Greenbriar project . . .?'

'That's what I was thinking, too.'

I heard him draw in a deep breath, the air whistling in his teeth.'

'It's not just Millville, then.'

'Maybe a whole lot more than Millville.'

'What are you going to do now, Brad?'

'Go down into my garden and have a hard look at some flowers.'

'Flowers?'

'Alf,' I told him, 'it's a long, long story. I'll tell you later. Are you staying on?'

'Of course I am,' said Alf. 'The greatest show on earth and me with a ringside seat.'

'I'll call you back in an hour or so.'

'I'll stay close,' he promised. 'I'll be waiting for your call.'

I put down the phone and stood there, trying to make some head or tail of it. The flowers, somehow, were important, and so was Tupper Tyler, but they were all mixed up together and there was no place one could start.

I went out of the house and down into the garden by the greenhouse. The trail that Tupper had left was still plain and I was considerably relieved, for I had been afraid that the wind that brought the seeds might have blown it away, that the flowers might have been so beaten and so twisted that the trail could well be lost.

I stood at the edge of the garden and looked around, as if I were seeing the place for the first time in my life. It wasn't really a garden. At one time it had been land on which we'd grown the stuff we sold, but when I quit the greenhouse business I'd simply let it go wild and the flowers had taken over. To one side stood the greenhouse, with its door hanging on the broken hinges and most of the panes gone from the windows. And at one corner of it stood the elm tree that had grown from seed – the one I'd been about to pull up when my father stopped me.

Tupper had talked wildly about flowers growing by the acre. All of them, he said, had been purple flowers and he had been most emphatic that my father should be told of them. The mystery voice, or one of the mystery voices on the phone had been well informed about my father's greenhouse and had asked if I still ran it. And there had been, less than an hour ago, a perfect storm of seeds.

All the little purple flower-heads with their monkey faces seemed to be nodding at me as if at a secret joke and I jerked my gaze away from them to stare up at the sky. Broken clouds still streamed across it, shutting out the sun. Although, once the clouds were gone, the day would be a scorcher. One could smell the heat in the very air.

I moved out into the garden, following Tupper's trail. At the end of the trail I stopped and told myself that it had been a witless thing – this belief of mine that I would find something in this flower patch that would make some sense.

Tupper Tyler had disappeared ten years ago and he'd disappeared today and how he'd managed it no man might ever know.

And yet the idea still went on banging in my skull that Tupper was the key to all this screwy business.

Yet I couldn't, for the life of me, explain the logic of my thinking. For Tupper wasn't the only one involved – if he was, in fact, involved. There was Stiffy Grant as well. And I realized, with a start, that I had not asked anyone how Stiffy might be doing.

Doc Fabian's house was on the hill just above the greenhouse and I could go up there and ask. Doc might not be home, of course, but I could wait around a while and eventually he'd show up. At the moment there was nothing else to do. And with Hiram and Tom Preston shooting off their mouths, it might be a good idea not to be found at home.

I had been standing at the end of Tupper's trail and now I took a step beyond it, setting out for Doc's. But I never got to Doc's. I took that single step and the sun came out and the houses went away. Doc's house and all the other houses, and the trees as well, and the bushes and the grass. Everything disappeared and there was nothing left but the purple flowers, which covered everything, and a sun that was blazing out of a cloudless sky.

11

I HAD TAKEN that one step and everything had happened. So now I took another one to bring my feet together and I stood there, stiff and scared, afraid to turn around – afraid, perhaps, of what I'd see behind me. Although I think I knew what I would see behind me. Just more purple flowers.

For this, I knew, in one dim corner of my curdled mind, was the place that Tupper had been telling me about.

Tupper had come out of this place and he'd gone back to this place and now I'd followed him.

Nothing happened.

And that was right, of course. For it seemed to me, somehow, that this would be the sort of place where nothing ever happened.

There were just the flowers and the sun blazing in the sky and there was nothing else. There wasn't a breath of wind and there was no sound. But there was a fragrance, the almost overpowering, cloying fragrance of all those little blossoms with their monkey faces.

At last I dared to move and I slowly turned around. And there was nothing but the flowers.

Millville had gone away somewhere, into some other world. Although that was wrong, I told myself. For somewhere, in its same old world, there yet must be a Millville. It had not been Millville, but myself, that had gone away. I had taken just one step and had walked clear out of Millville into another place.

Yet, while it was a different place, the terrain seemed to be identical with the old terrain. I still was standing in the dip of ground that lay behind my house and back of me the hill rose steeply to the now non-existent street where Doc's house had stood and a half a mile away loomed the hill where the Sherwood house should be.

This, then, was Tupper's world. It was the world into which he had gone ten years ago and again this morning. Which meant that, at this very moment, he must still be here.

And that meant, I told myself with a sudden rush of hope, that there was a chance of getting out, of getting back to Millville. For Tupper had gotten back again and thus must know the way. Although, I realized, one never could be sure. You never could be sure of anything with a dope like Tupper Tyler.

The first thing to do, of course, was find him. He could not be far off. It might take a while, but I was fairly confident that I could track him down.

I walked slowly up the hill that, back in my home village, would have taken me to Doc Fabian's place.

I reached the top of the hill and stopped and there, below me, lay the far sweep of land clothed by the purple flowers.

The land looked strange, robbed of all its landmarks, naked of its trees and roads and houses. But it lay, I saw, as it had lain. If there were any differences, they were minor ones. There, to the east, was the wet and swampy land below the little knoll where Stiffy's shack had stood – where Stiffy's shack still stood in another time or place.

What strange circumstances, or what odd combination of many circumstances, must occur, I wondered, to make it possible for a man to step from one world to another.

I stood, a stranger in an unknown land, with the perfume of the flowers clogging not my nostrils only, but every pore of me, pressing in upon me, as if the flowers themselves were rolling in great purple waves to bear me down and bury me for all eternity. The world was quiet; it was the quietest place I had ever been. There was no sound at all. And I realized that perhaps at no time in my life had I ever known silence. Always there had been something that had made some sort of noise – the chirring of a lone insect in the quiet of a summer noon, or the rustle of a leaf. Even in the dead of night there would have been the creaking of the timbers in the house, the murmur of the furnace, the slight keening of a wind that ran along the eaves.

But there was silence here. There was no sound at all. There was no sound, I knew, because there was nothing that could make a sound. There were no trees or bushes; there were no birds or insects. There was nothing here but the flowers and the soil in which they grew.

A silence and the emptiness that held the silence in its hand, and the purpleness that ran to the far horizon to meet the burnished, pale-blue brightness of a summer sky.

Now, for the first time, I felt panic stalking me – not a big and burly panic that would send one fleeing, howling as he fled, but a little, sneaky panic that circled all about me, like a pesky, yapping dog, bouncing on its pipestem legs, waiting for a chance to sink its needle teeth in me. Nothing one could fight, nothing one could stand against – a little yapping panic that set the nerves on edge.

There was no fear of danger, for there was no danger. One could see with half an eye that there was no danger. But there was, perhaps worse than any danger, the silence and the loneliness and the sameness and the not knowing where you were.

Down the slope was the wet and swampy area where Stiffy's shack should be, and there, a little farther off, the silver track of river that ran at the edge of town. And at the place where the river bent toward the south, a plume of smoke rose daintily against the blue wash of the sky – so faint and far a trickle that one could barely make it out.

'Tupper!' I shouted, running down the slope, glad of a chance to run, of some reason I should run, for I had been standing, determined not to run, determined not to allow the little yapping panic to force me into running, and all the time I'd stood there I had ached to run.

I crossed the little ridge that hid the river and the camp lay there before me – a tiny hut of crudely woven branches, a garden full of growing things, and all along the river bank little straggling, dying trees, with most of their branches dead and bearing only a few tassels of green leaves at their very tops.

A small campfire burned in front of the hut and squatting by the fire was Tupper. He wore the shirt and trousers I had given him and he still had the outrageous hat perched on his head.

'Tupper!' I shouted and he rose and came gravely up the slope to meet me. He wiped off his chin and held out his hand in greeting. It still was wet with slobber, but I didn't mind. Tupper wasn't much, but he was another human.

'Glad you could make it, Brad,' he said. 'Glad you could drop over.'

As if I'd been dropping over every day, for years.

'Nice place you have,' I said.

'They did it all for me,' he said, with a show of pride. 'The Flowers fixed it up for me. It wasn't like this to start with, but they fixed it up for me. They have been good to me.'

'Yes, they have,' I said.

I didn't know what it was all about, but I went along. I had to go along. There was just a chance that Tupper could get me back to Millville.

'They're the best friends I have,' said Tupper, slobbering in his happiness. 'That is, except for you and your papa. Until I found the Flowers, you and your papa were the only friends I had. All the rest of them just made fun of me. I let on I didn't know that they were making fun, but I knew they were and I didn't like it.'

'They weren't really unkind,' I assured him. 'They really didn't mean what they said or did. They were only being thoughtless.'

'They shouldn't have done it,' Tupper insisted. 'You never made any fun of me. I like you because you never made any fun of me.'

And he was right, of course. I'd not made fun of him. But not because I hadn't wanted to at times; there were times when I could have killed him. But my father had taken me off to the side one day and warned me that if he ever caught me making fun of Tupper, like the other kids, he would warm my bottom.

'This is the place you were telling me about,' I said. 'The place with all the flowers.'

He grinned delightedly, drooling from both corners of his mouth 'Ain't it nice?' he said.

We had been walking down the slope together and now we reached the fire. A crude clay pot was standing in the ashes and there was something bubbling in it.

'You'll stay and eat with me,' invited Tupper. 'Please, Brad, say you'll stay and eat with me. It's been so long since I've had anyone who would eat with me.'

Weak tears were running down his cheeks at the thought of how long it had been since he'd had someone who would stay and eat with him.

'I got corn and potatoes roasting in the coals,' he said, 'and I got peas and beans and carrots all cooked up together. That's them in the pot. There isn't any meat. You don't mind, do you, if there isn't any meat?'

'Not at all,' I told him.

'I miss meat something dreadful,' he confided. 'But they can't do anything about it. They can't turn themselves into animals.'

'They?' I asked.

'The Flowers,' he said, and the way he said it, he made them a proper noun. 'They can turn themselves into anything at all – plant things, that is. But they can't make themselves into things like pigs or rabbits. I never asked them to. That is, I mean I never asked them twice. I asked them once and they explained to me. I never asked again, for they've done a lot of things for me and I am grateful to them.'

'They explained to you? You mean you talk with them.'

'All the time,' said Tupper.

He got down on his hands and knees and crawled into the hut, scrabbling around for something, with his back end sticking out, like a busy dog digging out a woodchuck.

He backed out and he brought with him a couple of crude pottery plates, lopsided and uneven. He put them down upon the ground and laid on each of them a spoon carved out of wood.

'Made them myself,' he told me. 'Found some clay down in the river bank and at first I couldn't seem to do it, but then they found out for me and . . .'

'The Flowers found out for you?'

'Sure, the Flowers. They do everything for me.'

'And the spoons?'

'Used a piece of stone. Flint, I guess. Had a sharp edge on it. Nothing like a knife, but it did the job. Took a long time, though.'

I nodded.

'But that's all right,' he said. 'I had a lot of time.'

He did a mopping job and wiped his hands meticulously on his trouser seat.

'They grew flax for me,' he said, 'so I could make some clothes. But I couldn't get the hang of it. They told me and they told me, but I couldn't do it. So they finally quit. I went around without no clothes for quite a spell. Except for this hat,' he said. 'I did that myself, without no help at all. They didn't even tell me, I figured it all out and did it by myself. Afterwards they told me that I'd done real good.'

'They were right,' I said. 'It's magnificent.'

'You really think so, Brad?'

'Of course I do,' I said.

'I'm glad to hear you say so, Brad. I'm kind of proud of it. It's the first thing in my life I ever did alone, without no one telling me.'

'These flowers of yours . . .'

'They ain't my flowers,' said Tupper, sharply.

'You say these flowers can turn themselves into anything they want to. You mean they turned themselves into garden stuff for you.'

'They can turn themselves into any kind of plants. All I do is ask them.'

'Then, if they can be anything they want to be, why are they all flowers?'

'They have to be something, don't they?' Tupper demanded, rather heatedly. 'They might as well be flowers.'

'Well, yes,' I said. 'I suppose they might.'

He raked two ears of corn out of the coals and a couple of potatoes. He used a potlifter that looked as if it were fashioned out of bark to get the pot off the fire. He dumped the cooked vegetables that were in it out onto the plates.

'And the trees?' I asked.

'Oh, them are things they changed themselves into. I needed them for wood. There wasn't any wood to start with and I couldn't do no cooking and I told them how it was. So they made the trees and they made them special for me. They grow fast and die so that I can break branches off and have dry wood for fire. Slow burning, though, not like ordinary dry wood. And that's good, for I have to keep a fire burning all the time. I had a pocket full of matches when I came here, but I haven't had any for a long, long time.'

I remembered when he spoke about the pocket full of matches how entranced he had always been with fire. He always carried matches with him and he'd sit quietly by himself and light match after match, letting each burn down until it scorched his fingers, happy with the sight of flame. A lot of people had been afraid that he might burn some building down, but he never did. He was just a little jerk who liked the sight of fire.

'I haven't any salt,' said Tupper. 'The stuff may taste funny to you. I've got used to it.'

'But you eat vegetables all the time. You need salt for that kind of stuff.'

'The Flowers say I don't. They say they put things into the vegetables that takes the place of salt. Not that you can taste it, but it gives you the things you need just the same as salt. They studied me to find out what my body needed and they put in a lot of stuff they said I needed. And just down the river I have an orchard full of fruit. And I have raspberries and strawberries that bear almost all the time.'

I couldn't rightly understand what fruit had to do with the problem of nutrition if the Flowers could do all he said they could, but I let the matter stand. One never got anywhere trying to get Tupper straightened out. If you tried to reason with him, you just made matters worse.

'We might as well sit down,' said Tupper, 'and get started on this.'

I sat down on the ground and he handed me a plate, then sat down opposite me and took the other plate.

I was hungry and the saltless food didn't go so badly. Flat, of course, and tasting just a little strange, but it was all right. It took away the hunger.

'You like it here?' I asked.

'It is home to me,' said Tupper, solemnly. 'It is where my friends are.'

'You don't have anything,' I said. 'You don't have an axe or knife. You don't have a pot or pan. And there is no one you can turn to. What if you got sick?'

Tupper quit wolfing down his food and stared at me, as if I were the crazy one.

'I don't need any of those things,' he said. 'I make my dishes out of clay. I can break off the branches with my hands and I don't need an axe. I don't need to hoe the garden. There aren't ever any weeds. I don't even need to plant it. It's always there. While I use up one row of stuff, another row is growing. And if I got sick, the Flowers would take care of me. They told me they would.'

'OK,' I said. 'OK.'

He went back to his eating. It was a terrible sight to watch.

But he was right about the garden. Now that he had mentioned it, I could see that it wasn't cultivated. There were rows of growing vegetables – long, neat rows without the sign of ever being hoed and without a single weed. And that, of course, was the way it would be, for no weed would dare to grow here. There was nothing that could grow here except the Flowers themselves, or the things into which the Flowers had turned themselves, like the vegetables and trees.

The garden was a perfect garden. There were no stunted plants and no disease or blight. The tomatoes, hanging on the vines, were an even red and all were perfect globes. The corn stood straight and tall.

'You cooked enough for two,' I said. 'Did you know that I was coming?'

For I was fast reaching the point where I'd have believed almost anything. It was just possible, I told myself, that he (or the Flowers) had known that I was coming.

'I always cook enough for two,' he told me. 'There never is no telling when someone might drop in.'

'But no one ever has?'

'You're the first,' he said. 'I'm glad that you could come.'

I wondered if time had any meaning for him. Sometimes it seemed it didn't. And yet he had wept weak tears because it had been so long since anyone had broken bread with him.

We ate in silence for a while and then I took a chance. I'd humoured him long enough and it was time to ask some questions.

'Where is this place?' I asked. 'What kind of place is it? And if you want to get out of it, to get back home, how do you go about it?'

I didn't mention the fact that he had gotten out of it and returned to Millville. I sensed it might be something he would resent, for he'd been in a hurry to get back again – as if he'd broken some sort of rule or regulation and was anxious to return before anyone found out.

Carefully Tupper laid his plate on the ground and placed his spoon upon it, then he answered me. But he answered me in a different voice, in the measured voice of the businessman who had talked to me on the mystery phone.

'This,' said Tupper, in the voice of the businessman, 'is not Tupper Tyler speaking. This is Tupper speaking for the Flowers. What shall we talk about?'

'You're kidding me,' I said, but it wasn't that I really thought I was being kidded. What I said I said almost instinctively, to gain a little time.

'I can assure you,' said the voice, 'that we are very much in earnest. We are the Flowers and you want to talk with us and we want to talk with you. This is the only way to do it.'

Tupper wasn't looking at me; he didn't seem to be looking at anything at all. His eyes had gone all bleak and vacant and he had an indrawn look. He sat stiff and straight, with his hands dangling in his lap. He didn't look human, any more; he looked like a telephone.

'I've talked to you before,' I said.

'Oh, yes,' said the Flowers, 'but only very briefly. You did not believe in us.'

'I have some questions that I want to ask.'

'And we shall answer you. We'll do the best we can. We'll reply to you as concisely as we know.'

'What is this place?' I asked.

'This is an alternate Earth,' said the Flowers. 'It's no more than a clock-tick away from yours.'

'An alternate Earth?'

'Yes, there are many Earths. You did not know that, did you?'

'No,' I said, 'I didn't.'

'But you can believe it?'

'With a little practice, maybe.'

'There are billions of Earths,' the Flowers told me. 'We don't know how many, but there are many billions of them. There may be no end to them. There are some who think so.'

'One behind the other?'

'No. That's not the way to think of it. We don't know how to tell it. It becomes confused in telling.'

'So let's say there are a lot of Earths. It's a little hard to understand. If there were a lot of Earths, we'd see them.'

'You could not see them,' said the Flowers, 'unless you could see in time. The alternate Earths exist in a time matrix . . .'

'A time matrix? You mean . . .'

'The simplest way to say it is that time divides the many Earths. Each one is distinguished by its time-location. All that exists for you is the present moment. You cannot see into the past or future . . .'

'Then to get here I travelled into time.'

'Yes,' said the Flowers. 'That is exactly what you did.'

Tupper still was sitting there with the blank look on his face, but I'd forgotten him. It was his lips and tongue and larynx that formed the words I heard, but it was not Tupper speaking. I knew that I was talking with the Flowers; that, insane as it might seem, I was talking with the purpleness that flowed all around the camp.

'Your silence tells us,' said the Flowers, 'that you find it hard to digest what we are telling you.'

'I choke on it,' I told them.

'Let's try to say it another way. Earth is a basic structure but it progresses along the time path by a process of discontinuity.'

'Thanks,' I said, 'for trying, but it doesn't help too much.'

'We have known it for a long time,' said the Flowers. 'We discovered it many years ago. To us it is a natural law, but to you it's not. It'll take you a little time. You cannot swallow at a single gulp what it took us centuries to know.'

'But I walked through time,' I said. 'That's what's hard to take. How could I walk through time?'

'You walked through a very thin spot.'

'Thin spot?'

'A place where time was not so thick.'

'And you made this thin spot?'

'Let's say that we exploited it.'

'To try to reach our Earth?'

'Please, sir,' said the Flowers, 'not that tone of horror. For some years now, you people have been going into space.'

'We've been trying to,' I said.

'You're thinking of invasion. In that we are alike. You are trying to invade space; we're trying to invade time.'

'Let's just go back a ways,' I pleaded. 'There are boundaries between these many Earths?'

'That is right.'

'Boundaries in time? The worlds are separated by time phases?'

'That is indeed correct. You catch on very neatly.'

'And you are trying to break through this time barrier so you can reach my Earth?'

'To reach your Earth,' they told me.

'But why?'

'To co-operate with you. To form a partnership. We need living space and if you give us living space, we'll give our knowledge; we need technology, for we have no hands, and with our knowledge you can shape new technologies and those technologies can be used for the benefit of each of us. We can go together into other worlds. Eventually a long chain of many Earths will be linked together and the races in them linked, as well, in a common aim and purpose.'

A cold lump of lead blossomed in my guts, and despite the lump of lead I felt that I was empty and there was a vile metallic taste that coated tongue and mouth. A partnership, and who would be in charge? Living space, and how much would they leave for us? Other worlds, and what would happen in those other worlds?

'You have a lot of knowledge?'

'Very much,' they said. 'It is a thing we pay much attention to – the absorption of all knowledge.'

'And you're very busy collecting it from us. You are the people who are hiring all the readers?'

'It is so much more efficient,' they explained, 'than the way we used to do it, with results indifferent at best. This way is more certain and a great deal more selective.'

'Ever since the time,' I said, 'that you got Gerald Sherwood to make the telephones.'

'The telephones,' they told me, 'provide direct communication. All we had before was the tapping of the mind.'

'You mean you had mental contact with people of our Earth? Perhaps for a good long time?'

'Oh, yes,' they said, most cheerfully. 'With very many people, for many, many years. But the sad part of it was that it was a one-way business. We had contact with them, but by and large, they had none with us. Most of them were not aware of us at all and others, who were more sensitive, were aware of us only in a vague and fumbling way.'

'But you picked those minds.'

'Of course we did,' they said. 'But we had to content ourselves with what was in the minds. We could not manage to direct them to specific areas of interest.'

'You tried nudging them, of course.'

'There were some we nudged with fair success. There were others we could nudge, but they moved in wrong directions. And there were many, most of them perhaps, who stubbornly

113

remained unaware of us, no matter what we did. It was discouraging.

'You contact these minds through certain thin spots, I suppose. You could not have done it through the normal boundaries.'

'No, we had to make maximum usage of the thin spots that we found.'

'It was, I gather, somewhat unsatisfactory.'

'You are perceptive, sir. We were getting nowhere.'

'Then you made a breakthrough.'

'We are not quite sure we understand.'

'You tried a new approach. You concentrated on actually sending something physical through the boundary. A handful of seeds, perhaps.'

'You are right, of course. You follow us so closely and you understand so well. But even that would have failed if it had not been for your father. Only a very few of the seeds germinated and the resultant plants would have died out eventually if he'd not found them and taken care of them. You must understand that is why we want you to act as our emissary . . .'

'Now, just a minute there,' I told them. 'Before we get into that, there are a few more points I want cleared up. The barrier, for instance, that you've thrown around Millville.'

'The barrier,' said the Flowers, 'is a rather simple thing. It is a time bubble we managed to project outward from the thin spot in the boundary that separates our worlds. That one slight area of space it occupies is out of phase both with Millville and with the rest of your Earth. The smallest imaginable fraction of a second in the past, running that fraction of a second of time behind the time of Earth. So slight a fraction of a second, perhaps, that it would be difficult, we should imagine, for the most sophisticated of your instruments to take a measurement. A very little thing and yet, we imagine you'll agree, it is quite effective.'

'Yes,' I said, 'effective.'

And, of course, it would be – by the very nature of it, it would be strong beyond imagination. For it would represent the past, a filmy soap bubble of the past encapsulating Millville, so slight a thing that it did not interfere with either sight or sound, and yet was something no human could hope to penetrate.

'But sticks and stones,' I said. 'And raindrops . . .'

'Only life,' they said. 'Life at a certain level of sentience, of awareness of its surroundings, of feeling – how do you say it?'

'You've said it well enough,' I told them. 'And the inanimate . . .'

'There are many rules of time,' they told me, 'of the natural phenomenon which you call time. That is a part, a small part, of the knowledge we would share with you.'

'Anything at all,' I said, 'in that direction would be new knowledge for us. We have not studied time. We haven't even thought of it as a force that we could study. We haven't made a start. A lot of metaphysical mutterings, of course, but no real study of it. We have never found a place where we could start a study of it.'

'We know all that,' they said.

And was there a note of triumph in the way they said it? I could not be entirely sure.

A new sort of weapon, I thought. A devilish sort of weapon. It wouldn't kill you and it wouldn't hurt you. It would shove you along, herding you along, out of the way, crowding you together, and there wouldn't be a thing you could do about it.

What, Nancy had asked, if it swept all life from Earth, leaving only Millville? And that, perhaps, was possible, although it need not go that far. If it was living space alone that the Flowers were looking for, then they already had the instrument to get that living space. They could expand the bubble, gaining all the space they needed, holding the human race at bay while they settled down in that living space. The weapon was at once a weapon to be used against the people of the Earth and a protection for the Flowers against such reprisals as mankind might attempt.

The way was open to them if they wanted Earth. For Tupper had travelled the way that they must go and so had I and there was nothing now to stop them. They could simply move into the Earth, shielded by that wall of time.

'So,' I asked, 'what are you waiting for?'

'You are, on certain points, so slow to reach an understanding of what we intend,' they said. 'We do not plan invasion. We want co-operation. We want to come as friends in perfect understanding.'

'Well, that's fine,' I said. 'You are asking to be friends. First we must know our friends. What sort of things are you?'

'You are being rude,' they said.

'I am not being rude. I want to know about you. You speak of yourselves as plural, or perhaps collective.'

'Collective,' they said. 'You probably would describe us as an organism. Our root system is planet-wide and interconnected and you might want to think of it as our nervous system. At regular intervals there are great masses of our root material and these masses serve – we suppose you'd call them brains. Many, many brains and all of them connected by a common nervous system.'

'But it's all wrong,' I protested. 'It goes against all reason. Plants can't be intelligent. No plant could experience the survival pressure or the motivation to achieve intelligence.'

'Your reasoning,' they told me calmly, 'is beyond reproach.'

'So it is beyond reproach,' I said. 'Yet I am talking with you.'

'You have an animal on your Earth that you call a dog.'

'That is right. An animal of great intelligence.'

'Adopted by you humans as a pet and a companion. An animal that has associated with you people since before the dawning of your history. And, perhaps, the more intelligent because of that association. An animal that is capable of a great degree of training.'

'What has the dog to do with it?' I asked.

'Consider,' they said. 'If the humans of your Earth had devoted all their energies, through all their history, to the training of the dog, what might have been achieved?'

'Why, I don't know,' I said. 'Perhaps, by now, we'd have a dog that might be our equal in intelligence. Perhaps not intelligent in the same manner that we're intelligent, but . . .'

'There once was another race,' the Flowers told me, 'that did that very thing with us. It all began more than a billion years ago.'

'This other race deliberately made a plant intelligent?'

'There was a reason for it. They were a different kind of life than you. They developed us for one specific purpose. They needed a system of some sort that would keep the data they had collected continually correlated and classified and ready for their use.'

'They could have kept their records. They could have written it all down.'

'There were certain physical restrictions and, perhaps more important, certain mental blocks.'

'You mean they couldn't write.'

'They never thought of writing. It was an idea that did not occur to them. Not even speech, the way you speak. And even if they had had speech or writing, it would not have done the job they wanted.'

'The classification and the correlation?'

'That is part of it, of course. But how much ancient human knowledge, written down and committed to what seemed at that time to be safe keeping, is still alive today?'

'Not much of it. It has been lost or destroyed. Time has washed it out.'

'We still hold the knowledge of that other race,' they said. 'We proved better than the written record – although this other race, of course, did not consider written records.'

'This other race,' I said. 'The knowledge of this other race and how many other races?'

They did not answer me. 'If we had the time,' they said, 'we'd explain it all to you. There are many factors and considerations you'd find incomprehensible. Believe us when we say that the decision of this other race, to develop us into a data storage system, was the most reasonable and workable of the many alternatives they had under study.'

'But the time it took,' I said, dismayed. 'My God, how much

time would it take to make a plant intelligent! And how could they even start? What do you do to make a plant intelligent?'

'Time,' they said, 'was no great consideration. It wasn't any problem. They knew how to deal with time. They could handle time as you can handle matter. And that was a part of it. They compressed many centuries of our lives into seconds of their own. They had all the time they needed. They made the time they needed.'

'They made time?'

'Certainly. Is that so hard to understand?'

'For me, it is,' I told them. 'Time is a river. It flows on and on. There is nothing you can do about it.'

'It is nothing like a river,' said the Flowers, 'and it doesn't flow, and there's much that can be done with it. And, furthermore, we ignore the insult that you offer us.'

'The insult?'

'Your feeling that it would be so difficult for a plant to acquire intelligence.'

'No insult was intended. I was thinking of the plants of Earth. I can't imagine a dandelion . . .'

'A dandelion?'

'A very common plant.'

'You may be right,' they said. 'We may have been different, originally, than the plants of Earth.'

'You remember nothing of it all, of course.'

'You mean ancestral memory?'

'I suppose that's what I mean.'

'It was so long ago,' they said. 'We have the record of it. Not a myth, you understand, not a legend. But the actual record of how we became intelligent.'

'Which,' I said, 'is far more than the human race has got.'

'And now,' said the Flowers, 'we must say goodbye. Our enunciator is becoming quite fatigued and we must not abuse his strength, for he has served us long and faithfully and we have affection for him. We will talk with you again.'

'Whew!' said Tupper.

He wiped the slobber off his chin.

'That's the longest,' he said, 'I have ever talked for them. What did you talk about?'

'You mean you don't know?'

'Of course I don't,' snapped Tupper. 'I never listen in.'

He was human once again. His eyes had returned to normal and his face had become unstuck.

'But the readers,' I said. 'They read longer than we talked.'

'I don't have nothing to do with the reading that is done,' said Tupper. 'That ain't two-way talk. That's all mental contact stuff.'

'But the phones,' I said.

'The phones are just to tell them the things they should read.'

'Don't they read into the phones?'

'Sure they do,' said Tupper. 'That's so they'll read aloud. It's easier for the Flowers to pick it up if they read aloud. It's sharper in the reader's brain or something.'

He got up slowly.

'Going to take a nap,' he said.

He headed for the hut.

Halfway there, he stopped and turned back to face me.

'I forgot,' he said. 'Thanks for the pants and shirt.'

12

MY HUNCH had been correct. Tupper was a key, or at least one of the keys, to what was happening. And the place to look for clues, crazy as it had sounded, had been the patch of flowers in the garden down below the greenhouse.

For the flower patch had led, not alone to Tupper, but to all the rest of it – to that second self that had helped out Gerald Sherwood, to the phone set-up and the reader service, to the ones who employed Stiffy Grant and probably to the backers of that weird project down in Mississippi.

And to how many other projects and endeavours I had no idea.

It was not only now, I knew, that this was happening, but it had been happening for years. For many years, they'd told me, the Flowers had been in contact with many minds of Earth, had been stealing the ideas and the attitudes and knowledge which had existed in those minds, and even in those instances in which the minds were unaware of the prowlers in them, had persisted in the nudging of those minds, as they had nudged the mind of Sherwood.

For many years, they'd said, and I had not thought to ask them for a better estimate. For several centuries, perhaps, and that seemed entirely likely, for when they spoke of the lifetime of their intelligence they spoke of a billion years.

For several hundred years, perhaps, and could those centuries, I wondered, have dated from the Renaissance? Was it possible, I asked myself, that the credit for the flowering of man's culture, that the reason for his advancement might be due, at least in part, to the nudging of the Flowers? Not, of course, that they themselves would have placed their imprint upon the ways of man, but theirs could have been the nagging force which had driven man to much of his achievement.

In the case of Gerald Sherwood, the busybody nudging had resulted in constructive action. Was it too much to think, I wondered, that in many other instances the result had been the same – although perhaps not as pronounced as it had been in Sherwood's case? For Sherwood had recognized the otherness that had come to live with him and had learned that it was to his benefit to co-operate. In many other cases there would not have been awareness, but even with no awareness, the drive and urge were there and, in part, there would have been response.

In those hundreds of years, the Flowers must have learned a great deal of humanity and have squirrelled away much human knowledge. For that had been their original purpose, to serve as knowledge storage units. During the last several years man's knowledge had flowed to them in a steady stream, with dozens, perhaps hundreds, of readers busily engaged in pouring down their mental gullets the accumulated literary efforts of all of humankind.

I got off the ground where I was sitting and found that I was stiff and cramped. I stretched and slowly turned and there, on every side, reaching to the near horizons of the ridges that paralleled the river, swept the purple tide.

It could not be right, I told myself. I could not have talked with flowers. For of all the things on Earth, plants were the one thing that could never talk.

And yet this was not the Earth. This was another Earth – only one, they'd said, of many billion earths.

Could one measure, I asked myself, one earth by another? And the answer seemed to be one couldn't. The terrain appeared to be almost identical with the terrain I had known back on my own Earth, and the terrain itself might remain the same for all those multi-billion earths. For what was it they had said – that earth was a basic structure?

But when one considered life and evolution, then all the bets were off. For even if the life of my own Earth and this other Earth on which I stood had started out identically (and they might well have started out identically) there still would be, along the way, millions of little deviations, no one of which perhaps, by itself, would be significant, but the cumulative effects of all these deviations eventually would result in a life and culture that would bear no resemblance to any other Earth.

Tupper had begun to snore – great wet, slobbering snores, the very kind of snores that one might guess he'd make. He was lying on his back inside the hut, on a bed of leaves, but the hut was so small that his feet stuck out the doorway. They rested on his calloused heels and his spraddled toes pointed at the sky and they had a raw and vulgar look about them.

I picked up the plates and spoons from where they rested on the ground and tucked the bowl in which Tupper had cooked our meal underneath my arm. I found the trail that led down to the water's edge and followed it. Tupper had cooked the food; the least I could do, I told myself, was to wash the dishes.

I squatted by the river's edge and washed the awkward plates and pot, sluiced off the spoons and rubbed them clean between my fingers. I was careful with the plates, for I had the feeling they'd not survive much wetting. On both of them and on the pot there still were the marks of Tupper's great splayed fingers, where he had pressed them into shape.

For ten years he had lived and been happy here, happy with the purple flowers that had become his friends, secure at last from the unkindness and the cruelty of the world into which he was born. The world that had been unkind and cruel because he had been different, but which was capable of unkindness and of cruelty even when there was no difference.

To Tupper, I knew, this must seem a fairyland, for real. Here was the beauty and the simplicity to which his simple soul responded. Here he could live the uncomplicated and undisturbed sort of life for which he'd always yearned, perhaps not knowing that he yearned for it.

I set the plates and pot on the river bank and stooped above the water, scooping it up in my two hands, clasped together, drinking it. It had a smooth, clean taste and despite the heat of the summer sun, it had a touch of coldness.

As I straightened up, I heard the faint sound of crinkling paper and, with a sinking heart, suddenly remembered. I put my hand into my inside jacket pocket and pulled out the long, white envelope. I flipped back the flap and there was the sheaf of money, the fifteen hundred dollars that Sherwood had put on the desk for me.

I squatted there, with the envelope in my hand and I thought what a damn fool thing to do. I had meant to hide it somewhere in the house, since I intended leaving on the fishing trip with Alf before the bank had opened, and then, in the rush of events, had forgotten it. How in the world, I wondered, could one forget fifteen hundred dollars!

With a cold sweat breaking out on me, I ran through my mind all the things that could have happened to that envelope. Except for plain fool luck, I'd have lost it a dozen times or more. And yet, aghast as I might be that I should so utterly forget such a handsome sum of cash, as I sat there and looked at it, it seemed to have lost some of its significance.

Perhaps it was, I thought, a condition of Tupper's fairyland that I should not think so highly of it as I had at one time. Although I knew that if it were possible to get back into my world again it would assume its old importance. But here, for this little moment, a crude piece of pottery made out of river clay was an important thing, a hut made out of sticks and a bed made out of leaves. And more important than all the money in the world, the necessity to keep a little campfire burning once the matches were gone.

Although, I told myself, this was not my world. This was Tupper's world, his soft, short-sighted world – and tied in with it was his utter failure to grasp the overwhelming implications of this world of his.

For this was the day about which there had been speculation – although far too little speculation and too little done about it because it seemed so distant and so improbable. This was the day that the human race had come into contact (or perhaps, collision) with an alien race.

All the speculation, of course, had concerned an alien out of space, an alien on, or from, some other world in space. But here was the alien, not out of space, but time, or at least from behind a barrier in time.

It made no difference, I told myself. Out of either space or time, the involvement was the same. Man at this moment finally faced his greatest test, and one he could not fail.

I gathered up the pottery and went back up the trail again.

Tupper was still sleeping, but no longer snoring. He had not changed position and his toes still pointed at the sky.

The sun had moved far down the west, but the heat still held and there was no hint of breeze. The purple of the flowers lay unstirring on the hillsides.

I stood and looked at them and they were innocent and pretty and they held no promise and no threat. They were just a field of flowers, like a field of daisies or of daffodils. They were the sort of thing that we had taken for granted all our years on earth. They had no personality and they stood for nothing except a splotch of colour that was pleasing to the eye.

That was the hard thing about all this, I thought – the utter impossibility of thinking of the Flowers as anything but flowers. It was impossible to think of them as beings, as anything that had even a symbol of importance. One could not take them seriously and yet they must be taken seriously, for in their right they were as intelligent, perhaps more intelligent than the human race.

I put the dishes down beside the fire and slowly climbed the hill. My moving feet brushed the flowers aside and I crushed some of them, but there was no chance of walking without crushing some of them.

I'd have to talk to them again, I told myself. As soon as Tupper could get rested, I'd talk to them again. There were a lot of things that must be clarified, much to be explained. If the Flowers and the human race were to live together, there must be understanding. I ran through the conversation I'd had with them, trying to find the gentle threat that I knew was there. But from what I could remember, there had been no threat.

I reached the top of the hill and stopped there, gazing out across the undulating purple swales. At the bottom of the slope, a small creek ran between the hills to reach the river. From where I was I could hear the silver babble of it as it ran across the stones.

Slowly I made my way down the hill toward it and as I moved down the slope I saw the mound that lay across the creek, at the foot of the opposite slope. I had not seen it before and I supposed that my failure to see it was because it had been masked by the slant of light across the land.

There was nothing special about it except that it appeared slightly out of character. Here, in this place of flowing swales, it stood by itself, like a hump-backed monstrosity left over from another time.

I came down to the creek and waded across a shallow place

where the water ran no deeper than three inches over a shining gravel bar.

At the water's edge a large block of stone lay half-buried in the sharp rise of the bank. It offered a ready seat and I sat down upon it, looking down the stream. The sun glanced off the water, making diamonds out of every ripple, and the air was sprayed with the silver tinkle of the singing brook.

There was no creek here in the world where Millville lay, although there was a dry run in Jack Dickson's pasture, through which the swamp that lay back of Stiffy's shack sometimes drained. Perhaps there had been such a creek as this, I thought, in Millville's world before the farmer's plough and resultant erosion had reshaped the terrain.

I sat entranced by the flashing diamonds of the water and the tinkle of the stream. It seemed that a man could sit there forever, warm in the last rays of the sun and guarded by the hills.

I had put my hands on either side of me and had been idly rubbing them back and forth across the surface of the stone on which I sat. My hands must have told me almost instantly that there was something strange about the surface, but I was so engrossed with the sensations of sun and water that it took some minutes before the strangeness broke its way into my consciousness.

When it did, I still remained sitting there, still rubbing the surface of the stone with the tips of my fingers, but not looking at it, making sure that I had not been wrong, that the stone had the feel of artificial shaping.

When I got up and examined the block, there was no doubt of it. The stone had been squared into a block and there were places where the chisel marks could still be seen upon it. Around one corner of it still clung a brittle substance that could be nothing else than some sort of mortar in which the block had once been set.

I straightened up from my examination and stepped away, back into the stream, with the water tugging at my ankles.

Not a simple boulder, but a block of stone! A block of stone bearing chisel marks and with a bit of mortar still sticking to one edge.

The Flowers, then, were not the only ones upon this planet. There were others – or there had been others. Creatures that knew the use of stone and had the tools to chip the stone into convenient form and size.

My eyes travelled from the block of stone up the mound that stood at the water's edge, and there were other blocks of stone protruding from its face. Standing frozen, with the glint of water and the silver song forgotten, I traced out the blocks and could see that once upon a time they had formed a wall.

This mound, then, was no vagary of nature. It was the evidence of a work that at one time had been erected by beings that knew the use of tools.

I left the stream and clambered up the mound. None of the stones was large, none was ornamented; there were just the chisel marks and here and there the bits of mortar that had lain between the blocks. Perhaps, a building had stood here at one time. Or it may have been a wall. Or a monument.

I started down the mound, choosing a path a short way downstream from where I had crossed the creek, working my way along slowly and carefully, for the slope was steep, using my hands as brakes to keep myself from sliding or from falling.

And it was then, hugged close against the slope, that I found the piece of bone. It had weathered out of the ground, perhaps not too long ago, and it lay hidden there among the purple flowers. Under ordinary circumstances, I probably would have missed it. I could not see it well at first, just the dull whiteness of it lying on the ground. I had slid past it before I saw it and crawled back to pick it up.

The surface of it powdered slightly at the pressure of my fingers, but it did not break.

It was slightly curved and white, a ghostly, chalky white.

Turning it over in my hand, I made out that it was a rib bone and the shape and size of it was such that it could be human, although my knowledge was too slight to be absolutely sure.

If it were really humanoid, I told myself, then it meant that at one time a thing like man had lived here. And could it mean that something very similar to the human race still resided here?

A planet full of flowers – with nothing living on it except the purple flowers, and more lately Tupper Tyler. That was what I'd thought when I had seen the flowers spreading to the far horizons, but it had been supposition only. It was a conclusion I had jumped to without too much evidence. Although it was in part supported by the seeming fact that nothing else existed in this particular place – no birds, no insects or animals, not a thing at all, except perhaps some bacteria and viruses and even these, I thought, might be essential to the well-being of the Flowers.

Although the outer surface of the bone had chalked off when I picked it up, it seemed sound in structure. Not too long ago, I knew, it had been a part of a living thing. Its age probably would depend to a large extent upon the composition and the moistness of the soil and probably many other factors. It was a problem for an expert and I was no expert.

Now I saw something else, a little spot of whiteness just to the right of me. It could have been a white stone lying on the ground, but even as I looked at it I didn't think it was. It had that same chalky whiteness of the rib I had picked up.

I moved over to it and as I bent above it I could see it was no stone. I let the rib drop from my fingers and began to dig. The soil was loose and sandy and although I had no tools, my fingers served the purpose.

As I dug, the bone began to reveal its shape and in a moment I knew it was a skull – and only a little later that it was a human skull.

I dug it loose and lifted it and while I might have failed to identify the rib, there was no mistaking this.

I hunkered on the slope and felt pity well inside of me, pity for this creature that once had lived and died – and a growing fear, as well.

For by the evidence of the skull I held within my hands, I

knew for a certainty that this was not the home world of the Flowers. This was – this must be – a world that they had conquered, or at least had taken over. They might, indeed, I thought, be very far in time from that old home where another race (by their description of it, a non-human race) had trained them to intelligence.

How far back, I wondered, lay the homeland of the Flowers? How many conquered earths lay between this world and the one where they had risen? How many other earths lay empty, swept clean of any life that might compete with the Flowers?

And that other race, the race that had raised and elevated them above their vegetable existence – where was that old race today?

I put the skull back into the hole from which I'd taken it. Carefully, I brushed back the sand and dirt until it was covered once again, this time entirely covered, with no part of it showing. I would have liked to take it back to camp with me so I could have a better look at it. But I knew I couldn't, for Tupper must not know what I had found. His mind was an open book to his friends the Flowers, and I was sure mine wasn't, for they had had to use the telephone to get in touch with me. So long as I told Tupper nothing, the Flowers would never know that I had found the skull. There was the possibility, of course, that they already knew, that they had the sense of sight, or perhaps some other sense that was as good as sight. But I doubted that they had; there was so far no evidence they had. The best bet was that they were mental symbionts, that they had no awareness beyond the awareness they shared with minds in other kinds of life.

I worked my way around and down the mound and along the way I found other blocks of stone. It was becoming evident to me that at some other time a building had stood upon this site. A city, I wondered, or a town? Although whatever form it might have taken, it had been a dwelling place.

I reached the creek at the far end of the mound, where it ran close against the cutbank it had chewed out of the mound, and started wading back to the place where I had crossed.

The sun had set and with it had gone the diamond sparkle of the water. The creek ran dark and tawny in the shadow of the first twilight.

Teeth grinned at me out of the blackness of the bank that rose above the stream, and I stopped dead, staring at that row of snaggled teeth and the whiteness of the bone that arched above them. The water, tugging at my ankles, growled a little at me and I shivered in the chill that swept down from the darkening hills.

For, staring at that second skull, grinning at me out of the darkness of the soil that stood poised above the water, I knew that the human race faced the greatest danger it had ever known. Except for man himself, there had been, up to this moment, no threat against the continuity of humanity. But here, finally, that threat lay before my eyes.

13

I SIGHTED the small glowing of the fire before I reached the camp. When I stumbled down the hillside, I could see that Tupper had finished with his nap and was cooking supper.

'Out for a walk?' he asked.

'Just a look around,' I said. 'There isn't much to see.'

'The Flowers is all,' said Tupper.

He wiped his chin and counted the fingers on one hand, then counted them again to be sure he'd made no mistake.

'Tupper?'

'What is it, Brad?'

'Is it all like this? All over this Earth, I mean? Nothing but the Flowers?'

'There are others come sometimes.'

'Others?'

'From other worlds,' he said. 'But they go away.'

'What kind of others?'

'Fun people. Looking for some fun.'

'What kind of fun?'

'I don't know,' he said. 'Just fun, is all.'

He was surly and evasive.

'But other than that,' I said, 'there's nothing but the Flowers?'

'That's all,' he said.

'But you haven't seen it all.'

'They tell me,' Tupper said. 'And they wouldn't lie. They aren't like people back in Millville. They don't need to lie.'

He used two sticks to move the earthen pot off the hot part of the fire.

'Tomatoes,' he said. 'I hope you like tomatoes.'

I nodded that I did and he squatted down beside the fire to watch the supper better.

'They don't tell nothing but the truth,' he said, going back to the question I had asked. 'They couldn't tell nothing but the truth. That's the way they're made. They got all this truth wrapped up in them and that's what they live by. And they don't need to tell nothing but the truth. It's afraid of being hurt that makes people lie and there is nothing that can hurt them.'

He lifted his face to stare at me, daring me to disagree with him.

'I didn't say they lied,' I told him. 'I never for a moment questioned anything they said. By this truth they're wrapped up in, you mean their knowledge, don't you?'

'I guess that's what I mean. They know a lot of things no one back in Millville knows.'

I let it go at that. Millville was Tupper's former world. By saying Millville, he meant the human world.

Tupper was off on his finger-counting routine once again. I watched him as he squatted there, so happy and content, in a world where he had nothing, but was happy and content.

I wondered once again at his strange ability to communicate with the Flowers, to know them so well and so intimately that he could speak for them. Was it possible, I asked myself, that this slobbering, finger-counting village idiot possessed some sensory perception that the common run of mankind did not have? That this extra ability of his might be a form of compensation, to make up in some measure for what he did not have?

After all, I reminded myself, man was singularly limited in his perception, not knowing what he lacked, not missing what he lacked by the very virtue of not being able to imagine himself as anything other than he was. It was entirely possible that Tupper, by some strange quirk of genetic combination, might have abilities that no other human had, all unaware that he was gifted in any special way, never guessing that other men might lack what seemed entirely normal to himself. And could these extra-human abilities match certain unguessed abilities that lay within the Flowers themselves?

The voice on the telephone, in mentioning the diplomatic job, had said that I came highly recommended. And was it this man across the fire who had recommended me? I wanted very much to ask him, but I didn't dare.

'Meow,' said Tupper. 'Meow, meow, meow.'

I'll say this much for him. He sounded like a cat. He could sound like anything at all. He was always making funny noises, practising his mimicry until he had it pat.

I paid no attention to him. He had pulled himself back into his private world and the chances were he'd forgotten I was there.

The pot upon the fire was steaming and the smell of cooking stole upon the evening air. Just above the eastern horizon the first star came into being and once again I was conscious of the little silences, so deep they made me dizzy when I tried to listen to them, that fell into the chinks between the crackling of the coals and the sounds that Tupper made.

It was a land of silence, a great eternal globe of silence, broken only by the water and the wind and the little feeble noises that came from intruders like Tupper and myself. Although, by now, Tupper might be no intruder.

I sat alone, for the man across the fire had withdrawn

himself from me, from everything around him, retreating into a room he had fashioned for himself, a place that was his alone, locked behind a door that could be opened by no one but himself, for there was no other who had a key to it or, indeed, any idea as to what kind of key was needed.

Alone and in the silence, I sensed the purpleness – the formless, subtle personality of the things that owned this planet. There was a friendliness, I thought, but a repulsive friendliness, the fawning friendliness of some monstrous beast. And I was afraid.

Such a silly thing, I thought. To be afraid of flowers.

Tupper's cat was lone and lost. It prowled the dark and dripping woods of some other ogre-land and it mewed softly to itself, sobbing as it padded on and on, along a confusing world-line of uncertainties.

The fear had moved away a little beyond the circle of the firelight. But the purpleness still was there, hunched upon the hilltop.

An enemy, I wondered. Or just something strange?

If it were an enemy, it would be a terrible enemy, implacable and efficient.

For the plant world was the sole source of energy by which the animal world was able to survive.

Only plants could trap and convert and store the vital stuff of life. It was only by making use of the energy provided by the vegetable world that the animal kingdom could exist. Plants, by wilfully becoming dormant or by making themselves somehow inedible, could doom all other life.

And the Flowers were versatile, in a very nasty way. They could, as witness Tupper's garden and the trees that grew to supply him wood, be any kind of plant at all. They could be tree or grass, vine or bush or grain. They could not only masquerade as another plant, they could become that plant.

Suppose they were allowed into the human Earth and should offer to replace the native trees for a better tree, or perhaps the same old trees we had always known, only that they would grow faster and straighter and taller, for better shade or lumber. Or to replace wheat for a better wheat, with a higher yield and a fuller kernel, and a wheat that was resistant to drought and other causes that made a wheat crop fail. Suppose they made a deal to become all vegetables, all grass, all grain, all trees, replacing the native plants of Earth, giving men more food per acre, more lumber per tree, an improved productivity in everything that grew.

There would be no hunger in the world, no shortages of any kind at all, for the Flowers could adapt themselves to every human need.

And once man had come to rely upon them, once he had his entire economy based upon them, and his very life staked upon their carrying out their bargain, then they would have man at their mercy. Overnight they could cease being wheat and corn and grass; they could rob the entire Earth of its food supply. Or they might turn poisonous and thus kill more quickly and more mercifully. Or, if by that time, they had come to hate man sufficiently, they could develop certain types of pollen to which all Earthly life would be so allergic that death, when it came, would be a welcome thing.

Or let us say, I thought, playing with the thought, that man did not let them in, but they came in all the same, that man made no bargain with them, but they became the wheat and grass and all the other plants of Earth surreptitiously, killing off the native plants of Earth and replacing them with an identical plant life, in all its variations. In such a case, I thought, the result could be the same.

If we let them in, or if we didn't let them in (but couldn't keep them out), we were in their hands. They might kill us, or they might not kill us, but even if they didn't kill us, there'd still remain the fact they could at any time they wished.

But if the Flowers were bent on infiltrating Earth, if they planned to conquer Earth by wiping out all life, then why had they contacted me? They could have infiltrated without us knowing it. It would have taken longer, but the road was clear. There was nothing that would stop them, for we would not know. If certain purple flowers should begin escaping Millville gardens, spreading year by year, in fence corners and in ditches, in the little out-of-the-way places of the land, no one would pay attention to them. Year by year the flowers could have crept out and out and in a hundred years have been so well established that nothing could deny them.

And there was another thought that, underneath my thinking and my speculation, had kept hammering at me, pleading to be heard. And now I let it in: even if we could, should we keep them out? Even in the face of potential danger, should we bar the way to them? For here was an alien life, the first alien life we'd met. Here was the chance for the human race, if it would take the chance, to gain new knowledge, to find new attitudes, to fill in the gaps of knowing and to span the bridge of thought, to understand a non-human viewpoint, to sample new emotion, to face new motivation, to investigate new logic. Was this something we could shy away from? Could we afford to fail to meet this first alien life halfway and work out the differences that might exist between the two of us? For if we failed here, the first time, then we'd fail the second time, and perhaps forever.

Tupper made a noise like a ringing telephone and I wondered how a telephone had gotten in there with that lone, lost cat of his. Perhaps, I thought, the cat had found a telephone, maybe in a booth out in the dark and dripping woods, and would find out where it was and how it might get home.

The telephone rang again and there was a little wait. Then Tupper said to me, most impatiently, 'Go ahead and talk. This call is for you.'

'What's that?' I asked, astonished.

'Say hello,' said Tupper. 'Go ahead and answer.'

'All right,' I said, just to humour him. 'Hello.'

His voice changed to Nancy's voice, so perfect an imitation that I felt the presence of her.

'Brad!' she cried. 'Brad, where are you?'

Her voice was high and gasping, almost hysterical.

'Where are you, Brad?' she asked. 'Where did you disappear to?'

'I don't know,' I said, 'that I can explain. You see . . .'

'I've looked everywhere,' she said, in a rush of words. 'We've looked everywhere. The whole town was looking for you. And then I remembered the phone in Father's study, the one without a dial, you know. I knew that it was there, but I'd never paid attention to it. I thought it was a model of some sort, or maybe just a decoration for the desk or a gag of some sort. But there was a lot of talk about the phones in Stiffy's shack, and Ed Adler told me about the phone that was in your office. And it finally dawned on me that maybe this phone that Father had was the same as those other phones. But it took an awful long time for it to dawn on me. So I went into his study and I saw the phone and I just stood and looked at it – because I was scared, you see. I was afraid of it and I was afraid to use it because of what I might find out. But I screwed my courage up and I lifted the receiver and there was an open line and I asked for you. I knew it was a crazy thing to do, but . . . What did you say, Brad?'

'I said I don't know if I can explain exactly where I am. I know where I am, of course, but I can't explain it so I'll be believed.'

'Tell me. Don't you fool around. Just tell me where you are.'

'I'm in another world. I walked out of the garden . . .'

'You walked where!'

'I was just walking in the garden, following Tupper's tracks and . . .'

'What kind of track is that?'

'Tupper Tyler,' I said. 'I guess I forgot to tell you that he had come back.'

'But he couldn't,' she told me. 'I remember him. That was ten years ago.'

'He did come back,' I said. 'He came back this morning. And then he left again. I was following his tracks . . .'

'You told me,' she said. 'You were following him and you wound up in another world. Where is this other world?'

She was like any other woman. She asked the damndest questions.

'I don't know exactly, except that it's in time. Perhaps only a second away in time.'

'Can you get back?'

'I'm going to try,' I said. 'I don't know if I can.'

'Is there anything I can do to help – that the town can do to help?'

'Listen, Nancy, this isn't getting us anywhere. Tell me, where is your father?'

'He's down at your place. There are a lot of people there. Hoping that you will come back.'

'Waiting for me?'

'Well, yes. You see, they looked everywhere and they know you aren't in the village and there are a lot of them convinced that you know all about this . . .'

'About the barrier, you mean.'

'Yes, that's what I mean.'

'And they are pretty sore?'

'Some of them,' she said.

'Listen, Nancy . . .'

'Don't say that again. I am listening.'

'Can you go down and see your father?'

'Of course I can,' she said.

'All right. Go down and tell him that when I can get back – if I can get back – I'll need to talk with someone. Someone in authority. Someone high in authority. The President, perhaps, or someone who's close to the President. Maybe someone from the United Nations . . .'

'But, Brad, you can't ask to see the President!'

'Maybe not,' I said. 'But as high as I can get. I have something our government has to know. Not only ours, but all the governments. Your father must know someone he can talk to. Tell him I'm not fooling. Tell him it's important.'

'Brad,' she said. 'Brad, you're sure you aren't kidding? Because if you are, this could be an awful mess.'

'Cross my heart,' I said. 'I mean it, Nancy, it's exactly as

I've said. I'm in another world, an alternate world . . .'

'Is it a nice world, Brad?'

'It's nice enough,' I said. 'There's nothing here but flowers.'

'What kind of flowers?'

'Purple flowers. My father's flowers. The same kind that are back in Millville. The flowers are people, Nancy. They're the ones that put up the barrier.'

'But flowers can't be people, Brad.'

Like I was a kid. Like she had to humour me. Asking me if it was a nice world and telling me that flowers never could be people. All sweet reasonableness.

I held in my anger and my desperation.

'I know they can't,' I said. 'But just the same as people. They are intelligent and they can communicate.'

'You have talked with them?'

'Tupper talks for them. He's their interpreter.'

'But Tupper was a drip.'

'Not back here he isn't. He's got things we haven't.'

'What kind of things? Brad, you have to be . . .'

'You will tell your father?'

'Right away,' she said. 'I'll go down to your place . . .'

'And, Nancy . . .'

'Yes.'

'Maybe it would be just as well if you didn't tell where I am or how you got in touch. I imagine the village is pretty well upset.'

'They are wild,' said Nancy.

'Tell your father anything you want. Tell him everything. But not the rest of them. He'll know what to tell them. There's no use in giving the village something more to talk about.'

'All right,' she said. 'Take care of yourself. Come back safe and sound.'

'Sure,' I said.

'You can get back?'

'I think I can. I hope I can.'

'I'll tell Father what you said. Exactly what you said. He'll get busy on it.'

'Nancy. Don't worry. It'll be all right.'

'Of course I won't. I'll be seeing you.'

'So long, Nancy. Thanks for calling.'

I said to Tupper, 'Thank you, telephone.'

He lifted a hand and stretched out a finger at me, stroking it with the finger of the other hand, making the sign for shame.

'Brad has got a girl,' he chanted in a sing-song voice. 'Brad has got a girl.'

'I thought you never listened in,' I said, just a little nettled.

'Brad has got a girl! Brad has got a girl! Brad has got a girl!'

He was getting excited about it and the slobber was flying all about his face.

'Cut it out,' I yelled at him. 'If you don't cut it out, I'll break your God damn neck.'

He knew I wasn't fooling, so he cut it out.

14

I WOKE in a blue and silver night and wondered, even as I woke, what had wakened me. I was lying on my back and above me the sky was glimmering with stars. I was not confused. I knew where I was. There was no blind groping back to an old reality. I heard the faint chuckling of the river as it ran between its banks and I smelled the wood smoke that drifted from the campfire.

Something had awakened me. I lay still, for it seemed important that whatever had wakened me, if it were close at hand, should not know that I was awake. There was a sense of fear, or perhaps of expectation. But if it were a sense of fear, it was neither deep nor sharp.

Slowly I twisted my head a bit and when I did I could see the moon, bright and seeming very near, swimming just above the line of scrubby trees that grew on the river bank.

I was lying flat upon the ground, with nothing under me but

the hard-packed earth. Tupper had crawled into his hut to sleep, curling up so his feet did not stick out. And if he were still there and sleeping, he was very quiet about it, for I heard no sound from him.

Having turned my head, I lay quietly for a time, listening for a sound to tell me that something prowled the camp. But there was no sound and finally I sat up.

The slope of ground above the camp, silvered by the flood-light of the moon, ran up to touch the night-blue sky – a balanced piece of beauty hanging in the silence, so fragile that one was careful not to speak nor to make any sudden motion, for fear that one might break that beauty and that silence and bring it down, sky and slope together, in a shower of shards.

Carefully I got to my feet, standing in the midst of that fragile world, still wondering what had wakened me.

But there was nothing. The land and sky were poised, as if they stood on tiptoe in a single instant of retarded time. Here, it seemed, was the present frozen, with no past or future, a place where no clock would ever tick nor any word be spoken.

Then something moved upon the hilltop, a man or a man-like thing, running on the ridge crest, black against the sky, lithe and tall and graceful, running with abandon.

I was running, too. Without reason, without purpose, simply running up the slope. Simply knowing there was a man or a manlike thing up there and that I must stand face to face with it, hoping, perhaps, that in this land of empti-ness and flowers, in this land of silence and of fragile beauty, it might make some sense, might lend to this strange dimen-sion of space and time some sort of perspective that I could understand.

The manlike thing was still running on the hilltop and I tried to shout to it, but my throat would make no sound and so I kept on running.

The figure must have seen me, for suddenly it stopped and swung around to face me and stood there on the hilltop, look-ing down at me. And now I saw that while it undoubtedly was of human form, it had a crest of some sort above its head, giving it a birdlike look – as if the head of a cockatoo had been grafted on a human body.

I ran, panting, toward it, and now it moved down the hill to meet me, walking slowly and deliberately and with unconscious grace.

I stopped running and stood still, fighting to regain my breath. There was no need of running any more. I need not run to catch it.

It continued walking down the hill toward me and while its body still stayed black and featureless, I could see that the crest was white, or silver. In the moonlight it was hard to tell if it were white or silver.

My breath came more easily now and I climbed up the hill to meet it. We approached one another slowly, each of us, I suppose, afraid that any other manner of approach might give the other fright.

The manlike thing stopped ten feet or so away and I stopped as well, and now I saw that indeed it was humanoid and that it was a woman, either a naked or an almost naked woman. In the moonlight, the crest upon her head was a thing of shining wonder, but I could not make out if it were a natural appendage or some sort of eccentric hairdo, or perhaps a hat.

The crest was white, but the rest of her was black, a jet black with blue highlights that glinted in the moonlight. And there was about her body an alertness and an awareness and a sense of bubbling life that took my breath away.

She spoke to me in music. It must have been a music, for there seemed to be no words.

'I'm sorry,' I said. 'I do not understand.'

She spoke again and the trilling of the voice ran across the blue and silver world like a spray of crystal thought, but there was no understanding. I wondered, in despair, if any man of my race could ever understand a language that expressed itself in music, or if, in fact, it was meant to be understood as were the words we used.

I shook my head and she laughed, the laughter making her

without any doubt a human – a low and tinkling laugh that was happy and excited.

She held out her hand and took a few quick steps toward me and I took the outstretched hand. And as I took her hand, she turned and ran lightly up the hill and I went running with her. We reached the top of the ridge and continued running, hand in hand, down the other slope, a wild, ecstatic running that was sheer youth and craziness – a running into nothing, for the utter joy of being alive in that heady moonlight.

We were young and drunk with a strange happiness for which there seemed no reason or accounting – drunk with, at least for me, a wild exuberance.

Her grip upon my hand was hard, with a lithe, young strength, and we ran together as if we were one person running – and it seemed to me, indeed, that in some awesome manner I had become a part of her, and that somehow I knew where we were going and why we were going there, but my brain was so seething with this strange happiness that it could not translate the knowledge into terms I understood.

We came down to the creek and splashed across, then ran around the mound where I had found the skulls and on up the second ridge and there, at the top of it, we came upon the picnic.

There were other people there, at this midnight picnic, a half a dozen of them, all like this alien girl who had run with me. Scattered on the ground were hampers, or things that looked like hampers, and bottles, and these bottles and the hampers were arranged in a sort of circle. In the centre of the circle was a small, silvery contraption that was just slightly larger than a basketball.

We stopped at the edge of the circle and all the rest of them turned to look at us – but to look without surprise, as if it were not unusual at all for one of them to lead in an alien creature such as I.

The woman who was with me spoke in her singing voice and they answered back with music. All of them were watching me, but it was friendly watching.

Then all of them except one sat down in the circle and the one who remained standing stepped toward me, making a motion inviting me to join the circle with them.

I sat down, with the running woman on one side of me and the one who made the invitation sitting on the other.

It was, I gathered, some sort of holiday, although there was something in that circle which made it more than a holiday. There was a sense of anticipation in the faces and the bodies of these people sitting in the circle, as if they might be waiting for an event of great importance. They were happy and excited and vibrant with the sense of life to their fingertips.

Except for their crests, they were humanoid, and I could see now that they wore no clothing. I found time to wonder where they might have come from, for Tupper would have told me if there were people such as they. But he had told me that the Flowers were the only things which existed on this planet, although he had said sometimes there were others who came visiting.

Were these people, then, the ones who came visiting, or was it possible that they were the descendants of those people whose bones I had found down on the mound, now finally emerged from some secret hiding place? Although there was no sign in them of ever having hidden, of ever having skulked.

The strange contraption lay in the centre of the circle. At a picnic back in Millville it would have been a record player or a radio that someone had brought along. But these people had no need of music, for they talked in music, and the thing looked like nothing I had ever seen. It was round and seemed to be fashioned of many lenses, all tilted at different angles so that the surfaces caught the moonlight, reflecting it to make the ball itself a sphere of shining glory.

Some of the people sitting in the circle began an unpacking of the hampers and an uncorking of the bottles and I knew that more than likely they'd ask me to eat with them. It worried me to think of it, for since they'd been so kind I could not very well refuse, and yet it might be dangerous to eat the food they had. For although they were humanoid, there easily could

142

be differences in their metabolism and what might be food for them could be poisonous for me.

It was a little thing, of course, but it seemed a big decision, and I sat there in mental agony, trying to make up my mind. The food might be a loathsome and nauseating mess, but that I could have managed; for the friendship of these people I would have choked it down. It was the thought that it might be deadly that made me hesitate.

A while ago, I remembered, I had convinced myself that no matter how great a threat the Flowers might be, we still must let them in, must strive to find a common ground upon which any differences that might exist between us could somehow be adjusted. I had told myself that the future of the human race might easily hang upon our ability to meet and to get along with an alien race, for the time was coming, in a hundred years from now, or a thousand years from now, when we'd be encountering other alien races, and we could not fail this first time.

And here, I realized, was another alien race, sitting in this circle, and there could be no double standard as between myself and the world at large. I, in my own right, must act as I'd decided the human race must act – I must eat the food when it was offered me.

Perhaps I was not thinking very clearly. Events were happening much too fast and I had too little time. It was a snap decision at best and I hoped I was not wrong.

I never had a chance to know, for before the food could be passed around, the contraption in the centre of the circle began a little ticking – no more than the ticking of a clock in an empty room, but at the first tick it gave they all jumped to their feet and stood watching it.

I jumped up, too, and stood watching with them, and I could sense that they'd forgotten I was with them. All of their attentions were fastened on that shining basketball.

As it ticked, the glow of it became a shining mistiness and the mistiness spread out, like a fog creeping up the land from a river bottom.

The mistiness enveloped us and out of that mistiness strange shapes began to form. At first they were wavering and unstable forms, but in a while they steadied and became more substantial, although never quite substantial; there was about them a touch of fairyland, of a shape and time that one might see, but that was forever out of reach.

And now the mistiness went away – or perhaps it still remained and we did not notice it, for with the creation of the forms it had supplied another world, of which we were observers, if not an actual part.

It appeared that we were standing on the terrace of what on Earth might have been called a villa. Beneath our feet were rough-hewn flagstones, with thin lines of grass growing in the cracks between the stones, and back of us rose rough walls of masonry. But the walls had a misty texture, as if they were some sort of simulated backdrop that one was not supposed to inspect too closely.

In front of us spread a city, an ugly city with no beauty in it. It was utilitarian in its every aspect, a geometric mass of stone, reared without imagination, with no architectural concept beyond the principle that one stone piled atop another would achieve a place of shelter. The city was the drab colour of dried mud and it spread as far as the eye could see, a disorderly mass of rectilinear structures thrust together, cheek by jowl, with no breathing space provided.

And yet there was an insubstantiality about it; never for an instant did that massive city become solid masonry. Nor were the flagstones underneath our feet an actual flagstone terrace. Rather it was as though we floated, a fraction of an inch above the flagstones, never touching them.

We stood, it seemed, in the middle of a three-dimensional movie. And all around us the movie moved and went about its business and we knew that we were there, for we could see it on every side of us, but the actors in the movie were unaware of us and while we knew that we were there, there also was the knowledge that we were not a part of it, that we somehow stood aside from this magic world in which we were engulfed.

At first I'd seen only the city, but now I saw there was terror in the city. People were running madly in the streets, and from far off I could hear the screaming, the thin and frantic wailing of a lost and hopeless people.

Then the city and the screaming were blotted out in a searing flash of light, a blossoming whiteness that became so intense it suddenly went black. The blackness covered us and we stood in a world that had nothing in it except the darkness and the cataract of thunder that poured out of that place where the flash of light had blossomed.

I took a short step forward, groping as I went. My hands met emptiness and the feeling flooded over me that I stood in an emptiness that stretched on forever, that what I'd known before had been nothing but illusion and the illusion now was gone, leaving me to grope eternally through black nothingness.

I took no other step, but stood stiff and straight, afraid to move a muscle, sensing in all irrationality that I stood upon a platform and might fall from it into a great emptiness which would have no bottom.

As I stood there the blackness turned to grey and through the greyness I could see the city, flattened and sharded, swept by tornadic winds, with gouts of flame and ash twisting in the monstrous whirlwind of destruction. Above the city was a rolling cloud, as if a million thunderstorms had been rolled all into one. And from this maelstrom of fury came a deep-throated growling of death and fear and fate, a savage terrible sound that made one think of evil.

Around me I saw the others – the black-skinned people with the silver crests – standing transfixed and frozen, fascinated by the sight that lay before them, rigid as if with fear, but something more than just plain fear – superstitious fear, perhaps.

I stood there, rooted with them, and the growling died away. Thin wisps of smoke curled up above the rubble, and in the silence that came as the growling ceased I could hear the little cracklings and groanings and the tiny crashes as the splintered stone that still remained settled more firmly into place. But there was no sound of crying now, none of the thin, high screaming. There were no people and the only movements were the little ripples of settling rubble that lay beyond the bare and blackened and entirely featureless area where the light had blossomed.

The greyness faded and the city began to dim. Out in the centre of the picnic circle I could make out the glimmer of the lens-covered basketball. There were no signs of my fellow picnickers; they had disappeared. And from the thinning greyness came another screaming – but a different kind of screaming, not the kind I'd heard from the city before the bomb had struck.

For now I knew that I had seen a city destroyed by a nuclear explosion – as one might have watched it on a TV set. And the TV set, if one could call it that, could have been nothing other than the basketball. By some strange magic mechanism it had invaded time and brought back from the past a moment of high crisis.

The greyness faded out and the night came back again, with the golden moon and the dust of stars and the silver slopes that curved to meet the quicksilver of the creek.

Down the farther slope I could see the scurrying figures, with their silver topknots gleaming in the moonlight, running wildly through the night and screaming in simulated terror.

I stood looking after them and shivered, for there was something here, I knew, that had a sickness in it, a sickness of the mind, an illness of the soul.

Slowly I turned back to the basketball. It was, once again, just a thing of lenses. I walked over to it and knelt beside it and had a look at it. It was made of many lenses and in the interstices between the tilted lenses, I could catch glimpses of some sort of mechanism, although all the details of it were lost in the weakness of the moonlight.

I reached out a hand and touched it gingerly. It seemed fragile and I feared that I might break it, but I couldn't leave it here. It was something that I wanted and I told myself that if I could get it back to Earth, it would help to back up the story I had to tell.

I took off my jacket and spread it on the ground, and then carefully picked up the basketball, using both my hands to cradle it, and put it on the jacket. I gathered up the ends of the cloth and wrapped them all around the ball, then tied the sleeves together to help hold the folds in place.

I picked it up and tucked it securely underneath an arm, then got to my feet.

The hampers and the bottles lay scattered all about and it occurred to me that I should get away as quickly as I could, for these other people would be coming back to get the basketball and to gather up their picnic. But there was as yet no sign of them. Listening intently, it seemed to me that I could hear the faint sounds of their screaming receding in the distance.

I turned and went down the hill and crossed the creek. Halfway up the other slope I met Tupper coming out to hunt me.

'Thought you had got lost,' he said.

'I met a group of people. I had a picnic with them.'

'They have funny topknots?'

'They had that,' I said.

'Friends of mine,' said Tupper. 'They come here many times. They come here to be scared.'

'Scared?'

'Sure. It's fun for them. They like being scared.'

I nodded to myself. So that was it, I thought. Like a bunch of kids creeping on a haunted house and peeking through the windows so that they might run, shrieking from imagined horror at imagined stirrings they'd seen inside the house. And doing it time after time, never getting tired of the good time that they had, gaining some strange pleasure from their very fright.

'They have more fun,' said Tupper, 'than anyone I know.'

'You've seen them often?'

'Lots of times,' said Tupper.

'You didn't tell me.'

'I never had the time,' said Tupper. 'I never got around to it.'

'And they live close by?'

'No,' said Tupper. 'Very far away.'

'But on this planet.'

'Planet?' Tupper asked.

'On this world,' I said.

'No. On another world. In another place. But that don't make no difference. They go everywhere for fun.'

So they went everywhere for fun, I thought. And everywhen, perhaps. They were temporal ghouls, feeding on the past, getting their vicarious kicks out of catastrophe and disaster of an ancient age, seeking out those historic moments that were horrible and foul. Coming back again and yet again to one such scene that had a high appeal to their perverted minds.

A decadent race, I wondered, from some world conquered by the Flowers, free now to use the many gateways that led from world to world?

Conquered, in the light of what I knew, might not be the proper word. For I had seen this night what had happened to this world. Not depopulated by the Flowers, but by the mad suicide of the humans who had been native to it. More than likely it had been an empty and a dead world for years before the Flowers had battered down the time-phase boundary that let them into it. The skulls I had found had been those of the survivors – perhaps a relatively few survivors – who had managed to live on for a little time, but who had been foredoomed by the poisoned soil and air and water.

So the Flowers had not really conquered; they had merely taken over a world that had gone forfeit by the madness of its owners.

'How long ago,' I asked, 'did the Flowers come here?'

'What makes you think,' asked Tupper, 'that they weren't always here?'

'Nothing. Just a thought. They never talked to you about it?'

'I never asked,' said Tupper.

Of course he wouldn't ask; he'd have no curiosity. He would be simply glad that he had found this place, where he had friends who talked with him and provided for his simple needs, where there were no humans to mock or pester him.

We came down to the camping place and I saw that the moon had moved far into the west. The fire was burning low and Tupper fed it with some sticks, then sat down beside it. I sat down across from him and placed the wrapped basketball beside me.

'What you got there?' asked Tupper.

I unwrapped it for him.

He said, 'It's the thing my friends had. You stole it from my friends.'

'They ran away and left it. I want a look at it.'

'You see other times with it,' said Tupper.

'You know about this, Tupper?'

He nodded. 'They show me many times – not often, I don't mean that, but many other times. Time not like we're in.'

'You don't know how it works?'

'They told me,' Tupper said, 'but I didn't understand.'

He wiped his chin, but failed to do the job, so wiped it a second time.

They told me, he had said. So he could talk with them. He could talk with Flowers and with a race that conversed by music. There was no use, I knew, in asking him about it, because he couldn't tell me. Perhaps there was no one who could explain an ability of that sort – not to a human being. For more than likely there'd be no common terms in which an explanation could be made.

The basketball glowed softly, lying on the jacket.

'Maybe,' Tupper said, 'we should go back to bed.'

'In a little while,' I said. Anytime I wanted, it would be no trouble going back to bed, for the ground was bed.

I put out a hand and touched the basketball.

A mechanism that extended back in time and recorded for the viewer the sight and sound of happenings that lay deep in the memory of the space-time continuum. It would have, I thought, very many uses. It would be an invaluable tool in historical research. It would make crime impossible, for it could dig out of the past the details of any crime. And it would be a terrible device if it fell into unscrupulous hands or became the property of a government.

I'd take it back to Millville, if I could take it back, if I could get back myself. It would help to support the story I had to tell, but after I had told the story and had offered it as proof, what would I do with it? Lock it in a vault and destroy the combination? Take a sledge and smash it into smithereens? Turn it over to the scientists? What could one do with it?

'You messed up your coat,' said Tupper, 'carrying that thing.'

I said, 'It wasn't much to start with.'

And then I remembered that envelope with the fifteen hundred dollars in it. It had been in the breast pocket of the jacket and I could have lost it in the wild running I had done or when I used the jacket to wrap up the time contraption.

What a damn fool thing to do, I thought. What a chance to take. I should have pinned it in my pocket or put it in my shoe or something of the sort. It wasn't every day a man got fifteen hundred dollars.

I bent over and put my hand into the pocket and the envelope was there and I felt a great relief as my fingers touched it. But almost immediately I knew there was something wrong. My groping fingers told me the envelope was thin and it should have been bulging with thirty fifty-dollar bills.

I jerked it from my pocket and flipped up the flap. The envelope was empty.

I didn't have to ask. I didn't have to wonder. I knew just what had happened. That dirty, slobbering, finger-counting bum – I'd choke it out of him, I'd beat him to a pulp, I'd make him cough it up!

I was halfway up to nail him when he spoke to me and the voice that he spoke with was that of the TV glamour gal.

'This is Tupper speaking for the Flowers,' the voice said. 'And you sit back down and behave yourself.'

'Don't give me that,' I snarled. 'You can't sneak out of this by pretending . . .'

'But this is the Flowers,' the voice insisted sharply and even as it said the words, I saw that Tupper's face had taken on that wall-eyed, vacant look.

'But he took my roll,' I said. 'He sneaked it out of the envelope when I was asleep.'

'Keep quiet,' said the honeyed voice. 'Just keep quiet and listen.'

'Not until I get my fifteen hundred back.'

'You'll get it back. You'll get much more than your fifteen hundred back.'

'You can guarantee that?'

'We'll guarantee it.'

I sat down again.

'Look,' I said, 'you don't know what that money meant to me. It's part my fault, of course. I should have waited until the bank was open or I should have found a good safe place to hide it. But there was so much going on . . .'

'Don't worry for a moment,' said the Flowers. 'We'll get it back to you.'

'OK,' I said, 'and does he have to use that voice?'

'What's the matter with the voice?'

'Oh, hell,' I said, 'go ahead and use it. I want to talk to you, maybe even argue with you, and it's unfair, but I'll remember who is speaking.'

'We'll use another voice, then,' said the Flowers, changing in the middle of the sentence to the voice of the businessman.

'Thanks very much,' I said.

'You remember,' said the Flowers, 'the time we spoke to you on the phone and suggested that you might represent us?'

'Certainly I remember. But as for representing you . . .'

'We need someone very badly. Someone we can trust.'

'But you can't be certain I'm the man to trust.'

'Yes, we can,' they said. 'Because we know you love us.'

'Now, look here,' I said. 'I don't know what gives you that idea. I don't know if . . .'

'Your father found those of us who languished in your world. He took us home and cared for us. He protected us and tended us and he loved us and we flourished.'

'Yes, I know all that.'

'You're an extension of your father.'

'Well, not necessarily. Not the way you mean.'

'Yes,' they insisted. 'We have knowledge of your biology. We know about inherited characteristics. Like father, like son is a saying that you have.'

It was no use, I saw. You couldn't argue with them. From the logic of their race, from the half-assimilated, half-digested facts they had obtained in some manner in their contact with our Earth, they had it figured out. And it probably made good sense in their plant world, for an offspring plant would differ very little from the parents. It would be, I suspected, a fruitless battle to try to make them see that an assumption that was valid in their case need not extend its validity into the human race.

'All right,' I said, 'we'll let you have it your way. You're sure that you can trust me and probably you can. But in all fairness I must tell you I can't do the job.'

'Can't?' they asked.

'You want me to represent you back on Earth. To be your ambassador. Your negotiator.'

'That was the thought we had in mind.'

'I have no training for a job of that sort. I'm not qualified. I wouldn't know how to do it. I wouldn't even know how to make a start.'

'You have started,' said the Flowers. 'We are very pleased with the start you've made.'

I stiffened and jerked upright. 'The start I've made?' I asked.

'Why, yes, of course,' they told me. 'Surely you remember. You asked that Gerald Sherwood get in touch with someone. Someone, you stressed, in high authority.'

'I wasn't representing you.'

'But you could,' they said. 'We want someone to explain us.'

'Let's be honest,' I told them. 'How can I explain you? I know scarcely anything about you.'

'We would tell you anything you want to know.'

'For openers,' I said, 'this is not your native world.'

'No, it's not. We've advanced through many worlds.'

'And the people – no, not the people, the intelligences – what happened to the intelligences of those other worlds?'

'We do not understand.'

'When you get into a world, what do you do with the intelligence you find there?'

'It is not often we find intelligence – not meaningful intelligence, not cultural intelligence. Cultural intelligence does not develop on all worlds. When it does, we co-operate. We work with it. That is, when we can.'

'There are times when you can't?'

'Please do not misunderstand,' they pleaded. 'There has been a case or two where we could not contact a world's intelligence. It would not become aware of us. We were just another life form, another – what do you call it? – another weed, perhaps.'

'What do you do, then?'

'What can we do?' they asked.

It was not, it seemed to me, an entirely honest answer. There were a lot of things that they could do.

'And you keep on going.'

'Keep on going?'

'From world to world,' I said. 'From one world to another. When do you intend to stop?'

'We do not know,' they said.

'What is your goal? What are you aiming at?'

'We do not know,' they said.

'Now, just wait a minute. That's the second time you've said that. You must know . . .'

'Sir,' they asked, 'does your race have a goal – a conscious goal?'

'I guess we don't,' I said.

'So that would make us even.'

'I suppose it would.'

'You have on your world things you call computers.'

'Yes,' I said, 'but very recently.'

'And the function of computers is the storage of data and the correlation of that data and making it available whenever it is needed.'

'There still are a lot of problems. The retrieval of the data . . .'

'That is beside the point. What would you say is the goal of your computers?'

'Our computers have no purpose. They are not alive.'

'But if they were alive?'

'Well, in that case, I suppose the ultimate purpose would be the storage of a universal data and its correlation.'

'That perhaps is right,' they said. 'We are living computers.'

'Then there is no end for you. You'll keep on forever.'

'We are not sure,' they said.

'But . . .'

'Data,' they told me, pontifically, 'is the means to one end only – arrival at the truth. Perhaps we do not need a universal data to arrive at truth.'

'How do you know when you have arrived?'

'We will know,' they said.

I gave up. We were getting nowhere.

'So you want our Earth,' I said.

'You state it awkwardly and unfairly. We do not want your Earth. We want to be let in, we want some living space, we want to work with you. You give us your knowledge and we will give you ours.'

'We'd make quite a team,' I said.

'We would, indeed,' they said.

'And then?'

'What do you mean?' they asked.

'After we've swapped knowledge, what do we do then?'

'Why, we go on,' they said. 'Into other worlds. The two of us together.'

'Seeking other cultures? After other knowledge?'

'That is right,' they said.

They made it sound so simple. And it wasn't simple; it couldn't be that simple. There was nothing ever simple.

A man could talk with them for days and still be asking questions, getting no more than a bare outline of the situation.

'There is one thing you must realize,' I said. 'The people of my Earth will not accept you on blind faith alone. They must know what you expect of us and what we can expect of you. They must have some assurance that we can work together.'

'We can help,' they said, 'in many different ways. We need not be as you see us now. We can turn ourselves into any kind of plant you need. We can provide a great reservoir of economic resources. We can be the old things that you have relied upon for years, but better than the old things ever were. We can be better foodstuff and better building material; better fibre. Name anything you need from plants and we can be that thing.'

'You mean you'd let us eat you and saw you up for lumber and weave you into cloth? And you would not mind?'

They came very close to sighing. 'How can we make you understand? Eat one of us and we still remain. Saw one of us and we still remain. The life of us is one life – you could never kill us all, never eat us all. Our life is in our brains and our nervous systems, in our roots and bulbs and tubers. We would not mind your eating us if we knew that we were helping.

'And we would not only be the old forms of economic plant life to which you are accustomed. We could be different kinds of grain, different kinds of trees – ones you have never heard of. We could adapt ourselves to any soils or climates. We could grow anywhere you wanted. You want medicines or drugs. Let your chemists tell us what you want and we'll be that for you. We'll be made-to-order plants.'

'All this,' I said, 'and your knowledge, too.'

'That is right,' they said.

'And in return, what do we do?'

'You give your knowledge to us. You work with us to utilize all knowledge, the pooled knowledge that we have.

You give us an expression we cannot give ourselves. We have knowledge, but knowledge in itself is worthless unless it can be used. We want it used, we want so badly to work with a race that can use what we have to offer, so that we can feel a sense of accomplishment that is denied us now. And, also, of course, we would hope that together we could develop a better way to open the time-phase boundaries into other worlds.'

'And the time dome that you put over Millville – why did you do that?'

'To gain your world's attention. To let you know that we were here and waiting.'

'But you could have told some of your contacts and your contacts could have told the world. You probably did tell some of them. Stiffy Grant, for instance.'

'Yes, Stiffy Grant. And there were others, too.'

'They could have told the world.'

'Who would have believed them? They would have been thought of as – how do you say it – crackpots?'

'Yes, I know,' I said. 'No one would pay attention to anything Stiffy said. But surely there were others.'

'Only certain types of minds,' they told me, 'can make contact with us. We can reach many minds, but they can't reach back to us. And to believe in us, to know us, you must reach back to us.'

'You mean only the screwballs . . .'

'We're afraid that's what we mean,' they said.

It made sense when you thought about it. The most successful contact they could find had been Tupper Tyler and while there was nothing wrong with Stiffy as a human being, he certainly was not what one would call a solid citizen.

I sat there for a moment, wondering why they'd contacted me and Gerald Sherwood. Although that was a little different. They'd contacted Sherwood because he was valuable to them; he could make the telephones for them and he could set up a system that would give them working capital. And me?

Because my father had taken care of them? I hoped to heaven that was all it was.

'So, OK,' I said. 'I guess I understand. How about the storm of seeds?'

'We planted a demonstration plot,' they told me. 'So your people could realize, by looking at it, how versatile we are.'

You never won, I thought. They had an answer for everything you asked.

I wondered if I ever had expected to get anywhere with them or really wanted to get anywhere with them. Maybe, subconsciously, all I wanted was to get back to Millville.

And maybe it was all Tupper. Maybe there weren't any Flowers. Maybe it was simply a big practical joke that Tupper had dreamed up in his so-called mind, sitting here ten years and dreaming up the joke and getting it rehearsed so he could pull it off.

But, I argued with myself, it couldn't be just Tupper, for Tupper wasn't bright enough. His mind was not given to a concept of this sort. He couldn't dream it up and he couldn't pull it off. And besides, there was the matter of his being here and of my being here, and that was something a joke would not explain.

I came slowly to my feet and turned so that I faced the slope above the camp and there in the bright moonlight lay the darkness of the purple flowers. Tupper still sat where he had been sitting, but now he was hunched forward, almost doubled up, fallen fast asleep and snoring very softly.

The perfume seemed stronger now and the moonlight had taken on a trembling and there was a Presence out there somewhere on the slope. I strained my eyes to see it, and once I thought I saw it, but it faded out again, although I still knew that it was there.

There was a purpleness in the very night and the feel of an intelligence that waited for a word to come stalking down the hill to talk with me, as two friends might talk, with no need of an interpreter, to squat about the campfire and yarn the night away.

Ready? asked the Presence.

A word, I wondered, or simply something stirring in my brain – something born of the purpleness and moonlight?

'Yes,' I said, 'I'm ready. I will do the best I can.'

I bent and wrapped the time contraption in my jacket and tucked it underneath my arm and then went up the slope. I knew the Presence was up there, waiting for me, and there were quivers running up and down my spine. It was fear, perhaps, but it didn't feel like fear.

I came up to where the Presence waited and I could not see it, but I knew that it had fallen into step with me and was walking there beside me.

'I am not afraid of you,' I told it.

It didn't say a word. It just kept walking with me. We went across the ridge and down the slope into the dip where in another world the greenhouse and garden were.

A little to your left, said the thing that walked the night with me, and then go straight ahead.

I turned a little to my left and then went straight ahead.

A few more feet, it said.

I stopped and turned my head to face it and there was nothing there. If there had been anything, it was gone from there.

The moon was a golden gargoyle in the west. The world was lone and empty; the silvered slope had a hungry look. The blue-black sky was filled with many little eyes with a hard sharp glitter to them, a predatory glitter and the remoteness of uncaring.

Beyond the ridge a man of my own race drowsed beside a dying campfire, and it was all right for him, for he had a talent that I did not have, that I knew now I did not have – the talent for reaching out to grasp an alien hand (or paw or claw or pad) and being able in his twisted mind to translate that alien touch into a commonplace.

I shuddered at the gargoyle moon and took two steps forward and walked out of that hungry world straight into my garden.

15

RAGGED CLOUDS still raced across the sky, blotting out the moon. A faint lighting in the east gave notice of the dawn. The windows of my house were filled with lamplight and I knew that Gerald Sherwood and the rest of them were waiting there for me. And just to my left the greenhouse with the tree growing at its corner loomed ghostly against the rise of ground behind it.

I started to walk forward and fingers were scratching at my trouser leg. Startled, I looked down and saw that I had walked into a bush.

There had been no bush in the garden the last time I had seen it; there had been only the purple flowers. But I think I guessed what might have happened even before I stooped to have a look.

Squatting there, I squinted along the ground and in the first grey light of the coming day, I saw there were no flowers. Instead of a patch of flowers there was a patch of little bushes, perhaps a little larger, but not much larger than the flowers.

I hunkered there, with a coldness growing in me – for there was no explanation other than the fact that the bushes were the flowers, that somehow the Flowers had changed the flowers that once had grown there into little bushes. And, I wondered wildly, what could their purpose be?

Even here, I thought – even here they reach out for us. Even here they play their tricks on us and lay their traps for us. And they could do anything they wanted, I supposed, for if they did not own, at least they manipulated this corner of the Earth entrapped beneath the dome.

I put out a hand and felt along a branch and the branch had soft-swelling buds all along its length. Springtime buds, that in a day or so would be breaking into leaf. Springtime buds in the depth of summer!

I had believed in them, I thought. In that little space of time toward the very end, when Tupper had ceased his talking and had dozed before the fire and there had been something on the hillside that had spoken to me and had walked me home, I had believed in them.

Had there been something on that hillside? Had something walked with me? I sweated, thinking of it.

I felt the bulk of the wrapped time contraption underneath my arm, and that, I realized, was a talisman of the actuality of that other world. With that, I must believe.

They had told me, I remembered, that I'd get my money back – they had guaranteed it. And here I was, back home again, without my fifteen hundred.

I got to my feet and started for the house, then changed my mind. I turned around and went up the slope toward Doc Fabian's house. It might be a good idea, I told myself, to see what was going on outside the barrier. The people who were waiting at the house could wait a little longer.

I reached the top of the slope and turned around, looking toward the east. There, beyond the village, blazed a line of campfires and the lights of many cars running back and forth. A searchlight swung a thin blue finger of light up into the sky, slowly sweeping back and forth. And at one spot that seemed a little closer was a greater blob of light. A great deal of activity seemed to be going on around it.

Watching it, I made out a steam shovel and great black mounds of earth piled up on either side of it. I could hear, faintly, the metallic clanging of the mighty scoop as it dumped a load and then reached down into the hole to take another bite. Trying, I told myself, to dig beneath the barrier.

A car came rattling down the street and turned into the driveway of the house behind me.

Doc, I thought – Doc coming home after being routed out of bed on an early morning call.

I walked across the lawn and around the house. The car was parked on the concrete strip of driveway and Doc was getting out.

'Doc,' I said, 'it's Brad.'

He turned and peered at me.

'Oh,' he said, and his voice sounded tired, 'so you are back again. There are people waiting at the house, you know.'

Too tired to be surprised that I was back again; too all beat out to care.

He shuffled forward and I saw, quite suddenly, that Doc was old. Of course I had thought of him as old, but never before had he actually seemed old. Now I could see that he was – the slightly stooped shoulders, his feet barely lifting off the ground as he walked toward me, the loose, old-man hang of his trousers, the deep lines in his face.

'Floyd Caldwell,' he said. 'I was out to Floyd's. He had a heart attack – a strong, tough man like him and he has a heart attack.'

'How is he?'

'As well as I can manage. He should be in a hospital, getting complete rest. But I can't get him there. With that thing out there, I can't get him where he should be.

'I don't know, Brad. I just don't know what will happen to us. Mrs Jensen was supposed to go in this morning for surgery. Cancer. She'll die, anyhow, but surgery would give her months, maybe a year or two, of life. And there's no way to get her there. The little Hopkins girl has been going regularly to a specialist and he's been helping her a lot. Decker – perhaps you've heard of him. He's a top-notch man. We interned together.'

He stopped in front of me. 'Can't you see,' he said. 'I can't help these people. I can do a little, but I can't do enough. I can't handle things like this – I can't do it all alone. Other times I could send them somewhere else, to someone who could help them. And now I can't do that. For the first time in my life, I can't help my people.'

'You're taking it too hard,' I said.

He looked at me with a beaten look, a tired and beaten look. 'I can't take it any other way,' he said. 'All these years, they've depended on me.'

'How's Stiffy?' I asked. 'You have heard, of course.'

Doc snorted angrily. 'The damn fool ran away.'

'From the hospital?'

'Where else would he run from? Got dressed when their backs were turned and snuck away. He always was a sneaky old goat and he never had good sense. They're looking for him, but no one's found him yet.'

'He'd head back here,' I said.

'I suppose he would,' said Doc. 'What about this story I heard about some telephone he had?'

I shook my head. 'Hiram said he found one.'

Doc peered sharply at me. 'You don't know anything about it?'

'Not very much,' I said.

'Nancy said you were in some other world or something. What kind of talk is that?'

'Did Nancy tell you that?'

He shook his head. 'No, Gerald told me. He asked me what to do. He was afraid that if he mentioned it, he would stir up the village.'

'And?'

'I told him not to. The folks are stirred up enough. He told them what you said about the flowers. He had to tell them something.'

'Doc,' I said, 'it's a funny business. I don't rightly know myself. Let's not talk about it. Tell me what's going on. What are those fires out there?'

'Those are soldier fires,' he told me. 'There are state troops out there. They've got the town ringed in. Brad, it's crazier than hell. We can't get out and no one can get in, but they got troops out there. I don't know what they think they're doing. They evacuated everybody for ten miles outside the barrier and there are planes patrolling and they have some tanks. They tried to dynamite the barrier this morning and they didn't do a thing except blow a hole in Jake Fisher's pasture. They could have saved that dynamite.'

'They're trying to dig under the barrier,' I said.

'They've done a lot of things,' said Doc. 'They had some helicopters that flew above the town, then tried to come straight down. Figuring, I guess, that there are only walls out there, without any top to them. But they found there was a top. They fooled around all afternoon and they wrecked two 'copters, but they found out, I guess, that it's a sort of dome. It curves all the way above us. A kind of bubble, you might say.

'And there are all those fool newspapermen out there. I tell you, Brad, there's an army of them. There isn't anything but Millville on the TV and radio, or in the papers either.'

'It's big news,' I said.

'Yes, I suppose so. But I'm worried, Brad. This village is getting ready to blow up. The people are on edge. They're scared and touchy. The whole damn place could go hysterical if you snapped your fingers.'

He came a little closer.

'What are you planning, Brad?'

'I'm going down to my place. There are people down there. You want to come along?'

He shook his head. 'No, I was down there for a while and then I got this call from Floyd. I'm all beat out. I'm going in to bed.'

He turned and started to shuffle away and then he turned back.

'You be careful, boy,' he warned. 'There's a lot of talk about the flowers. They say if your father hadn't raised those flowers it never would have happened. They think it was a plot your father started and you are in on it.'

'I'll watch my step,' I said.

16

THEY WERE in the living-room. As soon as I came in the kitchen door, Hiram Martin saw me.

'There he is!' he bellowed, leaping up and charging out into the kitchen.

He stopped his rush and looked accusingly at me. 'It took you long enough,' he said.

I didn't answer him.

I put the time contraption, still wrapped in my jacket, on the kitchen table. A fold of cloth fell away from it and the many-angled lenses winked in the light from the ceiling fixture.

Hiram backed away a step. 'What's that?' he asked.

'Something I brought back,' I said. 'A time machine, I guess.'

The coffee pot was on the stove and the burner was turned low. Used coffee cups covered the top of the kitchen sink. The sugar canister had its lid off and there was spilled sugar on the counter top.

The others in the living-room were crowding through the door and there were a lot of them, more than I'd expected.

Nancy came past Hiram and walked up to me. She put out a hand and laid it on my arm.

'You're all right,' she said.

'It was a breeze,' I told her.

She was beautiful, I thought – more beautiful than I'd remembered her, more beautiful than back in the high school days when I'd looked at her through a haze of stars. More beautiful, here close to me, than my memory had made her.

I moved closer to her and put an arm around her. For an

instant she leaned her head against my shoulder, then straightened it again. She was warm and soft against me and I was sorry that it couldn't last, but all the rest of them were watching us and waiting.

'I made some phone calls,' Gerald Sherwood said. 'Senator Gibbs is coming out to see you. He'll have someone from the State Department. On short notice, Brad, that was the best I could do.'

'It'll do,' I said.

For, standing in my kitchen once again, with Nancy close beside me, with the lamplight soft in the coming dawn, with the old familiar things all around, that other world had retreated into the background and had taken on a softness that half obscured its threat – if it were a threat.

'What I want to know,' Tom Preston blurted, 'is what about this stuff that Gerald tells us about your father's flowers.'

'Yes,' said Mayor Higgy Morris, 'what have they to do with it?'

Hiram didn't say anything, but he sneered at me.

'Gentlemen,' said lawyer Nichols, 'this is not the way to go about it. You must be fair about it. Keep the questions until later. Let Brad tell us what he knows.'

Joe Evans said, 'Anything he has to say will be more than we know now.'

'OK,' said Higgy, 'we'll be glad to listen.'

'But first,' said Hiram, 'I want to know about that thing on the table. It might be dangerous. It might be a bomb.'

'I don't know what it is,' I said. 'It has to do with time. It can handle time. Maybe you would call it a time camera, some sort of time machine.'

Tom Preston snorted and Hiram sneered again.

Father Flanagan, the town's one Catholic priest, had been standing quietly in the doorway, side by side with Pastor Silas Middleton, from the church across the street. Now the old priest spoke quietly, so quietly that one could barely hear him, his voice one with the lamplight and the dawn. 'I would be the last,' he said, 'to hold that time might be manipulated or that flowers would have anything to do with what has happened here. These are propositions that go against the grain of my every understanding. But unlike some of the rest of you, I'm willing to listen before I reach a judgement.'

'I'll try to tell you,' I said. 'I'll try to tell you just the way it happened.'

'Alf Peterson has been trying to call you,' Nancy said. 'He's phoned a dozen times.'

'Did he leave a number?'

'Yes, I have it here.'

'That can wait,' said Higgy. 'We want to hear this story.'

'Perhaps,' suggested Nancy's father, 'you'd better tell us right away. Let's all go in the living-room where we'll be comfortable.'

We all went into the living-room and sat down.

'Now, my boy,' said Higgy, companionably, 'go ahead and spill it.'

I could have strangled him. When I looked at him, I imagine that he knew exactly how I felt.

'We'll keep quiet,' he said. 'We'll hear you out.'

I waited until they all were quiet and then I said, 'I'll have to start with yesterday morning when I came home, after my car had been wrecked, and found Tupper Tyler sitting in the swing.'

Higgy leaped to his feet. 'But that's crazy?' he shouted. 'Tupper has been lost for years.'

Hiram jumped up, too. 'You made fun of me,' he bellowed, 'when I told you Tom had talked to Tupper.'

'I lied to you,' I said. 'I had to lie to you. I didn't know what was going on and you were on the prod.'

The Reverend Silas Middleton asked, 'Brad, you admit you lied?'

'Yes, of course I do. That big ape had me pinned against the wall . . .'

'If you lied once, you'll lie again,' Tom Preston shrilled. 'How can we believe anything you tell us?'

'Tom,' I said, 'I don't give a damn if you believe me or not.'

They all sat down and sat there looking at me and I knew that I had been childish, but they burned me up.

'I would suggest,' said Father Flanagan, 'that we should start over and all of us make a heroic effort to behave ourselves.'

'Yes, please,' said Higgy, heavily, 'and everyone shut up.'

I looked around and no one said a word. Gerald Sherwood nodded gravely at me.

I took a deep breath and began.

'Maybe,' I said, 'I should go even farther back than that – to the time Tom Preston sent Ed Adler around to take out my telephone.'

'You were three months in arrears,' yelped Preston. 'You hadn't even . . .'

'Tom,' said lawyer Nichols, sharply.

Tom settled back into his chair and began to sulk.

I went ahead and told everything – about Stiffy Grant and the telephone I'd found in my office and about the story Alf Peterson had told me and then how I'd gone out to Stiffy's shack. I told them everything except about Gerald Sherwood and how he had made the phones. I somehow had the feeling that I had no right to tell that part of it.

I asked them, 'Are there any questions?'

'There are a lot of them,' said lawyer Nichols, 'but go ahead and finish. Is that all right with the rest of you?'

Higgy Morris grunted. 'It's all right with me,' he said.

'It's not all right with me,' said Preston, nastily. 'Gerald told us that Nancy talked with Brad. He never told us how. She used one of them phones, of course.'

'My phone,' said Sherwood. 'I've had one of them for years.'

Higgy said, 'You never told me, Gerald.'

'It didn't occur to me,' said Sherwood, curtly.

'It seems to me,' said Preston, 'there has been a hell of a lot going on that we never knew about.'

'That,' said Father Flanagan, 'is true beyond all question. But I have the impression that this young man has no more than started on his story.'

So I went ahead. I told it as truthfully as I could and in all the detail I could recall.

Finally I was finished and they sat not moving, stunned perhaps, and shocked, and maybe not believing it entirely, but believing some of it.

Father Flanagan stirred uneasily. 'Young man,' he asked, 'you are absolutely sure this is not hallucination?'

'I brought back the time contraption. That's not hallucination.'

'We must agree, I think,' said Nichols, 'that there are strange things going on. The story Brad has told us is no stranger than the barrier.'

'There isn't anyone,' yelled Preston, 'who can work with time. Why time is – well, it's . . .'

'That's exactly it,' said Sherwood. 'No one knows anything of time. And it's not the only thing of which we're wholly ignorant. There is gravitation. There is no one, absolutely no one, who can tell you what gravitation is.'

'I don't believe a word of it,' said Hiram, flatly. 'He's been hiding out somewhere . . .'

Joe Evans said, 'We combed the town. There was no place he could hide.'

'Actually,' said Father Flanagan, 'it doesn't matter if we believe all this or not. The important thing is whether the people who are coming out from Washington believe it.'

Higgy pulled himself straighter in his chair. He turned to Sherwood. 'You said Gibbs was coming out. Bringing others with him.'

Sherwood nodded. 'A man from the State Department.'

'What exactly did Gibbs say?'

'He said he'd be right out. He said the talk with Brad could only be preliminary. Then he'd go back and report. He said it might not be simply a national problem. It might be international. Our government might have to confer with other governments. He wanted to know more about it. All I could tell him was that a man here in the village had some vital information.'

'They'll be out at the edge of the barrier, waiting for us. The east road, I presume.'

'I suppose so,' Sherwood said. 'We didn't go into it. He'll phone me from some place outside the barrier when he arrives.'

'As a matter of fact,' said Higgy, lowering his voice as if he were speaking confidentially, 'if we can get out of this without being hurt, it'll be the best thing that ever happened to us. No other town in all of history has gotten the kind of publicity we're getting now. Why, for years there'll be tourists coming just to look at us, just to say they've been here.'

'It seems to me,' said Father Flanagan, 'that if this should all be true, there are far greater things involved than whether or not our town can attract some tourists.'

'Yes,' said Silas Middleton. 'It means we are facing an alien form of life. How we handle it may mean the difference between life and death. Not for us alone, I mean, the people in this village. But the life or death of the human race.'

'Now, see here,' piped Preston, 'you can't mean that a bunch of flowers . . .'

'You damn fool,' said Sherwood, 'it's not just a bunch of flowers.'

Joe Evans said, 'That's right. Not just a bunch of flowers. But an entirely different form of life. Not an animal life, but a plant life – a plant life that is intelligent.'

'And a life,' I said, 'that has stored away the knowledge of God knows how many other races. They'll know things we've never even thought about.'

'I don't see,' said Higgy, doggedly, 'what we've got to be afraid of. There never was a time that we couldn't beat a bunch of weeds. We can use sprays and . . .'

'If we want to kill them off,' I said, 'I don't think it's quite as easy as you try to make it. But putting that aside for the moment, do we want to kill them off?'

'You mean,' yelled Higgy, 'let them come in and take over?'

'Not take over. Come in and co-operate with us.'

'But the barrier!' yelled Hiram. 'Everyone forgets about the barrier!'

'No one has forgotten about it,' said Nichols. 'The barrier is no more than a part of the entire problem. Let's solve the problem and we can take care of the barrier as well.'

'My God,' groaned Preston, 'you all are talking as if you believe every word of it.'

'That isn't it,' said Silas Middleton. 'But we have to use what Brad has told us as a working hypothesis. I don't say that what he has told us is absolutely right. He may have misinterpreted, he may simply be mistaken in certain areas. But at the moment it's the only solid information we have to work with.'

'I don't believe a word of it,' said Hiram, flatly. 'There's a dirty plot afoot and I . . .'

The telephone rang, its signal blasting through the room.

Sherwood answered it.

'It's for you,' he told me. 'It's Alf again.'

I went across the room and took the receiver Sherwood held out to me.

'Hello, Alf,' I said.

'I thought,' said Alf, 'you were going to call me back. In an hour, you said.'

'I got involved,' I told him.

'They moved me out,' he said. 'They evacuated everybody. I'm in a motel just east of Coon Valley. I'm going to move over to Elmore – the motel here is pretty bad – but before I did, I wanted to get in touch with you.'

'I'm glad you did,' I said. 'There are some things I want to ask you. About that project down in Greenbriar.'

'Sure. What about the project?'

'What kind of problems did you have to solve?'

'Many different kinds.'

'Any of them have to do with plants?'

'Plants?'

'You know. Flowers, weeds, vegetables.'

'I see. Let me think. Yes, I guess there were a few.'

'What kind?'

'Well, there was one: could a plant be intelligent?'

'And your conclusion?'

'Now, look here, Brad!'

'This is important, Alf.'

'Oh, all right. The only conclusion I could reach was that it was impossible. A plant would have no motive. There's no reason a plant should be intelligent. Even if it could be, there'd be no advantage to it. It couldn't use intelligence or knowledge. It would have no way in which it could apply them. And its structure is wrong. It would have to develop certain senses it doesn't have, would have to increase its awareness of its world. It would have to develop a brain for data storage and a thinking mechanism. It was easy, Brad, once you thought about it. A plant wouldn't even try to be intelligent. It took me a while to get the reasons sorted out, but they made good solid sense.'

'And that was all?'

'No, there was another one. How to develop a foolproof method of eradicating a noxious weed, bearing in mind that the weed has high adaptability and would be able to develop immunity to any sort of threat to its existence in a relatively short length of time.'

'There isn't any possibility,' I guessed.

'There is,' said Alf, 'just a possibility. But not too good a one.'

'And that?'

'Radiation. But you couldn't count on it as foolproof if the plant really had high adaptability.'

'So there's no way to eradicate a thoroughly determined plant?'

'I'd say none at all – none in the power of man. What's this all about, Brad?'

'We may have a situation just like that,' I said. Quickly I told him something of the Flowers.

He whistled. 'You think you have this straight?'

'I can't be certain, Alf. I think so, but I can't be certain. That is, I know the Flowers are there, but . . .'

'There was another question. It ties right in with this. It wanted to know how you'd go about contacting and establishing relations with an alien life. You think the project . . .?'

'No question,' I said. 'It was run by the same people who ran the telephones.'

'We figured that before. When we talked after the barrier went up.'

'Alf, what about that question? About contact with an alien?'

He laughed, a bit uneasily. 'There are a million answers. The method would depend upon the kind of alien. And there'd always be some danger.'

'That's all you can think of? All the questions, I mean?'

'I can't think of any more. Tell me more of what's happened there.'

'I'd like to, but I can't. I have a group of people here. You're going to Elmore now?'

'Yeah. I'll call you when I get there. Will you be around?'

'I can't go anywhere,' I said.

There had been no talk among the others while I'd been on the phone. They were all listening. But as soon as I hung up, Higgy straightened up importantly.

'I figure,' he said, 'that maybe we should be getting ready to go out and meet the senator. I think most probably I should appoint a welcoming committee. The people in this room, of course, and maybe half a dozen others. Doc Fabian, and maybe . . .'

'Mayor,' said Sherwood, interrupting him, 'I think someone should point out that this is not a civic affair or a social visit. This is something somewhat more important and entirely unofficial. Brad is the one the senator must see. He is the only one who has pertinent information and . . .'

'But,' Higgy protested, 'all I was doing . . .'

'We know what you were doing,' Sherwood told him. 'What I am pointing out is that if Brad wants a committee to go along with him, he is the one who should get it up.'

'But my official duty,' Higgy bleated.

'In a matter such as this,' said Sherwood, flatly, 'you have no official duty.'

'Gerald,' said the mayor, 'I've tried to think the best of you. I've tried to tell myself . . .'

'Mayor,' said Preston, grimly, 'there's no use of pussy-footing. We might as well say it out. There's something going on, some sort of plot afoot. Brad is part of it and Stiffy's part of it and . . .'

'And,' said Sherwood, 'if you insist upon a plot, I'm part of it as well. I made the telephones.'

Higgy gulped. 'You did what?' he asked.

'I made the telephones. I manufactured them.'

'So you knew all about it all along.'

Sherwood shook his head. 'I didn't know anything at all. I just made the phones.'

Higgy sat back weakly. He clasped and unclasped his hands, staring down at them.

'I don't know,' he said. 'I just don't understand.'

But I am sure he did. Now he understood, for the first time, that this was no mere unusual natural happening which would, in time, quietly pass away and leave Millville a tourist attraction that each year would bring the curious into town by the thousands. For the first time, I am sure, Mayor Higgy Morris realized that Millville and the entire world was facing a problem that it would take more than good luck and the Chamber of Commerce to resolve.

'There is one thing,' I said.

'What's that?' asked Higgy.

'I want my phone. The one that was in my office. The phone, you remember, that hasn't any dial.'

The mayor looked at Hiram.

'No, I won't,' said Hiram. 'I won't give it back to him. He's done harm enough already.'

'Hiram,' said the mayor.

'Oh, all right,' said Hiram. 'I hope he chokes on it.'

'It appears to me,' said Father Flanagan, 'that we are all acting quite unreasonably. I would suggest we might take this entire matter up and discuss it point by point, and in that way . . .'

A ticking interrupted him, a loud and ominous ticking that beat a measure, as of doom, through the entire house. And as I heard it, I knew that the ticking had been going on for quite some time, but very softly, and that I'd been hearing it and vaguely wondering what it was.

But now, from one tick to another, it had grown loud and hard, and even as we listened to it, half hypnotized by the terror of it, the tick became a hum and the hum a roar of power.

We all leaped to out feet, startled now, and I saw that the kitchen walls were flashing, as if someone were turning on and off a light of intensive brilliance, a pulsing glow that filled the room with a flood of light, then shut off, then filled it once again.

'I knew it!' Hiram roared, charging for the kitchen. 'I knew it when I saw it. I knew it was dangerous!'

I ran after him.

'Look out!' I yelled. 'Keep away from it!'

It was the time contraption. It had floated off the table and was hovering in mid-air, with a pulse of tremendous power running through it in a regular beat, while from it came the roar of cascading energy. Below it, lying on the table, was my crumpled jacket.

I grabbed hold of Hiram's arm and tried to haul him back, but he jerked away and was hauling his pistol from its holster.

With a flash of light, the time contraption moved, rising swiftly toward the ceiling.

'No!' I cried, for I was afraid that if it ever hit the ceiling, the fragile lenses would be smashed.

Then it hit the ceiling and it did not break. Without slackening its pace, it bored straight through the ceiling. I stood gaping at the neat round hole it made.

I heard the stamp of feet behind me and the banging of a

door and when I turned around the room was empty, except for Nancy standing by the fireplace.

'Come on,' I yelled at her, running for the door that led onto the porch.

The rest of them were grouped outside, between the porch and hedge, staring up into the sky, where a light winked off and on, going very rapidly.

I glanced at the roof and saw the hole the thing had made, edged by the ragged, broken shingles that had been displaced when the machine broke through.

'There it goes,' said Gerald Sherwood, standing at my side. 'I wonder what it is.'

'I don't know,' I said. 'They slipped one over on me. They played me for a fool.'

I was shaken up and angry, and considerably ashamed. They had used me back there in that other world. They had fooled me into carrying back to my own world something they couldn't get there by themselves.

There was no way of knowing what it was meant to do, although in a little while, I feared, we would all find out.

Hiram turned to me in disgust and anger. 'You've done it now,' he blurted. 'Don't tell us you didn't mean to do it, don't pretend you don't know what it is. Whatever may be out there, you're hand in glove with them.'

I didn't try to answer him. There was no way I could.

Hiram took a step toward me.

'Cut it out!' cried Higgy. 'Don't lay a hand on him.'

'We ought to shake it out of him,' yelled Hiram. 'If we found out what it was, then we might be able . . .'

'I said cut it out,' said Higgy.

'I've had about enough of you,' I said to Hiram. 'I've had enough of you all your whole damn life. All I want from you is that phone of mine. And I want it fast.'

'Why, you little squirt?' Hiram bellowed, and he took another step toward me.

Higgy hauled off and kicked him in the shin. 'God damn it,' Higgy said, 'I said for you to stop it.'

Hiram jigged on one leg, lifting up the other so he could rub his shin.

'Mayor,' he complained, 'you shouldn't have done that.'

'Go and get him his phone,' Tom Preston said. 'Let him have it back. Then he can call them up and report how good a job he did.'

I wanted to clobber all three of them, especially Hiram and Tom Preston. But, of course, I knew I couldn't. Hiram had beaten me often enough when we were kids for me to know I couldn't.

Higgy grabbed hold of Hiram and tugged him toward the gate. Hiram limped a little as the mayor led him off. Tom Preston held the gate for them and then the three of them went stalking up the street, never looking back.

And now I noticed that the rest had left as well – all of them except Father Flanagan and Gerald Sherwood, and Nancy, standing on the porch. The priest was standing to one side and when I looked at him, he made an apologetic gesture.

'Don't blame them,' he said, 'for leaving. They were embarrassed and uneasy. They took their chance to get away.'

'And you?' I asked. 'You're not embarrassed?'

'Why, not at all,' he told me. 'Although I am a bit uneasy. The whole thing, I don't mind telling you, has a whiff of heresy about it.'

'Next,' I said, bitterly, 'you'll be telling me you think I told the truth.'

'I had my doubts,' he said, 'and I'm not entirely rid of them. But that hole in your roof is a powerful argument against wholesale scepticism. And I do not hold with the modern cynicism that seems so fashionable. There is still, I think, much room in the world today for a dash of mysticism.'

I could have told him it wasn't mysticism, that the other world had been a solid, factual world, that the stars and sun and moon had shown there, that I had walked its soil and drunk its water, that I had breathed its air and that even now I had its dirt beneath my fingernails from having dug a human skull from the slope above the stream.

'The others will be back,' said Father Flanagan. 'They had to get away for a little time to think, to get a chance to digest some of this evidence. It was too much to handle in one gulp. They will be back, and so will I, but at the moment I have a mass to think of.'

A gang of boys came running down the street. They stopped a half a block away and pointed at the roof. They milled around and pushed one another playfully and hollered.

The first edge of the sun had come above the horizon and the trees were the burnished green of summer.

I gestured at the boys. 'The word has gotten out,' I said. 'In another thirty minutes we'll have everyone in town out in the street, gawking at the roof.'

17

THE CROWD outside had grown.

No one was doing anything. They just stood there and looked, gaping at the hole in the roof, and talking quietly among themselves – not screaming, not shouting, but talking, as if they knew something else was about to happen and were passing away the time, waiting for it to happen.

Sherwood kept pacing up and down the floor.

'Gibbs should be phoning soon,' he said. 'I don't know what has happened to him. He should have called by now.'

'Maybe,' Nancy said, 'he got held up – maybe his plane was late. Maybe there was trouble on the road.'

I stood at the window watching the crowd. I knew almost all of them. They were friends and neighbours and there was not a thing to stop them, if they wanted to, from coming up the walk and knocking at the door and coming in to see me. But now, instead, they stood outside and watched and waited. It was, I thought, as if the house were a cage and I was some new, strange animal from some far-off land.

Twenty-four hours ago I had been another villager, a man who had lived and grown up with those people watching in the street. But now I was a freak, an oddity – perhaps, in the minds of some of them, a sinister figure that threatened, if not their lives, their comfort and their peace of mind.

For this village could never be the same again – and perhaps the world could never be the same again. For even if the barrier now should disappear and the Flowers withdraw their attention from our Earth, we still would have been shaken from the comfortable little rut which assumed that life as we knew it was the only kind of life and that our road of knowledge was the only one that was broad and straight and paved.

There had been ogres in the past, but finally the ogres had been banished. The trolls and ghouls and imps and all the others of the tribe had been pushed out of our lives, for they could survive only on the misty shores of ignorance and in the land of superstition. Now, I thought, we'd know an ignorance again (but a different kind of ignorance) and superstition, too, for superstition fed upon the lack of knowledge. With this hint of another world – even if its denizens should decide not to flaunt themselves, even if we should find a way to stop them – the trolls and ghouls and goblins would be back with us again. There'd be chimney corner gossip of this other place and a frantic, desperate search to rationalize the implied horror of its vast and unknown reaches, and out of this very search would rise a horror greater than any the other world could hold. We'd be afraid, as we had been before, of the darkness that lay beyond the little circle of our campfire.

There were more people in the street; they kept coming all the time. There was Pappy Andrews, cracking his cane upon the sidewalk, and Grandma Jones, with her sunbonnet socked upon her head, and Charley Hutton, who owned the Happy Hollow tavern. Bill Donovan, the garbage man, was in the front ranks of the crowd, but I didn't see his wife, and I wondered if Myrt and Jake had come to get the kids. And just as big and mouthy as if he'd lived in Millville all his life and known these folks from babyhood, was Gabe Thomas, the trucker who, after me, had been the first man to find out about the barrier.

Someone stirred beside me and I saw that it was Nancy. I knew now that she had been standing there for some little time.

'Look at them,' I said. 'It's a holiday for them. Any minute now the parade will be along.'

'They're just ordinary people,' Nancy said. 'You can't expect too much of them. Brad, I'm afraid you do expect too much of them. You even expected that the men who were here would take what you told them at face value, immediately and unquestioningly.'

'Your father did,' I said.

'Father's different. He's not an ordinary man. And, besides, he had some prior knowledge, he had a little warning. He had one of those telephones. He knew a little bit about it.'

'Some,' I said. 'Not much.'

'I haven't talked with him. There's been no chance for us to talk. And I couldn't ask him in front of all those people. But I know that he's involved. Is it dangerous, Brad?'

'I don't think so. Not from out there or back there or wherever that other world may be. No danger from the alien world – not now, not yet. Any danger that we have to face lies in this world of ours. We have a decision we must make and it has to be the right one.'

'How can we tell,' she asked, 'what is the right decision? We have no precedent.'

And that was it, of course, I thought. There was no way in which a decision – any decision – could be justified.

There was a shouting from outside and I moved closer to the window to see farther up the street. Striding down the centre of it came Hiram Martin and in one hand he carried a cordless telephone.

Nancy caught sight of him and said, 'He's bringing back your phone. Funny, I never thought he would.'

It was Hiram shouting and he was shouting in a chant, a deliberate, mocking chant.

'All right, come out and get your phone. Come on out and get your God damn phone.'

Nancy caught her breath and I brushed past her to the door. I jerked it open and stepped out on the porch.

Hiram reached the gate and he quit his chanting. The two of us stood there, watching one another. The crowd was getting noisy and surging closer.

Then Hiram raised his arm, with the phone held above his head.

'All right,' he yelled, 'here's your phone, you dirty . . .'

Whatever else he said was drowned out by the howling of the crowd.

Then Hiram threw the phone. It was an unhandy thing to throw and the throw was not too good. The receiver flew out to one side, with its trailing cord looping in the air behind it. When the cord jerked taut, the flying phone skidded out of its trajectory and came crashing to the concrete walk, falling about halfway between the gate and porch. Pieces of shattered plastic sprayed across the lawn.

Scarcely aware that I was doing it, acting not by any thought or consideration, but on pure emotion, I came down off the porch and headed for the gate. Hiram backed away to give me room and I came charging through the gate and stood facing him.

I'd had enough of Hiram Martin. I was filled up to here with him. He'd been in my hair for the last two days and I was sick to death of him. There was just one thought – to tear the man apart, to pound him to a pulp, to make certain he'd never sneer at me again, never mock me, never try again to bully me by the sole virtue of sheer size.

I was back in the days of childhood – seeing through the stubborn and red-shot veil of hatred that I had known then, hating this man I knew would lick me, as he had many times before, but ready, willing, anxious to inflict whatever hurt I could while he was licking me.

Someone bawled, 'Give 'em room!' Then I was charging at him and he hit me. He didn't have the time or room to take much of a swing at me, but his fist caught me on the side of the head and it staggered me and hurt. He hit me again almost immediately, but this one also was a glancing blow and didn't hurt at all – and this time I connected. I got my left into his belly just above the belt and when he doubled over I caught him in the mouth and felt the smart of bruised, cut knuckles as they smashed against his teeth. I was swinging again when a fist came out of nowhere and slammed into my head and my head exploded into a pinwheel of screaming stars. I knew that I was down, for I could feel the hardness of the street against my knees, but I struggled up and my vision cleared. I couldn't feel my legs. I seemed to be moving and bobbing in the air with nothing under me. I saw Hiram's face just a foot or so away and his mouth was a gash of red and there was blood on his shirt. So I hit his mouth again – not very hard, perhaps, for there wasn't much steam left behind my punches. But he grunted and he ducked away and I came boring in.

And that was when he hit me for keeps.

I felt myself going down, falling backwards and it seemed that it took a long time for me to fall. Then I hit and the street was harder than I thought it would be and hitting the street hurt me more than the punch that put me there.

I groped around, trying to get my hands in position to hoist myself erect, although I wondered vaguely why I bothered. For if I got up, Hiram would belt me another one and I'd be back down again. But I knew I had to get up, that I had to get up each time I was able. For that was the kind of game Hiram and I had always played. He knocked me down each time I got up and I kept on getting up until I couldn't any more and I never cried for quarter and I never admitted I was licked. And if, for the rest of my life, I could keep on doing that, then I'd be the one who won, not Hiram.

But I wasn't doing so well. I wasn't getting up. Maybe, I thought, this is the time I don't get up.

I still kept pawing with my hands, trying to lift myself, and that's how I got the rock. Some kid, perhaps, had thrown it, maybe days before – maybe at a bird, maybe at a dog, maybe just for the fun of throwing rocks. And it had landed in the street and stayed there and now the fingers of my right hand found it and closed around it and it fitted comfortably into my palm, for it was exactly fist size.

A hand, a great meaty paw of a hand, came down from above and grabbed my shirt front and hauled me to my feet.

'So,' screamed a voice, 'assault an officer, would you!'

His face swam in front of me, a red-smeared face twisted with his hatred, heavy with its meanness, gloating at the physical power he held over me.

I could feel my legs again and the face came clearer and the clot of faces in the background – the faces of the crowd, pressing close to be in at the kill.

One did not give up, I told myself, remembering back to all those other times I had not given up. As long as one was on his feet, he fought, and even when he was down and could not get up, he did not admit defeat.

Both of his hands were clutching at my shirt front, his face pushed close toward mine, I clenched my fist and my fingers closed hard around the rock and then I swung. I swung with everything I had, putting every ounce of strength I could muster behind the swinging fist – swinging from the waist in a jolting upward jab, and I caught him on the chin.

His head snapped back, pivoting on the thick, bull neck. He staggered and his fingers loosened and he crumpled, sprawling in the street.

I stepped back a pace and stood looking down at him and everything was clearer now and I knew I had a body, a bruised and beaten body that ached, it seemed, in every joint and muscle. But that didn't matter; it didn't mean a thing – for the first time in my life I'd knocked Hiram Martin down. I'd used a rock to do it and I didn't give a damn. I hadn't meant to pick up that rock – I'd just found it and closed my fingers on it. I had not planned to use it, but now that I had it made no difference to me. If I'd had time to plan, I'd probably have planned to use it.

Someone leaped out from the crowd toward me and I saw it was Tom Preston.

'You going to let him get away with it?' Preston was screaming at the crowd. 'He hit an officer! He hit him with a rock! He picked up a rock!'

Another man pushed out of the crowd and grabbed Preston by the shoulder, lifting him and setting him back in the forefront of the crowd.

'You keep out of this,' Gabe Thomas said.

'But he used a rock!' screamed Preston.

'He should have used a club,' said Gabe. 'He should have beat his brains out.'

Hiram was stirring, sitting up. His hand reached for his gun.

'Touch that gun,' I told him. 'Just one finger on it and, so help me, I'll kill you.'

Hiram stared at me. I must have been a sight. He'd worked me over good and he'd mussed me up a lot and still I'd knocked him down and was standing on my feet.

'He hit you with a rock,' yelped Preston. 'He hit . . .'

Gabe reached out and his fingers fitted neatly around Preston's skinny throat. He squeezed and Preston's mouth flapped open and his tongue came out.

'You keep out of it,' said Gabe.

'But Hiram's an officer of the law,' protested Charley Hutton. 'Brad shouldn't have hit an officer.'

'Friend,' Gabe told the tavern owner, 'he's a damn poor officer. No officer worth his salt goes picking fights with people.'

I'd never taken my eyes off Hiram and he'd been watching me, but now he flicked his eyes to one side and his hand dropped to the ground.

And in that moment I knew that I had won – not because I was the stronger, not because I fought the better (for I wasn't and I hadn't) but because Hiram was a coward, because he had no guts, because, once hurt, he didn't have the courage to chance being hurt again. And I knew, too, that I need not fear the gun he carried, for Hiram Martin didn't have it in him to face another man and kill him.

Hiram got slowly to his feet and stood there for a moment. His hand came up and felt his jaw. Then he turned his back and walked away. The crowd, watching silently, parted to make a path for him.

I stared at his retreating back and a fierce, bloodthirsty satisfaction rose up inside of me. After more than twenty years, I'd beaten this childhood enemy. But, I told myself, I had not beat him fair – I'd had to play dirty to triumph over him. But I found it made no difference. Dirty fight or fair, I had finally licked him.

The crowd moved slowly back. No one spoke to me. No one spoke to anyone.

'I guess,' said Gabe, 'there are no other takers. If there were, they'd have to fight me, too.'

'Thanks, Gabe,' I said.

'Thanks, hell,' he said. 'I didn't do a thing.'

I opened up my fist and the rock dropped to the street. In the silence, it made a terrible clatter.

Gabe hauled a huge red handkerchief out of his rear pocket and stepped over to me. He put a hand back of my head to hold it steady and began to wipe my face.

'In a month or so,' he said, by way of comfort, 'you'll look all right again.'

'Hey, Brad,' yelled someone, 'who's your friend?'

I couldn't see who it was who yelled. There were so many people.

'Mister,' yelled someone else, 'be sure you wipe his nose.'

'Go on!' roared Gabe. 'Go on! Any of you wisecrackers walk out here in plain sight and I'll dust the street with you.'

Grandma Jones said in a loud voice, so that Pappy Andrews could hear. 'He's the trucker fellow that smashed Brad's car. Appears to me if Brad has to fight someone, he should be fighting him.'

'Big mouth,' yelled back Pappy Andrews. 'He's got an awful big mouth.'

I saw Nancy standing by the gate and she had the same look on her face that she'd had when we were kids and I had fought Hiram Martin then. She was disgusted with me. She had never held with fighting; she thought that it was vulgar.

The front door burst open and Gerald Sherwood came running down the walk. He rushed over and grabbed me by the arm.

'Come on,' he shouted. 'The senator called. He's out there waiting for you, on the east end of the road.'

18

FOUR OF THEM were waiting for me on the pavement just beyond the barrier. A short distance down the road several cars were parked. A number of state troopers were scattered about in little groups. Half a mile or so to the north the steam shovel was still digging.

I felt foolish walking down the road toward them while they waited for me. I knew that I must look as if the wrath of God had hit me.

My shirt was torn and the left side of my face felt as though someone had sandpapered it. I had deep gashes on the knuckles of my right hand where I'd smacked Hiram in the teeth and my left eye felt as if it were starting to puff up.

Someone had cleared away the windrow of uprooted vegetation for several rods on either side of the road, but except for that, the windrow was still there.

As I got close, I recognized the senator. I had never met the man, but I'd seen his pictures in the papers. He was stocky and well-built and his hair was white and he never wore a hat. He was dressed in a double-breasted suit and he had a bright blue tie with white polka dots.

One of the others was a military man. He wore stars on his shoulders. Another was a little fellow with patent leather hair and a tight, cold face. The fourth man was somewhat under-sized and chubby and had eyes of the brightest china blue I had ever seen.

I walked until I was three feet or so away from them and it was not until then that I felt the first slight pressure of the barrier. I backed up a step and looked at the senator.

'You must be Senator Gibbs,' I said. 'I'm Bradshaw Carter. I'm the one Sherwood talked with you about.'

'Glad to meet you, Mr Carter,' said the senator. 'I had expected that Gerald would be with you.'

'I wanted him to come,' I said, 'but he felt he shouldn't. There was a conflict of opinion in the village. The mayor wanted to appoint a committee and Sherwood opposed it rather violently.'

The senator nodded. 'I see,' he said. 'So you're the only one we'll see.'

'If you want others . . .'

'Oh, not at all,' he said. 'You are the man with the information.'

'Yes, I am,' I said.

'Excuse me,' said the senator. 'Mr Carter, General Walter Billings.'

'Hello, General,' I said.

It was funny, saying hello and not shaking hands.

'Arthur Newcombe,' said the senator.

The man with the tight, cold face smiled frostily at me. One could see at a glance he meant to stand no nonsense. He was, I guessed, more than a little outraged that such a thing as the barrier could have been allowed to happen.

'Mr Newcombe,' said the senator, 'is from the State Department. And Dr Roger Davenport, a biologist – I might add, an outstanding one.'

'Good morning, young man,' said Davenport. 'Would it be out of line to ask what happened to you?'

I grinned at him, liking the man at once. 'I had a slight misunderstanding with a fellow townsman.'

'The town, I would imagine,' Billings said, 'is considerably

186

upset. In a little while law and order may become something of a problem.'

'I am afraid so, sir,' I said.

'This may take some time?' asked the senator.

'A little time,' I said.

'There were chairs,' the general said. 'Sergeant, where are . . .?'

Even as he spoke a sergeant and two privates, who had been standing by the roadside, came forward with some folding chairs.

'Catch,' the sergeant said to me.

He tossed a chair through the barrier and I caught it. By the time I had it unfolded and set up, the four on the other side of the barrier had their chairs as well.

It was downright crazy – the five of us sitting there in the middle of the road on flimsy folding chairs.

'Now,' said the senator, 'I suppose we should get started. General, how would you propose that we might proceed?'

The general crossed his knees and settled down. He considered for a moment.

'This man,' he finally said, 'has something we should hear. Why don't we simply sit here and let him tell it to us?'

'Yes, by all means,' said Newcombe. 'Let's hear what he has to say. I must say, Senator . . .'

'Yes,' the senator said, rather hastily. 'I'll stipulate that it is somewhat unusual. This is the first time I have ever attended a hearing out in the open, but . . .'

'It was the only way,' said the general, 'that seemed feasible.'

'It's a longish story,' I warned them. 'And some of it may appear unbelievable.'

'So is this,' said the senator. 'This, what do you call it, barrier.'

'And,' said Davenport, 'you seem to be the only man who has any information.'

'Therefore,' said the senator, 'let us proceed forthwith.'

So, for the second time, I told my story. I took my time and told it carefully, trying to cover everything I'd seen. They did not interrupt me. A couple of times I stopped to let them ask some questions, but the first time Davenport simply signalled that I should go on and the second time all four of them just waited until I did continue.

It was an unnerving business – worse than being interrupted. I talked into a silence and I tried to read their faces, tried to get some clues as to how much of it they might be accepting. But there was no sign from them, no faintest flicker of expression on their faces. I began to feel a little silly over what I was telling them.

I finished finally and leaned back in my chair.

Across the barrier, Newcombe stirred uneasily. 'You'll excuse me, gentlemen,' he said, 'if I take exception to this man's story. I see no reason why we should have been dragged out here . . .'

The senator interrupted him. 'Arthur,' he said, 'my good friend, Gerald Sherwood, vouched for Mr Carter. I have known Gerald Sherwood for more than thirty years and he is, I must tell you, a most perceptive man – a hard-headed businessman with a tinge of imagination. Hard as this account, or parts of it, may be to accept, I still believe we must accept it as a basis for discussion. And, I must remind you, this is the first sound evidence we have been offered.'

'I,' said the general, 'find it hard to believe a word of it. But with the evidence of this barrier, which is wholly beyond any present understanding, we undoubtedly stand in a position where we must accept further evidence beyond our understanding.'

'Let us,' suggested Davenport, 'pretend just for the moment that we believe it all. Let's try to see if there may not be some basic . . .'

'But you can't!' exploded Newcombe. 'It flies in the face of everything we know.'

'Mr Newcombe,' said the biologist, 'man has flown in the face of everything he knew time after time. He knew, not too many hundreds of years ago, that the Earth was the centre of the universe. He knew, less than thirty years ago, that man could never travel to the other planets. He knew, a hundred years ago, that the atom was indivisible. And what have we here – the knowledge that time never can be understood or manipulated, that it is impossible for a plant to be intelligent. I tell you, sir . . .'

'Do you mean,' the general asked, 'that you accept all this?'

'No,' said Davenport, 'I'll accept none of it. To do so would be very unobjective. But I'll hold judgement in abeyance. I would, quite frankly, jump at the chance to work on it, to make observations and perform experiments and . . .'

'You may not have the time,' I said.

The general swung toward me. 'Was there a time limit set?' he asked. 'You didn't mention it.'

'No. But they have a way to prod us. They can exert some convincing pressure any time they wish. They can start this barrier to moving.'

'How far can they move it?'

'Your guess is as good as mine. Ten miles. A hundred miles. A thousand. I have no idea.'

'You sound as if you think they could push us off the Earth.'

'I don't know. I would rather think they could.'

'Do you think they would?'

'Maybe. If it became apparent that we were delaying. I don't think they'd do it willingly. They need us. They need someone who can use their knowledge, who can make it meaningful. It doesn't seem that, so far, they've found anyone who can.'

'But we can't hurry,' the senator protested. 'We will not be rushed. There is a lot to do. There must be discussions at a great many different levels – at the governmental level, at the international level, at the economic and scientific levels.'

'Senator,' I told him, 'there is one thing no one seems to grasp. We are not dealing with another nation, nor with other humans. We are dealing with an alien people . . .'

189

'That makes no difference,' said the senator. 'We must do it our way.'

'That would be fine,' I said, 'if you can make the aliens understand.'

'They'll have to wait,' said Newcombe, primly.

And I knew that it was hopeless, that here was a problem which could not be solved, that the human race would bungle its first contact with an alien people. There would be talk and argument, discussion, consultation – but all on the human level, all from the human viewpoint, without a chance that anyone would even try to take into account the alien point of view.

'You must consider,' said the senator, 'that they are the petitioners, they are the ones who made the first approach, they are asking access to our world, not we to theirs.'

'Five hundred years ago,' I said, 'white men came to America. They were the petitioners then . . .'

'But the Indians,' said Newcombe, 'were savages, barbarians . . .'

I nodded at him. 'You make my point exactly.'

'I do not,' Newcombe told me frostily, 'appreciate your sense of humour.'

'You mistake me,' I told him. 'It was not said in humour.'

Davenport nodded. 'You may have something there, Mr Carter. You say these plants pretend to have stored knowledge, the knowledge, you suspect, of many different races.'

'That's the impression I was given.'

'Stored and correlated. Not just a jumble of data.'

'Correlated, too,' I said. 'You must bear in mind that I cannot swear to this. I have no way of knowing it is true. But their spokesman, Tupper, assured me that they didn't lie . . .'

'I know,' said Davenport. 'There is some logic in that. They wouldn't need to lie.'

'Except,' said the general, 'that they never did give back your fifteen hundred dollars.'

'No, they didn't,' I said.

'After they said they would.'

'Yes. They were emphatic on that point.'

'Which means they lied. And they tricked you into bringing back what you thought was a time machine.'

'And,' Newcombe pointed out, 'they were very smooth about it.'

'I don't think,' said the general, 'we can place a great deal of trust in them.'

'But look here,' protested Newcombe, 'we've gotten around to talking as if we believed every word of it.'

'Well,' said the senator, 'that was the idea, wasn't it? That we'd use the information as a basis for discussion.'

'For the moment,' said the general, 'we must presume the worst.'

Davenport chuckled. 'What's so bad about it? For the first time in its history, humanity may be about to meet another intelligence. If we go about it right, we may find it to our benefit.'

'But you can't know that,' said the general.

'No, of course we can't. We haven't sufficient data. We must make further contact.'

'If they exist,' said Newcombe.

'If they exist,' Davenport agreed.

'Gentlemen,' said the senator, 'we are losing sight of something. A barrier does exist. It will let nothing living through it . . .'

'We don't know that,' said Davenport. 'There was the instance of the car. There would have been some micro-organisms in it. There would have had to be. My guess is that the barrier is not against life as such, but against sentience, against awareness. A thing that has awareness of itself . . .'

'Well, anyhow,' said the senator, 'we have evidence that something very strange has happened. We can't just shut our eyes. We must work with what we have.'

'All right, then,' said the general, 'let's get down to business. Is it safe to assume that these things pose a threat?'

I nodded. 'Perhaps. Under certain circumstances.'

'And those circumstances?'

'I don't know. There is no way of knowing how they think.'

'But there's the potentiality of a threat?'

'I think,' said Davenport, 'that we are placing too much stress upon the matter of a threat. We should first . . .'

'My first responsibility,' said the general, 'is consideration of a potential danger . . .'

'And if there were a danger?'

'We could stop them,' said the general, 'if we moved fast enough. If we moved before they'd taken in too much territory. We have a way to stop them.'

'All you military minds can think of,' Davenport said angrily, 'is the employment of force. I'll agree with you that a thermonuclear explosion could kill all the alien life that has gained access to the Earth, possibly might even disrupt the timephase barrier and close the Earth to our alien friends . . .'

'Friends!' the general wailed. 'You can't know . . .'

'Of course I can't,' said Davenport. 'And you can't know that they are enemies. We need more data; we need to make a further contact . . .'

'And while you're getting your additional data, they'll have the time to strengthen the barrier and move it . . .'

'Some day,' said Davenport, angrier than ever, 'the human race will have to find a solution to its problems that does not involve the use of force. Now might be the time to start. You propose to bomb this village. Aside from the moral issue of destroying several hundred innocent people . . .'

'You forget,' said the general, speaking gruffly, 'that we'd be balancing those several hundred lives against the safety of all the people of the Earth. It would be no hasty action. It would be done only after some deliberation. It would have to be a considered decision.'

'The very fact that you can consider it,' said the biologist, 'is enough to send a cold shiver down the spine of all humanity.'

The general shook his head. 'It's my duty to consider distasteful things like this. Even considering the moral issue involved, in the case of necessity I would . . .'

'Gentlemen,' the senator protested weakly.

The general looked at me. I am afraid they had forgotten I was there.

'I'm sorry, sir,' the general said to me. 'I should not have spoken in this manner.'

I nodded dumbly. I couldn't have said a word if I'd been paid a million dollars for it. I was all knotted up inside and I was afraid to move.

I had not been expecting anything like this, although now that it had come, I knew I should have been. I should have known what the world reaction would be and if I had failed to know, all I had to do would have been to remember what Stiffy Grant had told me as he lay on the kitchen floor.

They'll want to use the bomb, he'd said. *Don't let them use the bomb . . .*

Newcombe stared at me coldly. His eyes stabbed out at me. 'I trust,' he said, 'that you'll not repeat what you have heard.'

'We have to trust you, boy,' said the senator. 'You hold us in your hands.'

I managed to laugh. I suppose that it came out as an ugly laugh. 'Why should I say anything?' I asked. 'We're sitting ducks. There would be no point in saying anything. We couldn't get away.'

For a moment I thought wryly that perhaps the barrier would protect us even from a bomb. Then I saw how wrong I was. The barrier concerned itself with nothing except life – or, if Davenport were right (and he probably was) only with a life that was aware of its own existence. They had tried to dynamite the barrier and it had been as if there had been no barrier. The barrier had offered no resistance to the explosion and therefore had not been affected by it.

From the general's viewpoint, the bomb might be the answer. It would kill all life; it was an application of the conclusion Alf Peterson had arrived at on the question of how one killed a noxious plant that had great adaptability. A nuclear explosion might have no effect upon the time-phase mechanism, but it would kill all life and would so irradiate and poison the area that for a long, long time the aliens would be unable to re-occupy it.

'I hope,' I said to the general, 'you'll be as considerate as you're asking me to be. If you find you have to do it, you'll make no prior announcement.'

The general nodded, thin-lipped.

'I'd hate to think,' I said, 'what would happen in this village . . .'

The senator broke in. 'Don't worry about it now. It's just one of many alternatives. For the time we'll not even consider it. Our friend, the general, spoke a little out of turn.'

'At least,' the general said, 'I am being honest. I wasn't pussy-footing. I wasn't playing games.'

He seemed to be saying that the others were.

'There is one thing you must realize,' I told them. 'This can't be any cloak-and-dagger operation. You have to do it honestly – whatever you may do. There are certain minds the Flowers can read. There are minds, perhaps many minds, they are in contact with at this very moment. The owners of those minds don't know it and there is no way we can know to whom those minds belong. Perhaps to one of you. There is an excellent chance the Flowers will know, at all times, exactly what is being planned.'

I could see that they had not thought of that. I had told them, of course, in the telling of my story, but it hadn't registered. There was so much that it took a man a long time to get it straightened out.

'Who are those people down there by the cars?' asked Newcombe.

I turned and looked.

Half the village probably was there. They had come out to watch. And one couldn't blame them, I told myself. They had a right to be concerned; they had the right to watch. This was their life. Perhaps a lot of them didn't trust me, not after what Hiram and Tom had been saying about me, and here I was, out here, sitting on a chair in the middle of the road, talking with the men from Washington. Perhaps they felt shut out.

Perhaps they felt they should be sitting in a meeting such as this.

I turned back to the four across the barrier.

'Here's a thing,' I told them, urgently, 'that you can't afford to muff. If we do, we'll fail all the other chances as they come along . . .'

'Chances?' asked the senator.

'This is our first chance to make contact with another race. It won't be the last. When man goes into space . . .'

'But we aren't out in space,' said Newcombe.

I knew then that there was no use. I'd expected too much of the men in my living-room and I'd expected too much of these men out here on the road.

They would fail. We would always fail. We weren't built to do anything but fail. We had the wrong kind of motives and we couldn't change them. We had a built-in short-sightedness and an inherent selfishness and a self-concern that made it impossible to step out of the little human rut we travelled.

Although, I thought, perhaps the human race was not alone in this. Perhaps this alien race we faced, perhaps any alien race, travelled a rut that was as deep and narrow as the human rut. Perhaps the aliens would be as arbitrary and as unbending and as blind as was the human race.

I made a gesture of resignation, but I doubt that they ever saw it. All of them were looking beyond me, staring down the road.

I twisted around and there, halfway up the road, halfway between the barrier and the traffic snarl, marched all those people who had been out there waiting. They came on silently and with great deliberation and determination. They looked like the march of doom, bearing down upon us.

'What do they want, do you suppose?' the senator asked, rather nervously.

George Walker, who ran the Red Owl butcher department, was in the forefront of the crowd, and walking just behind him was Butch Ormsby, the service station operator, and Charley Hutton of the Happy Hollow. Daniel Willoughby was there, too, looking somewhat uncomfortable, for Daniel wasn't the kind of man who enjoyed being with a mob. Higgy wasn't there and neither was Hiram, but Tom Preston was. I looked for Sherwood, thinking it unlikely that he would be there. And I was right; he wasn't. But there were a lot of others, people I knew. Their faces all wore a hard and determined look.

I stepped off to one side, clear of the road, and the crowd tramped past me, paying no attention.

'Senator,' said George Walker in a voice that was louder than seemed necessary. 'You are the senator, ain't you?'

'Yes,' said the senator. 'What can I do for you?'

'That,' said Walker, 'is what we're here to find out. We are a delegation, sort of.'

'I see,' said the senator.

'We got trouble,' said George Walker, 'and all of us are taxpayers and we got a right to get some help. I run the meat department at the Red Owl store and without no customers coming into town, I don't know what will happen. If we can't get any out-of-town trade, we'll have to close our doors. We can sell to the people here in town, of course, but there ain't enough trade in town to make it worth our while and in a little while the people here in town won't have any money to pay for the things they buy, and our business isn't set up so we can operate on credit. We can get meat, of course. We've got that all worked out, but we can't go on selling it and . . .'

'Now, just a minute,' said the senator. 'Let's take this a little slow. Let's not go so fast. You have problems and I know you have them and I aim to do all I can . . .'

'Senator,' interrupted a man with a big, bull voice, 'there are others of us have problems that are worse than George's. Take myself, for example. I work out of town and I depend on my pay cheque, every week, to buy food for the kids, to keep them in shoes and to pay the other bills. And now I can't get to work and there won't be any cheque. I'm not the only one. There are a lot of others like me. It isn't like we had some money laid by to take care of emergencies. I tell you, Senator, there isn't hardly anyone in town got anything laid by. We all are . . .'

'Hold on,' pleaded the senator. 'Let me get a word in edgewise. Give me a little time. The people in Washington know what is going on. They know what you folks are facing out here. They'll do what they can to help. There'll be a relief bill in the Congress to help out you folks and I, for one, will work unceasingly to see that it is passed without undue delay. And that isn't all. There are two or three papers in the east and some television stations that have started a drive for funds to be turned over to this village. And that's just a start. There will be a lot of . . .'

'Hell, Senator,' yelled a man with a scratchy voice, 'that isn't what we want. We don't want relief. We don't ask for charity. We just want to be able to get back to our jobs.'

The senator was flabbergasted, 'You mean you want us to get rid of the barrier?'

'Look, Senator,' said the man with the bull-like voice, 'for years the government has been spending billions to send a man up to the moon. With all them scientists you got, you can spend some time and money to get us out of here. We been paying taxes for a long time now, without getting anything . . .'

'But that,' said the senator, 'will take a little time. We'll have to find out what this barrier is and then we'll have to figure out what can be done with it. And I tell you, frankly, we aren't going to be able to do that overnight.'

Norma Shepard, who worked as receptionist for Doc Fabian, wriggled through the press of people until she faced the senator.

'But something has to be done,' she said. 'Has to be done, do you understand? Someone has to find a way. There are people in this town who should be in a hospital and we can't get them there. Some of them will die if we can't get them there. We have one doctor in this town and he's no longer young. He's been a good doctor for a long, long time, but he hasn't got the skill or the equipment to take care of the people who are terribly sick. He never has had, he never pretended that he had . . .'

'My dear,' said the senator, consolingly. 'I recognize your concern and I sympathize with it, and you may rest assured . . .'

It was apparent that my interview with the men from Washington had come to an end. I walked slowly down the road, not actually down the road, but along the edge of it, walking in the harrowed ground out of which, already, thin points of green, were beginning to protrude. The seeds which had been sown in that alien whirlwind had in that short time germinated and were pushing toward the light.

I wondered bitterly, as I walked along, what kind of crops they'd bear.

And I wondered, too, how angry Nancy might be at me for my fight with Hiram Martin. I had caught that one look on her face and then she'd turned her back and gone up the walk. And she had not been with Sherwood when he had come charging down the walk to announce that Gibbs had phoned.

For that short moment in the kitchen, when I had felt her body pressing close to mine, she had been once again the sweetheart out of time – the girl who had walked hand in hand with me, who had laughed her throaty laugh and been an unquestioned part of me, as I had been of her.

Nancy, I almost cried aloud, *Nancy, please let it be the same.*

But maybe it could never be the same, I told myself. Maybe it was Millville – a village that had come between us – for she had grown away from Millville in the years she'd been away, and I, remaining here, had grown more deeply into it.

You could not dig back, I thought, through the dust of years, through the memories and the happenings and the changes in yourself – in both yourselves – to rescue out of time another day and hour. And even if you found it, you could not dust it clean, you could never make it shine as you remembered it. For perhaps it never had been quite the shining thing that you remembered, perhaps you had burnished it in your longing and your loneliness.

And perhaps it was only once in every lifetime (and perhaps not in every lifetime) that a shining moment came. Perhaps there was a rule that it could never come again.

'Brad,' a voice said.

I had been walking, not looking where I went, staring at the ground. Now, at the sound of the voice, I jerked up my head, and saw that I had reached the tangle of parked cars.

Leaning against one of them was Bill Donovan.

'Hi there, Bill,' I said. 'You should be up there with the rest of them.'

He made a gesture of disgust. 'We need help,' he said. 'Sure we do. All the help we can get. But it wouldn't hurt to wait a while before you ran squealing for it. You can't cave in the first time you are hit. You have to hang onto at least a shred or two of your self-respect.'

I nodded, not quite agreeing with him. 'They're scared,' I said.

'Yes,' he said, 'but there isn't any call for them to act like a bunch of bleating sheep.'

'How about the kids?' I asked.

'Safe and sound,' he told me. 'Jake got to them just before the barrier moved. Took them out of there. Jake had to chop down the door to reach them and Myrt carried on all the time he was chopping it. You never heard so much uproar in your life about a God damn door.'

'And Mrs Donovan?'

'Oh, Liz – she's all right. Cries for the kids and wonders what's to become of us. But the kids are safe and that's all that counts.'

He patted the metal of the car with the flat of his hand. 'We'll work it out,' he said. 'It may take a little time, but there isn't anything that men can't do if they set their minds to it. Like as not they'll have a thousand of them scientists working on this thing and, like I say, it may take a while, but they'll get her figured out.'

'Yes,' I said, 'I suppose they will.'

If some muddle-headed general didn't push the panic

button first. If, instead of trying to solve the problem, we didn't try to smash it.

'What's the matter, Brad?'

'Not a thing,' I said.

'You got your worries, too, I guess,' he said. 'What you did to Hiram, he had it coming to him for a long time now. Was that telephone he threw . . .?'

'Yes,' I said. 'It was one of the telephones.'

'Heard you went to some other world or something. How do you manage to get into another world? It sounds screwy to me, but that's what everyone is saying.'

A couple of yelling kids came running through the cars and went pelting up the road toward where the crowd was still arguing with the senator.

'Kids are having a great time,' said Donovan. 'Most excitement they've ever had. Better than a circus.'

Some more kids went past, whooping as they ran.

'Say,' asked Donovan, 'do you think something might have happened?'

The first two kids had reached the crowd and were tugging at people's arms and shouting something at them.

'Looks like it,' I said.

A few of the crowd started back down the road, walking to start with, then breaking into a trot, heading back for town.

As they came close, Donovan darted out to intercept them.

'What's the matter?' he yelled. 'What's going on?'

'Money,' one of them shouted back at him. 'Someone's found some money.'

By now the whole crowd had left the barrier and was running down the road.

As they swept past, Mae Hutton shouted at me, 'Come on, Brad! Money in your garden!'

Money in my garden! For the love of God, what next?

I took one look at the four men from Washington, standing beyond the barrier. Perhaps they were thinking that the town was crazy. They had every right to think so.

I stepped out into the road and jogged along behind the crowd, heading back for town.

19

WHEN I came back that morning I had found that the purple flowers growing in the swale behind my house, through the wizardry of that other world, had been metamorphosed into tiny bushes. In the dark I had run my fingers along the bristling branches and felt the many swelling buds. And now the buds had broken and where each bud had been was, not a leaf, but a miniature fifty-dollar bill!

Len Streeter, the high school science teacher, handed one of the tiny bills to me.

'It's impossible,' he said.

And he was right. It *was* impossible. No bush in its right mind would grow fifty-dollar bills – or any kind of bills.

There were a lot of people there – all the crowd that had been out in the road shouting at the senator, and as many more. It looked to me as if the entire village might be there. They were tramping around among the bushes and yelling at one another, all happy and excited. They had a right to be. There probably weren't many of them who had ever seen a fifty-dollar bill, and here were thousands of them.

'You've looked close at it,' I asked the teacher. 'You're sure it actually is a bill?'

He pulled a small magnifying glass out of his shirt pocket and handed it to me.

'Have a look,' he said.

I had a look and there was no question that it looked like a fifty-dollar bill – although the only fifty-dollar bills I had ever seen were the thirty of them in the envelope Sherwood had given me. And I hadn't had a chance to more than glance at those. But through the glass I could see that the little bills had the fabric-like texture one finds in folding money and everything else, including the serial number, looked authentic.

And I knew, even as I squinted through the lens, that it was authentic. For these were (how would one say it – the descendants?) of the money Tupper Tyler had stolen from me.

I knew exactly what had happened and the knowledge was a chill that bit deep into my mind.

'It's possible,' I told Streeter. 'With that gang back there, it's entirely possible.'

'You mean the gang from your other world?'

'Not my other world,' I shouted. 'Your other world. This world's other world. When you get it through your damn thick skulls . . .'

I didn't say the rest of it. I was glad I didn't.

'I'm sorry,' Streeter said. 'I didn't mean it quite the way it sounded.'

Higgy, I saw, was standing halfway up the slope that led to the house and he was yelling for attention.

'Listen to me!' he was shouting. 'Fellow citizens, won't you listen to me.'

The crowd was beginning to quiet down and Higgy went on yelling until everyone was quiet.

'Stop pulling off them leaves,' he told them. 'Just leave them where they are.'

Charley Hutton said, 'Hell, Higgy, all that we was doing was picking a few of them to have a better look.'

'Well, quit it,' said the mayor, sternly. 'Every one that you pull off is fifty dollars less. Give them leaves a little time and they'll grow to proper size and then they'll drop off and all we need to do is to pick them up and every one of them will be money in our pocket.'

'How do you know that?' Grandma Jones shrilled at him.

'Well,' the mayor said, 'it stands to reason, don't it? Here we have these marvellous plants growing money for us. The least we can do is let them be, so they can grow it for us.'

He looked around the crowd and suddenly saw me.

'Brad,' he asked me, 'isn't that correct?'

'I'm afraid it is,' I said.

For Tupper had stolen the money and the Flowers had used the bills as patterns on which to base the leaves. I would have bet, without looking further, that there were no more than thirty different serial numbers in the entire crop of money.

'What I want to know,' said Charley Hutton, 'is how you figure we should divide it up – once it's ripe, that is.'

'Why,' said the mayor, 'that's something I hadn't even thought of. Maybe we could put it in a common fund that could be handed out to people as they have the need of it.'

'That don't seem fair to me,' said Charley. 'That way some people would get more of it than others. Seems to me the only way is to divide it evenly. Everyone should get his fair share of it, to do with as he wants.'

'There's some merit,' said the mayor, 'in your point of view. But it isn't something on which we should make a snap decision. This afternoon I'll appoint a committee to look into it. Anyone who has any ideas can present them and they'll get full consideration.'

'Mr Mayor,' piped up Daniel Willoughby, 'there is one thing I think we've overlooked. No matter what we say, this stuff isn't money.'

'But it looks like money. Once it's grown to proper size, no one could tell the difference.'

'I know,' the banker said, 'that it looks like money. It probably would fool an awful lot of people. Maybe everyone. Maybe no one could ever tell that it wasn't money. But if the source of it should be learned, how much value do you think it would have then? Not only that, but all the money in this village would be suspect. If we can grow fifty-dollar bills, what is there to stop us from growing tens and twenties?'

'I don't see what this fuss is all about,' shouted Charley Hutton. 'There isn't any need for anyone to know. We can keep quiet about it. We can keep the secret. We can pledge ourselves that we'll never say a word about it.'

The crowd murmured with approval. Daniel Willoughby

looked as if he were on the verge of strangling. The thought of all that phony money shrivelled up his prissy soul.

'That's something,' said the mayor, blandly, 'that my committee can decide.'

The way the mayor said it one knew there was no doubt at all in his mind as to how the committee would decide.

'Higgy,' said lawyer Nichols, 'there's another thing we've overlooked. The money isn't ours.'

The mayor stared at him, outraged that anyone could say a thing like that.

'Whose is it, then?' he bellowed.

'Why,' said Nichols, 'it belongs to Brad. It's growing on his land and it belongs to him. There is no court anywhere that wouldn't make the finding.'

All the people froze. All their eyes swivelled in on me. I felt like a crouching rabbit, with the barrels of a hundred shotguns levelled at him.

The mayor gulped. 'You're sure of this?' he asked.

'Positive,' said Nichols.

The silence held and the eyes were still trained upon me.

I looked around and the eyes stared back. No one said a word.

The poor, misguided, blinded fools, I thought. All they saw here was money in their pockets, wealth such as not a single one of them had ever dared to dream. They could not see in it the threat (or promise?) of an alien race pressed close against the door, demanding entrance. And they could not know that because of this alien race, blinding death might blossom in a terrible surge of unleashed energy above the dome that enclosed the town.

'Mayor,' I said, 'I don't want the stuff.'

'Well, now,' the mayor said, 'that's a handsome gesture, Brad. I'm sure the folks appreciate it.'

'They damm well should,' said Nichols.

A woman's scream rang out – and then another scream. It seemed to come from behind me and I spun around.

A woman was running down the slope that led to Doc

204

Fabian's house – although running wasn't quite the word for it. She was trying to run when she was able to do little more than hobble. Her body was twisted with the terrible effort of her running and she had her arms stretched out so they would catch her if she fell – and when she took another step, she fell and rolled and finally ended up a huddled shape lying on the hillside.

'Myra!' Nichols yelled. 'My God, Myra, what's wrong?'

It was Mrs Fabian, and she lay there on the hillside with the whiteness of her hair shining in the sunlight, a startling patch of brilliance against the green sweep of the lawn. She was a little thing and frail and for years had been half-crippled by arthritis, and now she seemed so small and fragile, crumpled on the grass, that it hurt to look at her.

I ran toward her and all the others were running toward her, too.

Bill Donovan was the first to reach her and he went down on his knees to lift her up and hold her.

'Everything's all right,' he told her. 'See – everything's all right. All your friends are here.'

Her eyes were open and she seemed to be all right, but she lay there in the cradle of Bill's arms and she didn't try to move. Her hair had fallen down across her face and Bill brushed it back, gently, with a big, grimed, awkward hand.

'It's the doctor,' she told us. 'He's gone into a coma . . .'

'But,' protested Higgy, 'he was all right an hour ago. I saw him just an hour ago.'

She waited until he'd finished, then she said, as if he hadn't spoken, 'He's in a coma and I can't wake him up. He lay down for a nap and now he won't wake up.'

Donovan stood up, lifting her, holding her like a child. She was so little and he was so big that she had the appearance of a doll, a doll with a sweet and wrinkled face.

'He needs help,' she said. 'He's helped you all his life. Now he needs some help.'

Norma Shepard touched Bill on the arm. 'Take her up to the house,' she said. 'I'll take care of her.'

'But my husband, ' Mrs Fabian insisted. 'You'll get some help for him? You'll find some way to help him?'

'Yes, Myra,' Higgy said. 'Yes, of course we will. We can't let him down. He's done too much for us. We'll find a way to help him.'

Donovan started up the hill, carrying Mrs Fabian. Norma ran ahead of him.

Butch Ormsby said, 'Some of us ought to go, too, and see what we can do for Doc.'

'Well,' asked Charley Hutton, 'how about it, Higgy? You were the one who shot off his big fat face. How are you going to help him?'

'Somebody's got to help him,' declared Pappy Andrews, thumping his cane upon the ground by way of emphasis. 'There never was a time we needed Doc more than we need him now. There are sick people in this village and we've got to get him on his feet somehow.'

'We can do what we can,' said Streeter, 'to make him comfortable. We'll take care of him, of course, the best that we know how. But there isn't anyone who has any medical knowledge . . .'

'I'll tell you what we'll do,' said Higgy. 'Someone can get in touch with some medical people and tell them what's happened. We can describe the symptoms and maybe they can diagnose the illness and then tell us what to do. Norma is a nurse – well, sort of, she's been helping out in Doc's office for the last four years or so – and she'd be some help to us.'

'I suppose it's the best we can do,' said Streeter, 'but it's not very good.'

'I tell you, men,' said Pappy, loudly, 'we can't stay standing here. The situation calls for action and it behooves us to get started.'

What Streeter had said, I told myself, was right. Maybe it was the best that we could do, but it wasn't good enough. There was more to medicine than word-of-mouth advice or telephoned instructions. And there were others in the village in need of medical aid, more specialized aid than a stricken doctor – even if he could be gotten on his feet – was equipped to give them.

Maybe, I thought, there was someone else who could help – and if they could, they'd better, or I'd go back somehow into that other world and start ripping up their roots.

It was time, I told myself, that this other world was getting on the ball. The Flowers had put us in this situation and it was time they dug us out. If they were intent on proving what great tasks they could perform, there were more important ways of proving it than growing fifty-dollar bills on bushes and all their other hocus-pocus.

There were phones down at the village hall, the ones that had been taken from Stiffy's shack, and I could use one of those, of course, but I'd probably have to break Hiram's skull before I could get at one of them. And another round with Hiram, I decided, was something I could get along without.

I looked around for Sherwood, but he wasn't there, and neither was Nancy. One of them might be home and they'd let me use the phone in Sherwood's study.

A lot of the others were heading up toward Doc's house, but I turned and went the other way.

20

No one answered the bell. I rang several times and waited, then finally tried the door and it was unlocked.

I went inside and closed the door behind me. The sound of its closing was muffled by the hushed solemnity of the hall that ran back to the kitchen.

'Anyone home?' I called.

Somewhere a lone fly buzzed desperately, as if trying to escape, trapped against a window perhaps, behind a fold of drape. The sun spilled through the fanlights above the door to make a ragged pattern on the floor.

There was no answer to my hail, so I went down the hall and walked into the study. The phone stood on the heavy desk. The walls of books still seemed rich and wondrous. A half-empty whisky bottle and an unwashed glass stood on the liquor cabinet.

I went across the carpeting to the desk and reached out, pulling the phone toward me.

I lifted the receiver and immediately Tupper said, in his businessman's voice, 'Mr Carter, it's good to hear from you at last. Events are going well, we hope. You have made, we would presume, preliminary contact.'

As if they didn't know!

'That's not what I called about,' I snapped.

'But that was the understanding. You were to act for us.'

The unctuous smugness of the voice burned me up.

'And it was understood, as well,' I asked, 'that you were to make a fool of me?'

The voice was startled. 'We fail to understand. Will you please explain?'

'The time machine,' I said.

'Oh, that.'

'Yes, oh, that,' I said.

'But, Mr Carter, if we had asked you to take it back you would have been convinced that we were using you. You'd probably have refused.'

'And you weren't using me?'

'Why, I suppose we were. We'd have used anyone. It was important to get that mechanism to your world. Once you know the pattern . . .'

'I don't care about the pattern,' I said angrily. 'You tricked me and you admit you tricked me. That's a poor way to start negotiations with another race.'

'We regret it greatly. Not that we did it, but the way we did it. If there is anything we can do . . .'

'There's a lot that you can do. You can cut out horsing around with fifty-dollar bills . . .'

'But that's repayment,' wailed the voice. 'We told you

you'd get back your fifteen hundred. We promised you'd get back much more than your fifteen hundred . . .'

'You've had your readers read economic texts?'

'Oh, certainly we have.'

'And you've observed, for a long time and at first hand, our economic practices?'

'As best we can,' the voice said. 'It's sometimes difficult.'

'You know, of course, that money grows on bushes.'

'No, we don't know that, at all. We know how money's made. But what is the difference? Money's money, isn't it, no matter what its source?'

'You couldn't be more wrong,' I said. 'You'd better get wised up.'

'You mean the money isn't good?'

'Not worth a damn,' I said.

'We hope we've done no wrong,' the voice said, crestfallen.

I said, 'The money doesn't matter. There are other things that do. You've shut us off from the world and we have sick people here. We had just one poor fumbling doctor to take care of them. And now the doctor's sick himself and no other doctor can get in . . .'

'You need a steward,' said the voice.

'What we need,' I told them, 'is to get this barrier lifted so we can get out and others can get in. Otherwise there are going to be people dying who don't have to die.'

'We'll send a steward,' said the voice. 'We'll send one right away. A most accomplished one. The best that we can find.'

'I don't know,' I said, 'about this steward. But we need help as fast as we can get it.'

'We,' the voice pledged, 'will do the best we can.'

The voice clicked off and the phone went dead. And suddenly I realized that I'd not asked the most important thing of all – why had they wanted to get the time machine into our world?

I jiggled the connection. I put the receiver down and lifted it again. I shouted in the phone and nothing happened.

I pushed the phone away and stood hopeless in the room. For all of it, I knew, was a very hopeless mess.

Even after years of study, they did not understand us or our institutions. They did not know that money was symbolic and not simply scraps of paper. They had not, for a moment, taken into consideration what could happen to a village if it were isolated from the world.

They had tricked me and had used me and they should have known that nothing can arouse resentment quite so easily as simple trickery. They should have known, but they didn't know, or if they knew, had discounted what they knew – and that was as bad or worse than if they had not known.

I opened the study door and went into the hall. And as I started down the hall, the front door opened and Nancy stepped inside.

I stopped at the foot of the stairway that rose out of the hall and for a moment we simply stood there, looking at one another, neither of us finding anything to say.

'I came to use the phone,' I said.

She nodded.

'I suppose,' I said, 'I should say I'm sorry for the fight with Hiram.'

'I'm sorry, too,' she said, misunderstanding me, or pretending that she misunderstood. 'But I suppose there was no way you could help it.'

'He threw the phone,' I told her.

But of course it had not been the phone, not the phone alone. It had been all the times before the phone was thrown.

'You said the other night,' I reminded her, 'that we could go out for drinks and dinner. I guess that will have to wait. Now there's no place we can go.'

'Yes,' she said, 'so we could start over.'

I nodded, feeling miserable.

'I was to dress up my prettiest,' she said, 'and we would have been so gay.'

'Like high school days,' I said.

'Brad.'

'Yes,' I said, and took a step toward her.

Suddenly she was in my arms.

'We don't need drinks and dinner,' she said. 'Not the two of us.'

No, I thought, not the two of us.

I bent and kissed her and held her close and there was only us. There was no closed-off village and no alien terror. There was nothing that mattered now except this girl who long ago had walked the street, hand in hand with me, and had not been ashamed.

21

THE STEWARD came that afternoon, a little, wizened humanoid who looked like a bright-eyed monkey. With him was another – also humanoid – but great, lumbering and awkward, gaunt and austere, with a horse-like face. He looked, at first sight, the perfect caricature of a career diplomat. The scrawny humanoid wore a dirty and shapeless piece of cloth draped about him like a robe, and the other wore a breech-clout and a sort of vest, equipped with massive pockets that bulged with small possessions.

The entire village was lined up on the slope behind my house and the betting had been heavy that nothing would show up. I heard whispers, suddenly cut off, everywhere I went.

Then they came, the two of them, popping out of nowhere and standing in the garden.

I walked down the slope and across the garden to meet them. They stood waiting for me and behind me, on that slope covered by a crowd of people, there was utter silence.

As I came near, the big one stepped forward, the little wizened character trailing close behind.

'I speak your language newly,' said the big one. 'If you don't know, ask me once again.'

'You're doing well,' I told him.

'You be Mr Carter?'

'That is right. And you?'

'My designation,' he told me, solemnly, 'is to you great gibberish. I have decided you can call me only Mr Smith.'

'Mr Smith,' I said, 'we are glad to have you here. You are the steward I was told about?'

'No. This other personage is he. But he has no designation I can speak to you. He makes no noise at all. He hears and answers only in his brain. He is a queerish thing.'

'A telepath,' I said.

'Oh, yes, but do not mistake me. Of much intelligence. Also very smart. We are of different worlds, you know. There be many different worlds, many different peoples. We welcome you to us.'

'They sent you along as an interpreter?'

'Interpreter? I do not share your meaning. I learn your words very fast from a mechanism. I do not have much time. I fail to catch them all.'

'Interpreter means you speak for him. He tells you and you tell us.'

'Yes, indeed. Also you tell me and I tell him. But interpreter is not all I am. Also diplomat, very highly trained.'

'Huh?'

'Help with negotiations with your race. Be helpful as I can. Explain very much, perhaps. Aid you as you need.'

'You said there are many different worlds and many different people. You mean a long, long chain of worlds and of people, too?'

'Not all worlds have people,' he told me. 'Some have nothing. No life of any sort. Some hold life, but no intelligence. Some once had intelligence, but intelligence is gone.' He made a strange gesture with his hand. 'It is pity what can happen to intelligence. It is frail; it does not stay forever.'

'And the intelligences? All humanoid?'

He hesitated. 'Humanoid?'

'Like us. Two arms, two legs, one head . . .'

'Most humanoid,' he said. 'Most like you and me.'

The scrawny little being tugged excitedly at his vest. The being I had been talking with turned around to face him, gave him close attention.

Then he turned back to me. 'Him much upset,' he told me. 'Says all people here are sick. Him prostrated with great pity. Never saw such terrible thing.'

'But that is wrong,' I cried. 'The sick ones are at home. This bunch here is healthy.'

'Can't be so,' said Mr Smith. 'Him aghast at situation. Can look inside of people, see everything that's wrong. Says them that isn't sick will be sick in little time, says many have inactive sickness in them, others still have garbage of ancient sicknesses still inside of them.'

'He can fix us up?'

'No fix. Repair complete. Make body good as new.'

Higgy had been edging closer and behind him several others. The rest of the crowd still stayed up on the bank, out of all harm's way. And now they were beginning to buzz a little. At first they had been stricken silent, but now the talk began.

'Higgy,' I said, 'I'd like you to meet Mr Smith.'

'Well, I'll be darned,' said Higgy. 'They got names just the same as ours.'

He stuck out his hand and after a moment of puzzlement, Mr Smith put out his hand and the two men shook.

'The other one,' I said, 'can't talk. He's a telepath.'

'That's too bad,' said Higgy, full of sympathy. 'Which one of them's the doctor?'

'The little one,' I told him, 'and I don't know if you can say he's a doctor. Seems that he repairs people, fixes them like new.'

'Well,' said Higgy, 'that's what a doctor's supposed to do, but never quite makes out.'

'He says we're all sick. He wants to fix us up.'

'Well, that's all right,' said Higgy. 'That's what I call service. We can set up a clinic down at the village hall.'

'But there's Doc and Floyd and all the others who are really sick. That's what he's here for.'

'Well, I tell you, Brad, we can take him to them first and he can get them cured, then we'll set up the clinic. The rest of us might just as well get in on it as long as he is here.'

'If,' said Mr Smith, 'you but merge with the rest of us, you can command the services of such as he whenever you have need.'

'What's this merger?' Higgy asked of me.

'He means if we let the aliens in and join the other worlds that the Flowers have linked.'

'Well, now,' said Higgy, 'that makes a lot of sense. I don't suppose there'll be any charges for his services.'

'Charges?' asked Mr Smith.

'Yeah,' said Higgy. 'Pay. Fees. Money.'

'Those be terms,' said Mr Smith, 'that ring no bell for me. But we must proceed with swiftness, since my fellow creature has other rounds to make. He and his colleagues have many worlds to cover.'

'You mean that they are doctors to the other worlds?' I asked.

'You grasp my meaning clear.'

'Since there isn't any time to waste,' said Higgy, 'leave us be about our business. Will you two come with me?'

'With alacrity,' cried Mr Smith, and the two of them followed Higgy as he went up the slope and out toward the street. I followed slowly after them and as I climbed the bank, Joe Evans came charging out of the back door of my house.

'Brad,' he shouted, 'there's a call for you from the State Department.'

It was Newcombe on the phone.

'I'm over here at Elmore,' he told me in his cold, clipped voice, 'and we've given the Press a rundown on what you told us. But now they're clamouring to see you; they want to talk with you.'

'It's all right with me,' I said. 'If they'll come out to the barrier . . .'

'It's not all right with me,' said Newcombe, sourly, 'but the pressure is terrific. I have to let them see you. I trust you'll be discreet.'

'I'll do my best,' I told him.

'All right,' he said. 'There's not much I can do about it. Two hours from now. At the place we met.'

'OK,' I said. 'I suppose it'll be all right if I bring a friend along.'

'Yes, of course,' said Newcombe. 'And for the love of Christ be careful!'

22

MR SMITH caught onto the idea of a Press conference with very little trouble. I explained it to him as we walked toward the barrier where the newsmen waited for us.

'You say all these people are communicators,' he said, making sure he had it straight. 'We say them something and they say other people. Interpreters, like me.'

'Well, something like that.'

'But all your people talk the same. The mechanism told me one language only.'

'That was because the one language is all that you would need. But the people of the Earth have many languages. Although that is not the reason for newspapermen. You see, all the people can't be here to listen to what we have to say. So these newsmen spread the news . . .'

'News?'

'The things that we have said. Or that other people have said. Things that happen. No matter where anything may happen, there are newsmen there and they spread the word. They keep the world informed.'

Mr Smith almost danced a jig. 'How wonderful!' he cried.

'What's so wonderful about it?'

'Why, the ingenuity,' said Mr Smith. 'The thinking of it up. This way one person talks to all the persons. Everybody knows about him. Everyone hears what he has to talk.'

We reached the barrier and there was quite a crowd of newsmen jammed on the strip of highway on the other side. Some of them were strung along the barrier on either side of the road. As we walked up, the cameramen were busy.

When we came up to the barrier, a lot of men started yelling at us, but someone quickly shushed them, then one man spoke to us.

'I'm Judson Barnes, of Associated Press,' he said. 'I suppose you're Carter.'

I told him that I was. 'And this gentleman you have with you?'

'His name is Smith,' I said.

'And,' said someone else, 'he's just got home from a masquerade.'

'No,' I told them, 'he's a humanoid from one of the alternate worlds. He is here to help with negotiations.'

'Howdy, sirs,' said Mr Smith, with massive friendliness.

Someone howled from the back: 'We can't hear back here.'

'We have a microphone,' said Barnes, 'if you don't mind.'

'Toss it here,' I told him.

He tossed it and I caught it. The cord trailed through the barrier. I could see where the speakers had been set up to one side of the road.

'And now,' said Barnes, 'perhaps we can begin. State filled us in, of course, so we don't need to go over all that you have told them. But there are some questions. I'm sure there are a lot of questions.'

A dozen hands went up.

'Just pick out one of them,' said Barnes.

I made a motion toward a great, tall, scrawny man.

'Thank you, sir,' he said. 'Caleb Rivers, Kansas City Star. We understand that you represent the – how do you say it? – people, perhaps, the people of this other world. I wonder if you would outline your position in somewhat more detail. Are you an official representative, or an unofficial spokesman, or a sort of go-between? It's not been made quite clear.'

'Very unofficial, I might say. You know about my father?'

'Yes,' said Rivers, 'we've been told how he cared for the flowers he found. But you'd agree, wouldn't you, Mr Carter, that this is, to say the least, a rather strange sort of qualification for your role?'

'I have no qualifications at all,' I told him. 'I can tell you quite frankly that the aliens probably picked one of the poorest representatives they could have found. There are two things to consider. First, I was the only human who seemed available – I was the only one who went back to visit them. Secondly, and this is important, they don't think, can't think, in the same manner that we do. What might make good sense to them may seem silly so far as we are concerned. On the other hand, our most brilliant logic might be gibberish to them.'

'I see,' said Rivers. 'But despite your frankness in saying you're not qualified to serve, you still are serving. Would you tell us why?'

'There's nothing else I can do,' I said. 'The situation has gotten to a point where there had to be an attempt at some sort of intelligent contact between the aliens and ourselves. Otherwise, things might get out of hand.'

'How do you mean?'

'Right now,' I said, 'the world is scared. There has to be some explanation of what is happening. There is nothing worse than a senseless happening, nothing worse than reasonless fear, and the aliens, so long as they know something's being done, may leave this barrier as it is. For the moment, I suspect, they'll do no more than they've already done. I hope it may work out that the situation gets no worse and that in the meantime some progress can be made.'

Other hands were waving and I pointed to another man.

'Frank Roberts, Washington Post,' he said. 'I have a question about the negotiations. As I understand it, the aliens want to be admitted to our world and in return are willing to provide us with a great store of knowledge they have accumulated.'

'That is right,' I said.

'Why do they want admission?'

'It's not entirely clear to me,' I told him. 'They need to be here so they can proceed to other worlds. It would seem the alternate worlds lie in some sort of progression, and they must be arrived at in a certain order. I confess quite willingly I understand none of this. All that can be done now is to reach proposals that we and the aliens can negotiate.'

'You know of no terms beyond the broad proposal you have stated?'

'None at all,' I said. 'There may be others. I am not aware of them.'

'But now you have – perhaps you would call him an advisor. Would it be proper to direct a question at this Mr Smith of yours?'

'A question,' said Mr Smith. 'I accept your question.'

He was pleased that someone had noticed him. Not without some qualms, I handed him the mike.

'You talk into it,' I said.

'I know,' he said. 'I watch.'

'You talk our language very well,' said the Washington Post.

'Just barely. Mechanism teach me.'

'Can you add anything about specific conditions?'

'I do not catch,' said Smith.

'Are there any conditions that your different people will insist upon before they reach an agreement with us?'

'Just one alone,' said Smith.

'And what would that one be?'

'I elucidate,' said Smith. 'You have a thing called war. Very bad, of course, but not impossible. Soon or late peoples get over playing war.'

He paused and looked around and all those reporters waited silently.

'Yes,' said one of the reporters finally, not the Post, 'yes, war is bad, but what . . . ?'

'I tell you now,' said Smith. 'You have a great amount of fission . . . I am at loss for word.'

'Fissionable material,' said a helpful newsman.

'That correct. Fissionable material. You have much of it. Once in another world there was same situation. When we arrive, there was nothing left. No life. No nothing. It was very sad. All life had been wiped out. We set him up again, but sad to think upon. Must not happen here. So we must insist such fissionable material be widely dispersed.'

'Now, wait,' a newsman shouted. 'You are saying that we must disperse fissionable material. I suppose you mean break up all the stockpiles and the bombs and have no more than a very small amount at any one place. Not enough, perhaps, to assemble a bomb of any sort.'

'You comprehend it fast,' said Smith.

'But how can you tell that it *is* dispersed? A country might say it complied when it really hadn't. How can you really know? How can you police it?'

'We monitor,' said Smith.

'You have a way of detecting fissionable material?'

'Yes, most certainly,' said Smith.

'All right, then, even if you knew – well, let's say it this way – you find there are concentrations still remaining; what do you do about them?'

'We blow them up,' said Smith. 'We detonate them loudly.'

'But . . .'

'We muster up a deadline. We edict all concentrations be gone by such a time. Time come and some still here, they auto . . . auto . . .'

'Automatically.'

'Thank you, kindly person. That is the word I grope for. They automatically blow up.'

An uneasy silence fell. The newsmen were wondering, I knew, if they were being taken in; if they were being, somehow, tricked by a phony actor decked out in a funny vest.

'Already,' Smith said, rather casually, 'we have a mechanism pinpointing all the concentrations.'

Someone shouted in a loud, hoarse voice: 'I'll be damned! The flying time machine!'

Then they were off and running, racing pell-mell for their cars parked along the road. With no further word to us, with no leave-taking whatsoever, they were off to tell the world.

And this was it, I thought, somewhat bitterly and more than a little limp.

Now the aliens could walk in any time they wanted, any way they wanted, with full human blessing. There was nothing else that could have turned the trick – no argument, no logic, no inducement short of this inducement. In the face of the worldwide clamour which this announcement would stir up, with the public demand that the world accept this one condition of an alien compact, all sane and sober counsel would have no weight at all.

Any workable agreement between the aliens and ourselves would necessarily have been a realistic one, with checks and balances. Each side would have been pledged to some contribution and each would have had to face some automatic, built-in penalty if the agreement should be broken. But now the checks and balances were gone and the way was open for the aliens to come in. They had offered the one thing that the people – not the governments, but the people – wanted, or that they thought they wanted, above every other thing and there'd be no stopping them in their demand for it.

And it had all been trickery, I thought bitterly. I had been tricked into bringing back the time machine and I had been forced into a situation where I had asked for help and Smith had been the help, or at least a part of it. And his announcement of the one demand had been little short of trickery in itself. It was the same old story. Human or alien, it made no difference. You wanted something bad enough and you went out to get it any way you could.

They'd beat us all the way, I knew. All the time they'd been that one long jump ahead of us and now the situation was entirely out of hand and the Earth was licked.

Smith stared after the running reporters.

'What proceeds?' he asked.

Pretending that he didn't know. I could have broken his neck.

'Come on,' I said. 'I'll escort you back to the village hall. Your pal is down there, doctoring up the folks.'

'But all the galloping,' he said, 'all the shouting? What occasions it?'

'You should know,' I said. 'You just hit the jackpot.'

23

WHEN I got back home, Nancy was waiting for me. She was sitting on the steps that led up to the porch, huddled there, crouched against the world. I saw her from a block away and hurried, gladder at the sight of her than I had ever been before. Glad and humble, and with a tenderness I never knew I had welling up so hard inside of me that I nearly choked.

Poor kid, I thought. It had been rough on her. Just one day home and the world of Millville, the world that she remembered and thought of as her home, had suddenly come unstuck.

Someone was shouting in the garden where tiny fifty-dollar bills presumably were still growing on the little bushes.

Coming in the gate, I stopped short at the sound of bellowing.

Nancy looked up and saw me.

'It's nothing, Brad,' she said. 'It's just Hiram down there. Higgy has him guarding all that money. The kids keep sneaking in, the little eight- and ten-year-olds. They only want to count the money on each bush. They aren't doing any harm.

But Hiram chases them. There are times,' she said, 'when I feel sorry for Hiram.'

'Sorry for him?' I asked, astonished. He was the last person in the world I'd suspected anyone might feel sorry for. 'He's just a stupid slob.'

'A stupid slob,' she said, 'who's trying to prove something and is not entirely sure what he wants to prove.'

'That he has more muscle . . .'

'No,' she told me, 'that's not it at all.'

Two kids came tearing out of the garden and vanished down the street. There was no sign of Hiram. And no more hollering. He had done his job; he had chased them off.

I sat down on the step beside her.

'Brad,' she said, 'it's not going well. I can feel it isn't going well.'

I shook my head, agreeing with her.

'I was down at the village hall,' she said. 'Where that terrible, shrivelled creature is conducting a clinic. Daddy's down there, too. He's helping out. But I couldn't stay. It's awful.'

'What's so bad about it? That thing – whatever you may call it – fixed up Doc. He's up and walking around and he looks as good as new. And Floyd Caldwell's heart and . . .'

She shuddered. 'That's the terrible thing about it. They are as good as new. They're better than new. They aren't cured, Brad; they are repaired, like a machine. It's like witchcraft. It's indecent. This wizened thing looks them over and he never makes a sound, but just glides around and looks them over and you can see that he's not looking at the outside of them but at their very insides. I don't know how you know this, but you do. As if he were reaching deep inside of them and . . .'

She stopped. 'I'm sorry,' she said. 'I shouldn't talk this way. It's not very decent talk.'

'It's not a very decent situation,' I said. 'We may have to change our minds a great deal about what is decent and in-

222

decent. There are a lot of ways we may have to change. I don't suppose that we will like it . . .'

'You talk as if it's settled.'

'I'm afraid it is,' I said, and I told her what Smith had told the newsmen. It felt good to tell her. There was no one else I could have told right then. It was a piece of news so weighted with guilt I would have been ashamed to tell it to anyone but Nancy.

'But now,' said Nancy, 'there can't be war – not the kind of war the whole world feared.'

'No,' I said, 'there can't be any war.' But I couldn't seem to feel too good about it. 'We may have something now that's worse than war.'

'There is nothing worse than war,' she said.

And that, of course, would be what everyone would say. Maybe they'd be right. But now the aliens would come into this world of ours and once we'd let them in we'd be entirely at their mercy. They had tricked us and we had nothing with which we could defend ourselves. Once here they could take over and supersede all plant life upon the Earth, without our knowing it, without our ever being able to find out. Once we let them in we never could be sure. And once they'd done that, then they'd own us. For all the animal life on Earth, including man, depended on the plants of Earth for their energy.

'What puzzles me,' I said, 'is that they could have taken over, anyhow. If they'd had a little patience, if they had taken a little time, they could have taken over and we never would have known. For there are some of them right here, their roots in Millville ground. They needn't have stayed as flowers. They could have been anything. In a hundred years they could have been every branch and leaf, every blade of grass . . .'

'Maybe there was a time factor of some sort,' said Nancy. 'Maybe they couldn't afford to wait.'

I shook my head. 'They had lots of time. If they needed more, they could have made it.'

'Maybe they need the human race,' she said. 'Perhaps we

have something they want. A plant society couldn't do a thing itself. They can't move about and they haven't any hands. They can store a lot of knowledge and they can think long thoughts – they can scheme and plan. But they can't put any of that planning into execution. They would need a partner to carry out their plans.'

'They've had partners,' I reminded her. 'They have a lot of partners even now. There are the people who made the time machine. There's this funny little doctor and that big windbag of a Smith. The Flowers have all the partners they need. It must be something else.'

'These people that you mention,' she said, 'may not be the right kind of people. Perhaps they searched world after world for the right kind of human beings. For the right kind of partner. Maybe that's us.'

'Perhaps,' I said, 'the others weren't mean enough. They may be looking for a deadly race. And a deadly race, that's us. Maybe they want someone who'll go slashing into parallel world after parallel world, in a sort of frenzy; brutal, ruthless, terrible. For when you come right down to it, we are pretty terrible. They may figure that, working with us, there's nothing that can stop them. Probably they are right. With all their accumulated knowledge and their mental powers, plus our understanding of physical concepts and our flair for technology, there probably is no limit to what the two of us could do.'

'I don't think that's it,' she said. 'What's the matter with you? I gained the impression to start with that you thought the Flowers might be all right.'

'They still may be,' I told her, 'but they used so many tricks and I fell for all the tricks. They used me for a fall guy.'

'So that's what bothers you.'

'I feel like a heel,' I said.

We sat quietly side by side upon the step. The street was silent and empty. During all the time we had sat there, no one had passed.

Nancy said, 'It's strange that anyone could submit himself

to that alien doctor. He's a creepy sort of being, and you can't be sure . . .'

'There are a lot of people,' I told her, 'who run most willingly to quackery.'

'But this isn't quackery,' she said. 'He did cure Doc and the rest of them. I didn't mean he was a faker, but only that he's horrid and repulsive.'

'Perhaps we appear the same to him.'

'There's something else,' she said. 'His technique is so different. No drugs, no instruments, no therapy. He just looks you over and probes into you with nothing, but you can see him probing, and then you're whole again – not only well, but whole. And if he can do that to our bodies, what about our minds? Can he change our minds, can he re-orient our thoughts?'

'For some people in this village,' I told her, 'that might be a good idea. Higgy, for example.'

She said, sharply, 'Don't joke about it, Brad.'

'All right,' I said. 'I won't.'

'You're just talking that way to keep from being scared.'

'And you,' I said, 'are talking seriously about it in an effort to reduce it to a commonplace.'

She nodded. 'But it doesn't help,' she said. 'It isn't commonplace.'

She stood up. 'Take me home,' she said.

So I walked her home.

24

TWILIGHT was falling when I walked downtown. I don't know why I went there. Restlessness, I guess. The house was too big and empty (emptier than it had ever been before) and the neighbourhood too quiet. There was no noise at all except for the occasional snatch of voices either excited or pontifical, strained through the electronic media. There was not a house in the entire village, I was certain, that did not have a television set or radio turned on.

But when I turned on the TV in the living-room and settled back to watch, it did no more than make me nervous and uneasy.

A commentator, one of the better known ones, was holding forth with a calm and deep assurance.

'. . . no way of knowing whether this contraption which is circling the skies can really do the job which our Mr Smith from the other world has announced to be its purpose. It has been picked up on a number of occasions by tracking stations which do not seem to be able, for one reason or another, to keep it in their range, and there have been instances, apparently verified, of visual sightings of it. But it is something about which it is difficult to get any solid news.

'Washington, it is understood, is taking the position that the word of an unknown being – unknown by either race or reputation – scarcely can be taken as undisputed fact. The capital tonight seems to be waiting for more word and until something of a solid nature can be deduced, it is unlikely there will be any sort of statement. That is the public position, of course; what is going on behind the scenes may be any-body's guess. And the same situation applies fairly well to all other capitals throughout the entire world.

'But this is not the situation outside the governmental circles. Everywhere the news has touched off wild celebration. There are joyous, spontaneous marches breaking out in London, and in Moscow a shouting, happy mob has packed Red Square. The churches everywhere have been filled since the first news broke, people thronging there to utter prayers of thankfulness.

'In the people there is no doubt and not the slightest hesitation. The man in the street, here in the United States and in Britain and in France – in fact, throughout the world – has accepted this strange announcement at face value. It may be simply a matter of believing what one chooses to believe, or it may be for some other reason, but the fact remains that there has been a bewildering suspension of the disbelief which characterized mass reaction so short a time ago as this morning.

'There seems, in the popular mind, to be no consideration of all the other factors which may be involved. The news of the end of any possibility of nuclear war has drowned out all else. It serves to underline the quiet and terrible, perhaps subconscious, tension under which the world has lived . . .'

I shut off the television and prowled about the house, my footsteps echoing strangely in the darkening rooms.

It was well enough, I thought, for a smug, complacent commentator to sit in the bright-lit studio a thousand miles away and analyse these happenings in a measured and well-modulated manner. And it was well enough, perhaps, for people other than myself, even here in Millville, to sit and listen to him. But I couldn't listen – I couldn't stand to listen.

Guilt, I asked myself? And it might be guilt, for I had been the one who'd brought the time machine to Earth and I had been the one who had taken Smith to meet the newsmen at the barrier. I had played the fool – the utter, perfect fool – and it seemed to me the entire world must know.

Or might it be the conviction that had been growing since I talked with Nancy that there was some hidden incident or fact – some minor motive or some small point of evidence – that I had failed to see, that we all had failed to grasp, and that if one could only put his finger on this single truth then all that had happened might become simpler of understanding and all that was about to happen might make some sort of sense?

I sought for it, for this hidden factor, for this joker in the deck, for the thing so small it had been overlooked and yet held within it a vast significance, and I did not find it.

I might be wrong, I thought. There might be no saving factor. We might be trapped and doomed and no way to get out.

I left the house and went down the street. There was no place I really wanted to go, but I had to walk, hoping that the freshness of the evening air, the very fact of walking might somehow clear my head.

A half a block away I caught the tapping sound. It appeared to be moving down the street toward me and in a little while I saw a bobbing halo of white that seemed to go with the steady tapping. I stopped and stared at it and it came bobbing closer and the tapping sound went on. And in another moment I saw that it was Mrs Tyler with her snow-white hair and cane.

'Good evening, Mrs Tyler,' I said as gently as I could, not to frighten her.

She stopped and twisted around to face me.

'It's Bradshaw, isn't it?' she asked. 'I can't see you well, but I recognize your voice.'

'Yes, it is,' I said. 'You're out late, Mrs Tyler.'

'I came to see you,' she said, 'but I missed your house. I am so forgetful that I walked right past it. Then I remembered and I was coming back.'

'What can I do for you?' I asked.

'Why, they tell me that you've seen Tupper. Spent some time with him.'

'That's true,' I said, sweating just a little, afraid of what might be coming next.

She moved a little closer, head tilted back, staring up at me.

'Is it true,' she asked, 'that he has a good position?'

'Yes,' I said, 'a very good position.'

'He holds the trust of his employers?'

'That is the impression that I gained. I would say he held a post of some importance.'

'He spoke of me?' she asked.

'Yes,' I lied. 'He asked after you. He said he'd meant to write, but he was too busy.'

'Poor boy,' she said, 'he never was a hand to write. He was looking well?'

'Very well, indeed.'

'Foreign service, I understand,' she said. 'Who would ever have thought he'd wind up in foreign service. To tell the truth, I often worried over him. But that was foolish, wasn't it?'

'Yes, it was,' I said. 'He's making out all right.'

'Did he say when he would be coming home?'

'Not for a time,' I told her. 'It seems he's very busy.'

'Well, then,' she said, quite cheerfully, 'I won't be looking for him. I can rest content. I won't be having to go out every hour or so to see if he's come back.'

She turned away and started down the street.

'Mrs Tyler,' I said, 'can't I see you home? It's getting dark and . . .'

'Oh, my, no,' she said. 'There is no need of it. I won't be afraid. Now that I know Tupper's all right, I'll never be afraid again.'

I stood and watched her go, the white halo of her head bobbing in the darkness, her cane tapping out the way as she moved down the long and twisting path of her world of fantasy.

And it was better that way, I knew, better that she could take harsh reality and twist it into something that was strange and beautiful.

I stood and watched until she turned the corner and the tapping of the cane grew dim, then I turned about and headed downtown.

In the shopping district the street lamps had turned on, but all the stores were dark and this, when one saw it, was a bit upsetting, for most of them stayed open until nine o'clock. But now even the Happy Hollow tavern and the movie house were closed.

The village hall was lighted and a small group of people loitered near the door. The clinic, I imagined, must be coming to a close. I wondered, looking at the hall, what Doc Fabian might think of all of this. His testy old medic's soul, I knew, would surely stand aghast despite the fact he'd been the first to benefit.

I turned from looking at the hall, and plodded down the street, hands plunged deep into my trouser pockets, walking aimlessly and restlessly, not knowing what to do. On a night like this, I wondered, what was a man to do? Sit in his living-room and watch the flickering rectangle of a television screen? Sit down with a bottle and methodically get drunk? Seek out a friend or neighbour for endless speculation and senseless conversation? Or find some place to huddle, waiting limply for what would happen next?

I came to an intersection and up the side street to my right I saw a splash of light that fell across the sidewalk from a lighted window. I looked at it, astonished, then realized that the light came from the window of the *Tribune* office, and that Joe Evans would be there, talking on the phone, perhaps, with someone from the Associated Press or the New York *Times* or one of the other papers that had been calling him for news. Joe was a busy man and I didn't want to bother him, but perhaps he wouldn't mind, I thought, if I dropped in for a minute.

He was busy on the phone, crouched above his desk, with the receiver pressed against his ear. The screen door clicked behind me and he looked up and saw me.

'Just a minute,' he said into the phone, holding the receiver out to me.

'Joe, what's the matter?'

For something was the matter. His face wore a look of shock and his eyes were stiff and staring. Little beads of sweat trickled down his forehead and ran into his eyebrows.

'It's Alf,' he said, lips moving stiffly.

'Alf,' I said into the phone, but I kept my eyes on Joe Evans' face. He had the look of a man who had been hit on the head with something large and solid.

'Brad!' cried Alf. 'Is that you, Brad?'

'Yes,' I said, 'it is.'

'Where have you been? I've been trying to get in touch with you. When your phone didn't answer . . .'

'What's the matter, Alf? Take it easy, Alf.'

'All right,' he said. 'I'll try to take it easy. I'll take it from the top.'

I didn't like the sound of his voice. He was scared and he was trying not to be.

'Go ahead,' I said.

'I finally got to Elmore,' he told me. 'The traffic's something awful. You can't imagine what the traffic is out here. They have military check points and . . .'

'But you finally got to Elmore. You told me you were going.'

'Yes, I finally got here. On the radio I heard about this delegation that came out to see you. The senator and the general and the rest of them, and when I got to Elmore I found that they were stopping at the Corn Belt hotel. Isn't that the damndest name . . . ?

'But, anyhow, I figured that they should know more about what was going on down in Mississippi. I thought it might throw some light on the situation. So I went down to the hotel to see the senator – that is, to try to see him. It was a madhouse down there. There were great crowds of people and the police were trying to keep order, but they had their hands full. There were television cameras all over the place and newsmen and the radio people – well, anyhow, I never saw the senator. But I saw someone else. Saw him and recognized him from the pictures in the paper. The one called Davenport . . .'

'The biologist,' I said.

'Yes, that's it. The scientist. I got him cornered and I tried to explain I had to see the senator. He wasn't too much help. I'm not even sure he was hearing what I was saying. He seemed to be upset and he was sweating like a mule and he was paper-white. I thought he might be sick and I asked him if he was, if there was anything I could do for him. Then he told me. I don't think he meant to tell me. I think maybe he was sorry that he did after he had told me. But he was so full of anger it was spilling out of him and for the moment he didn't care. The man was in anguish, I tell you. I never saw a man as upset as he was. He grabbed me by the lapels and he stuck his face up close to mine and he was so excited and he talked so fast that he spit all over me. He wouldn't have done a thing like that for all the world; he's not that sort of man . . .'

'Alf,' I pleaded. 'Alf, get down to facts.'

'I forgot to tell you,' Alf said, 'that the news had just broken about that flying saucer you brought back. The radio was full of it. About how it was spotting the nuclear concentrations. Well, I started to tell the scientist about why I had to see the senator, about the project down in Greenbriar. And that was when he began to talk, grabbing hold of me so I couldn't get away. He said the news of the aliens' one condition, that we disperse our nuclear capacity, was the worst thing that could have happened. He said the Pentagon is convinced the aliens are a threat and that they must be stopped . . .'

'Alf,' I said, suddenly weak, guessing what was coming.

'And he said they know they must be stopped before they control more territory and the only way to do it is an H-bomb right on top of Millville.'

He stopped, half out of breath.

I didn't say a thing. I couldn't say a word, I was too paralysed. I was remembering how the general had looked when I'd talked with him that morning and the senator saying, 'We have to trust you, boy. You hold us in your hands.'

'Brad,' Alf asked, anxiously, 'are you there? Did you hear me?'

'Yes,' I said, 'I'm here.'

'Davenport told me he was afraid this new development of the nuclear pinpointing might push the military into action without due consideration – knowing that they had to act or they'd not have anything to use. Like a man with a gun, he said, facing a wild beast. He doesn't want to kill the beast unless he has to and there is always the chance the beast will slink away and he won't have to fire. But suppose he knows that in the next two minutes his gun will disappear into thin air – well, then he has to take a chance and shoot before the gun can disappear. He has to kill the beast while he still has a gun.'

'And now,' I said, speaking more levelly than I would have thought possible, 'Millville is the beast.'

'Not Millville, Brad. Just . . .'

'Yes,' I said, 'most certainly not Millville. Tell that to the people when the bomb explodes.'

'This Davenport was beside himself. He had no business talking to me . . .'

'You think he knows what he is talking about? He had a row with the general this morning.'

'I think he knows more than he told me, Brad. He talked for a couple of minutes and then he buttoned up. As though he knew he had no business talking. But he's obsessed with one idea. He thinks the only thing that can stop the military is the force of public opinion. He thinks that if what they plan is known, there'll be such an uproar they'd be afraid to move. Not only, he pointed out, would the public be outraged at such cold-bloodedness, but the public wants these aliens in; they're for anyone who can break the bomb. And this biologist of yours is going to plant this story. He didn't say he would, but that's what he was working up to. He'll tip off some news-paperman, I'm sure of that.'

I felt my guts turn over and my knees were weak. I pressed my legs hard against the desk to keep from keeling over.

'This village will go howling mad,' I said. 'I asked the general this morning . . .'

'You asked the general! For Christ sake, did you know?'

'Of course I knew. Not that they would do it. Just that they were thinking of it.'

'And you didn't say a word?'

'Who could I tell? What good would it have done? And it wasn't certain. It was just an alternative – a last alternative. Three hundred lives against three billion . . .'

'But you, yourself! All your friends . . .'

'Alf,' I pleaded, 'there was nothing I could do. What would you have done? Told the village and driven everyone stark mad?'

'I don't know,' said Alf. 'I don't know what I'd have done.'

'Alf, is the senator at the hotel? I mean, is he there right now?'

'I think he is. You mean to call him, Brad?'

'I don't know what good it'll do,' I said, 'but perhaps I should.'

'I'll get off the line,' said Alf. 'And Brad . . .'

'Yes.'

'Brad, the best of luck. I mean – oh, hell, just the best of luck.'

'Thanks, Alf.'

I heard the click of the receiver as he hung up and the line droned empty in my ear. My hand began to shake and I laid the receiver carefully on the desk, not trying to put it back into the cradle.

Joe Evans was looking at me hard. 'You knew,' he said. 'You knew all the time.'

I shook my head. 'Not that they meant to do it. The general mentioned it as a last resort. Davenport jumped on him . . .'

I didn't finish what I meant to say. The words just dwindled off. Joe kept on staring at me.

I exploded at him. 'Damn it, man,' I shouted, 'I couldn't tell anyone. I asked the general, if he had to do it, to do it without notice. Not to let us know. That way there'd be a flash we'd probably never see. We'd die, of course, but only once. Not a thousand deaths . . .'

Joe picked up the phone. 'I'll try to raise the senator,' he said.

I sat down in a chair.

I felt empty. There was nothing in me. I heard Joe talking into the telephone, but I didn't really hear his words, for it seemed that I had, for the moment, created a small world all of my own (as though there were no longer room for me in the normal world) and had drawn it about me as one would draw a blanket.

I was miserable and at the same time angry, and perhaps considerably confused.

Joe was saying something to me and I became aware of it only after he had almost finished speaking.

'What was that?' I asked.

'The call is in,' said Joe. 'They'll call us back.'

I nodded.

'I told them it was important.'

'I wonder if it is,' I said.

'What do you mean? Of course it . . .'

'I wonder what the senator can do. I wonder what difference it will make if I, or you, or anyone, talks to him about it.'

'The senator has a lot of weight,' said Joe. 'He likes to throw it around.'

We sat in silence for a moment, waiting for the call, waiting for the senator and what he knew about it.

'If no one will stand up for us,' asked Joe, 'if no one will fight for us, what are we to do?'

'What can we do?' I asked. 'We can't even run. We can't get away. We're sitting ducks.'

'When the village knows . . .'

'They'll know,' I said, 'as soon as the news leaks out. If it does leak out. It'll be bulletined on TV and radio and everyone in this village is plastered to a set.'

'Maybe someone will get hold of Davenport and hush him up.'

I shook my head. 'He was pretty sore this morning. Right down the general's throat.'

And who was right? I asked myself. How could one tell in this short space of time who was right or wrong?

For years man had fought insects and blights and noxious weeds. He'd fought them any way he could. He'd killed them any way he could. Let one's guard down for a moment and the weeds would have taken over. They crowded every fence corner, every hedgerow, sprang up in every vacant lot. They'd grow anywhere. When drought killed the grain and sickened the corn, the weeds would keep on growing, green and tough and wiry.

And now came another noxious weed, out of another time,

235

a weed that very possibly could destroy not only corn and grain but the human race. If this should be the case, the only thing to do was to fight it as one fought any weed, with everything one had.

But suppose that this was a different sort of weed, no ordinary weed, but a highly adaptive weed that had studied the ways of man and weed, and out of its vast knowledge and adaptability could manage to survive anything that man might throw at it. Anything, that is, except massive radiation.

For that had been the answer when the problem had been posed in that strange project down in Mississippi.

And the Flowers' reaction to that answer would be a simple one. Get rid of radiation. And while you were getting rid of it, win the affection of the world.

If that should be the situation, then the Pentagon was right.

The phone buzzed from the desk.

Joe picked up the receiver and handed it to me.

My lips seemed to be stiff. The words I spoke came out hard and dry.

'Hello,' I said. 'Hello. Is this the senator?'

'Yes.'

'This is Bradshaw Carter. Millville. Met you this morning. At the barrier.'

'Certainly, Mr Carter. What can I do for you?'

'There is a rumour . . .'

'There are many rumours, Carter. I've heard a dozen of them.'

'About a bomb on Millville. The general said this morning . . .'

'Yes,' said the senator, far too calmly. 'I have heard that rumour, too, and am quite disturbed by it. But there is no confirmation. It is nothing but a rumour.'

'Senator,' I said. 'I wish you'd level with me. To you it's a disturbing thing to hear. It's personal with us.'

'Well,' said the senator. You could fairly hear him debating with himself.

'Tell me,' I insisted. 'We're the ones involved . . .'

'Yes. Yes,' said the senator. 'You have the right to know. I'd not deny you that.'

'So what is going on?'

'There is only one solid piece of information,' said the senator. 'There are top level consultations going on among the nuclear powers. Quite a blow to them, you know, this condition of the aliens. The consultations are highly secret, as you might imagine. You realize, of course . . .'

'It's perfectly all right,' I said. 'I can guarantee . . .'

'Oh, it's not that so much,' said the senator. 'One of the newspaper boys will sniff it out before the night is over. But I don't like it. It sounds as if some sort of mutual agreement is being sought. In view of public opinion, I am very much afraid . . .'

'Senator! Please, not politics.'

'I'm sorry,' said the senator. 'I didn't mean it that way. I won't try to conceal from you that I am perturbed. I'm trying to get what facts I can . . .'

'Then it's critical.'

'If that barrier moves another foot,' said the senator, 'if anything else should happen, it's not inconceivable that we might act unilaterally. The military can always argue that they moved to save the world from invasion by an alien horde. They can claim, as well, that they had information held by no one else. They could say it was classified and refuse to give it out. They would have a cover story and once it had been done, they could settle back and let time take its course. There would be hell to pay, of course, but they could ride it out.'

'What do you think?' I asked. 'What are the chances?'

'God,' said the senator, 'I don't know. I don't have the facts. I don't know what the Pentagon is thinking. I don't know the facts they have. I don't know what the chiefs of staff have told the President. There is no way of knowing the attitudes of Britain or Russia, or of France.'

The wire sang cold and empty.

'Is there,' asked the senator, 'anything that you can do from the Millville end?'

'An appeal,' I said. 'A public appeal. The newspapers and the radio . . .'

I could almost see him shake his head. 'It wouldn't work,' he said. 'No one has any way of knowing what's happening there behind the barrier. There is always the possibility of influence by the aliens. And the pleading of special favour even when that would be prejudicial to the world. The communications media would snap it up, of course, and would play it up and make a big thing of it. But it would not influence official opinion in the least. It would only serve to stir up the people – the people everywhere. And there is enough emotionalism now. What we need are some solid facts and some common sense.'

He was fearful, I thought, that we'd upset the boat. He wanted to keep everything all quiet and decent.

'And, anyhow,' he said, 'there is no real evidence . . .'

'Davenport thinks there is.'

'You have talked with him?'

'No,' I said, quite truthfully, 'I haven't talked with him.'

'Davenport,' he said, 'doesn't understand. He stepped out of the isolation of his laboratory and . . .'

'He sounded good to me,' I said. 'He sounded civilized.'

And was sorry I'd said it, for now I'd embarrassed him as well as frightened him.

'I'll let you know,' he said, a little stiffly. 'As soon as I hear anything I'll let you or Gerald know. I'll do the best I can. I don't think you need to worry. Just keep that barrier from moving, just keep things quiet. That's all you have to do.'

'Sure, Senator,' I said, disgusted.

'Thanks for calling,' said the senator. 'I'll keep in touch.'

'Goodbye, Senator,' I said.

I put the receiver back into the cradle. Joe looked at me inquiringly.

I shook my head. 'He doesn't know and he isn't talking. And I gather he is helpless. He can't do anything for us.'

Footsteps sounded on the sidewalk and a second later the

door came open. I swung around and there stood Higgy Morris.

Of all the people who would come walking in at this particular moment, it would be Higgy Morris.

He looked from one to the other of us.

'What's the matter with you guys?' he asked.

I kept on looking at him, wishing that he'd go away, but knowing that he wouldn't.

'Brad,' said Joe, 'we've got to tell him.'

'All right,' I said. 'You go ahead and tell him.'

Higgy didn't move. He stood beside the door while Joe told him how it was. Higgy got wall-eyed and seemed to turn into a statue. He never moved a muscle; he didn't interrupt.

For a long moment there was silence, then Higgy said to me, 'What do you think? Could they do a thing like that to us?'

I nodded. 'They could. They might. If the barrier moves again. If something else should happen.'

'Well, then,' said Higgy, springing into action, 'what are we standing here for? We must start to dig.'

'Dig?'

'Sure. A bomb shelter. We've got all sorts of manpower. There's no one in the village who's doing anything. We could put everyone to work. There's road equipment in the shed down by the railroad station and there must be a dozen or more trucks scattered here and there. I'll appoint a committee and we'll . . . Say, what's the matter with you fellows?'

'Higgy,' said Joe, almost gently, 'you just don't understand. This isn't fallout – this would be a hit with the village as ground zero. You can't build a shelter that would do any good. Not in a hundred years, you couldn't.'

'We could try,' said Higgy, stubbornly.

'You can't dig deep enough,' I said, 'or build strong enough to withstand the blast. And even if you could, there'd be the oxygen . . .'

'But we got to do something,' Higgy shouted. 'We can't simply sit and take it. Why, we'd all be killed!'

'Chum,' I told him, 'that's too damned bad.'

'Now, see here . . .' said Higgy.

'Cut it out!' yelled Joe. 'Cut it out, both of you. Maybe you don't care for one another, but we have to work together. And there is a way. We do have a shelter.'

I stared at him for a moment, then I saw what he was getting at.

'No!' I shouted. 'No, we can't do that. Not yet. Don't you see? That would be throwing away any chance we have for negotiation. We can't let them know.'

'Ten to one,' said Joe, 'they already know.'

'I don't get it at all,' Higgy pleaded. 'What shelter have we got?'

'The other world,' said Joe. 'The parallel world, the one that Brad was in. We could go back there if we had to. They would take care of us, they would let us stay. They'd grow food for us and there'd be stewards to keep us healthy and . . .'

'You forget one thing,' I said. 'We don't know how to go. There's just that one place in the garden and now it's all changed. The flowers are gone and there's nothing there but the money bushes.'

'The steward and Smith could show us,' said Joe. 'They would know the way.'

'They aren't here,' said Higgy. 'They went home. There was no one at the clinic and they said they had to go, but they'd be back again if we needed them. I drove them down to Brad's place and they didn't have no trouble finding the door or whatever you call it. They just walked a ways across the garden and then they disappeared.'

'You could find it, then?' asked Joe.

'I could come pretty close.'

'We can find it if we have to, then,' said Joe. 'We can form lines, arm in arm, and march across the garden.'

'I don't know,' I said. 'It may not be always open.'

'Open?'

'If it stayed open all the time,' I said, 'we'd have lost a lot of people in the last ten years. Kids played down there and other people used it for a short cut. I went across it to go over to Doc Fabian's, and there were a lot of people who walked back and forth across it. Some of them would have hit that door if it had been open.'

'Well, anyhow,' said Higgy, 'we can call them up. We can pick up one of those phones . . .'

'Not,' I said, 'until we absolutely have to. We'd probably be cutting ourselves off forever from the human race.'

'It would be better,' Higgy said, 'than dying.'

'Let's not rush into anything,' I pleaded with them. 'Let's give our own people time to try to work it out. It's possible that nothing will happen. We can't go begging for sanctuary until we know we need it. There's still a chance that the two races may be able to negotiate. I know it doesn't look too good now, but if it's possible, humanity has to have a chance to negotiate.'

'Brad,' said Joe, 'I don't think there'll be any negotiations. I don't think the aliens ever meant there should be any.'

'And,' said Higgy, 'this never would have happened if it hadn't been for your father.'

I choked down my anger and I said, 'It would have happened somewhere. If not in Millville, then it would have happened some place else. If not right now, then a little later.'

'But that's the point,' said Higgy, nastily. 'It wouldn't have happened here; it would have happened somewhere else.'

I had no answer for him. There was an answer, certainly, but not the kind of answer that Higgy would accept.

'And let me tell you something else,' said Higgy. 'Just a friendly warning. You better watch your step. Hiram's out to get you. The beating you gave him didn't help the situation any. And there are a lot of hotheads who feel as Hiram does about it. They blame you and your family for what has happened here.'

'Higgy,' protested Joe, 'no one has any right . . .'

'I know they don't,' said Higgy, 'but that's the way it is. I'll try to uphold law and order, but I can't guarantee it now.'

241

He turned and spoke directly to me. 'You better hope,' he said, 'that this thing gets straightened out and soon. And if it doesn't, you better find a big, deep hole to hide in.'

'Why, you . . .' I said. I jumped to my feet and I would have slugged him, but Joe came fast around the desk and grabbed hold of me and pushed me back.

'Cut it out!' he said, exasperated. 'We got trouble enough without you two tangling.'

'If the bombing rumour does get out,' said Higgy, viciously, 'I wouldn't give a nickel for your life. You're too mixed up in it. Folks will begin to wonder . . .'

Joe grabbed hold of Higgy and shoved him against the wall. 'Shut your mouth,' he said, 'or I'll shut it for you.' He balled up a fist and showed it to Higgy and Higgy shut his mouth.

'And now,' I said to Joe, 'since you've restored law and order and everything is peaceable and smooth, you won't be needing me. I'll run along.'

'Brad,' said Joe, between his teeth, 'just a minute, there . . .'

But I went out and slammed the door behind me.

Outside, the dusk had deepened and the street was empty. Light still burned in the village hall, but the few loungers at the door were gone.

Maybe, I told myself, I should have stayed. If for no other reason than to help Joe keep Higgy from making some fool move.

But there had, it seemed to me, been no point in staying. Even if I had something to offer (which I didn't), it would have been suspect. For by now, apparently, I was fairly well discredited. More than likely Hiram and Tom Preston had been busy all afternoon lining people up in the Hate Bradshaw Carter movement.

I turned off Main Street and headed back toward home. All along the street lay a sense of peacefulness. Shadows flickered on the lawns quartering the intersections as a light summer breeze set the street lamps, hung on their arms, to swaying. Windows were open against the heat and to catch the breeze and soft lights shone within the houses, while from the open windows came snatches of muttering from the TV or radio.

Peaceful, and yet I knew that beneath that quiet exterior lay the fear and hate and terror that could turn the village into a howling bedlam at a single word or an unexpected action.

There was resentment here, a smouldering resentment that one little group of people should be penned like cattle while all the others in the world were free. And a feeling of rebellion against the cosmic unfairness that we, of all the people in the world, should have been picked for penning. Perhaps, as well, a strange unquiet at being stared at by the world and talked of by the world, as if we were something monstrous and unkempt. And perhaps the shameful fear that the world might think we had brought all this on ourselves through some moral or mental relapse.

Thrown into this sort of situation, it was only natural that the people of the village should be avid to grasp at any sort of interpretation that might clear their names and set them right, not only with themselves, but with the aliens and the world; that they should be willing to believe anything at all (the worst or best), to embrace all rumours, to wallow in outlandish speculation, to attempt to paint the entire picture in contrasting black and white (even when they knew that all of it was grey), because in this direction of blackness and of whiteness lay the desired simplicity that served an easier understanding and a comfortable acceptance.

They could not be blamed, I told myself. They were not equipped to take a thing like this in stride. For years they had lived unspectacularly in a tiny backwash off the mainstream of the world. The small events of village life were their great events, the landmarks of their living – that time the crazy Johnson kid had rammed his beat-up jalopy into the tree on Elm Street, the day the fire department had been called to rescue Grandma Jones' cat, marooned on the roof of the Presbyterian parsonage (and to this day no one could figure out how the cat had got there), the afternoon Pappy Andrews had fallen asleep while fishing on the river bank, and had tumbled

243

down into the stream, to be hauled out, now thoroughly awakened, but with water in his lungs, spewing and gasping, by Len Streeter (and the speculation as to why Len Streeter should have been walking along the river bank). Of such things had their lives been made, the thin grist of excitement.

But now they faced a bigger thing, something they could not comprehend, a happening and a situation that was, for the moment, too big for the world to comprehend. And because they could not reduce this situation to the simple formula of aimless wonder that could be accorded a cat that had somehow attained the parsonage roof, they were uneasy and upset and their tempers were on edge, ready to flare into an antagonistic attitude, and very probably into violence – if they could find something or someone against which such a violence could be aimed. And now I knew that Tom Preston and Hiram Martin had provided them with a target for their violence – if and when the violence came.

I saw now that I was almost home. I was in front of the house of Daniel Willoughby, a big brick house, upstanding and foursquare, the kind of house you'd know, without even thinking of it, that a man like Daniel Willoughby would own. Across the street, on the corner, was the old Perkins house. New people had moved into the place a week or so ago. It was one of the few houses in the village that was put up for rent, and people moved in and out of it every year or so. No one ever went out of their way to get acquainted with these renters; it wasn't worth one's while. And just down the street was Doc Fabian's place.

A few minutes more, I thought, and I would be home, back in the house with the hole punched in the roof, back with the echoing emptiness and the lonely question, with the hatred and suspicion of the town performing sentry-go just outside the gate.

Across the street a screen door slammed and feet tramped across the porch boards.

A voice yelled: 'Wally, they're going to bomb us! It was on television!'

A shadow hunched up out of the darkness of the earth – a man who had been lying on the grass or sitting in a low-slung lawn chair, invisible until the cry had jerked him upright.

He gurgled as he tried to form some word, but it came out wrong.

'There was a bulletin!' the other one shouted from the porch. 'Just now. On television.'

The man out in the yard was up and running, heading for the house.

And I was running, too. Heading for home, as fast as I could go, my legs moving of their own accord, unprompted by the brain.

I'd expected I'd have a little time, but there'd been no time. The rumour had broken sooner than I had anticipated.

For the bulletin, of course, had been no more than rumour, I was sure of that – that a bombing might take place; that, as a last resort, a bomb might be dropped on Millville. But I also knew that so far as this village was concerned, it would make no difference. The people in the village would not differentiate between fact and rumour.

This was the trigger that would turn this village into a hate-filled madhouse. I might be involved and so might Gerald Sherwood – and Stiffy, too, if he were here.

I ran off the street and plunged down the slope back of the Fabian house, heading for the little swale where the money crop was growing. It was not until I was halfway down the slope that I thought of Hiram. Earlier in the day he had been guarding the money bushes and he might still be there. I skidded to a halt and crouched against the ground. Quickly I surveyed the area below me, then went slowly over it, looking for any hunch of darkness, any movement that might betray a watcher.

From far away I heard a shout and on the street above someone ran, feet pounding on the pavement. A door banged and somewhere, several blocks away, a car was started and the driver gunned the engine. The excited voice of a news commentator floated thinly through an open window, but I could not make out the words.

There was no sign of Hiram.

I rose from my crouch and went slowly down the slope. I reached the garden and made my way across it. Ahead of me loomed the shattered greenhouse, and growing at its corner the seedling elm tree.

I came up to the greenhouse and stood beside it for a moment, taking one last look for Hiram, to make sure he wasn't sneaking up on me. Then I started to move on, but a voice spoke to me and the sound of the voice froze me.

Although, even as I stood frozen, I realized there'd been no sound.

Bradshaw Carter, said the voice once again, speaking with no sound.

And there was a smell of purpleness – perhaps not a smell, exactly, but a sense of purpleness. It lay heavy in the air and it took me back in sharp and crystal memory to Tupper Tyler's camp where the Presence had waited on the hillside to walk me back to Earth.

'Yes,' I said. 'Where are you?'

The seedling elm at the corner of the greenhouse seemed to sway, although there was not breeze enough to sway it.

I am here, it said. I have been here all the years. I have been looking forward to this time when I could talk with you.

'You know?' I asked, and it was a foolish question, for somehow I was sure it knew about the bomb and all the rest of it.

We know, said the elm tree, but there can be no despair.

'No despair?' I asked, aghast.

If we fail this time, it said, we will try again. Another place, perhaps. Or we may have to wait the – what do you call it?

'The radiation,' I said. 'That is what you call it.'

Until, said the purpleness, the radiations leave.

'That will be years,' I said.

We have the years, it said. We have all the time there is. There is no end of us. There is no end of time.

'But there is an end of time for us,' I said, with a gush of pity for all humanity, but mostly for myself. 'There is an end for me.'

Yes, we know, said the purpleness. We feel much sorrow for you.

And now, I knew, was the time to ask for help, to point out that we were in this situation through no choice and no action of our own, and that those who had placed us in it should help to get us out.

But when I tried to say the words, I couldn't make them come. I couldn't admit to this alien thing our complete helplessness.

It was, I suppose, stubbornness and pride. But I had not known until I tried to speak the words that I had the stubbornness and pride.

We feel much sorrow for you, the elm tree had said. But what kind of sorrow – a real and sincere sorrow, or the superficial and pedantic sorrow of the immortal for a frail and flickering creature that was about to die?

I would be bone and dust and eventually neither bone nor dust but forgetfulness and clay, and these things would live on and on, forever.

And it would be more important, I knew, for us who would be bone and dust to have a stubborn pride than it would be for a thing of strength and surety. It was the one thing we had, the one thing we could cling to.

A purpleness, I thought, and what was the purpleness? It was not a colour; it was something more than that. It was, perhaps, the odour of immortality, the effluvium of that great uncaring which could not afford to care since anything it cared for could only last a day, while it went on into an eternal future toward other things and other lives for which it could not allow itself to care.

And this was loneliness, I thought, a never-ending and hopeless loneliness such as the human race would never be called upon to face.

Standing there, touching the hard, cold edge of that

loneliness, I felt pity stir in me and it seemed strange that one should feel pity for a tree. Although, I knew, it was not the tree nor the purple flowers but the Presence that had walked me home and that was here as well – the same life stuff of which I myself was made – that I felt pity for.

'I am sorry for you, too,' I said, but even as I spoke I knew it would not understand the pity any more than it would have understood the pride if it had known about the pride.

A car came screeching around the curve on the street above the swale and the illumination of its headlights slashed across the greenhouse. I flinched away, but the lights were gone before the flinch had finished.

Somewhere out in the darkness someone was calling me, speaking softly, almost fearfully.

Another car came around the curve, turning fast, its tyres howling on the turn. The first car was stopping at my house, skidding on the pavement as the brakes spun it to a halt.

'Brad!' said the soft and fearful voice. 'Are you out there, Brad?'

'Nancy,' I said. 'Nancy, over here.'

There was something wrong, I knew, something terribly wrong. There was a tenseness in her voice, as if she were speaking through a haze of terror. And there was a wrongness, too, about those speeding cars stopping at the house.

'I thought I heard you talking,' Nancy said, 'but I couldn't see you. You weren't in the house and . . .'

A man was running around the back of the house, a dark shadow outlined briefly by the street lamp at the corner. Out in front were other men; I could hear their running and the angry mumble of them.

'Brad,' said Nancy.

'Hold it,' I cautioned. 'There's something wrong.'

I could see her now. She was stumbling toward me through the darkness.

Up by the house a voice yelled: 'We know you're in there, Carter! We're coming in to get you if you don't come out!'

248

I turned and ran toward Nancy and caught her in my arms. She was shivering.

'Those men,' she said.

'Hiram and his pals,' I said.

Glass crashed and a streak of fire went arcing through the night.

'Now, damn it,' someone yelled, triumphantly, 'maybe you'll come out.'

'Run,' I said to Nancy. 'Up the hill. Get in among the trees . . .'

'It's Stiffy,' she whispered back. 'I saw him and he sent me . . .'

A sudden glow of fire leaped up inside the house. The windows in the dining-room flared like gleaming eyes. And in the light cast by the flame I saw the dark figures gambolling, screaming now in a mindless frenzy.

Nancy turned and ran and I pelted after her, and behind us a voice boomed above the bawling of the mob.

'There he goes!' the voice shouted. 'Down there in the garden!'

Something caught my foot and tripped me and I fell, sprawling among the money bushes. The scraggly branches raked across my face and clawed at my clothes as I struggled to my feet.

A tongue of whipping flame leaped above the house, funnelled through the hole the time machine had punched in the roof, and the windows all were glowing now. In the sudden silence I could hear the sucking roar of fire eating through the structure.

They were running down the slope toward the garden a silent group of men. The pounding of their feet and the ugly gasping of their breath came across the space between us.

I stooped and ran my hand along the ground and in the darkness found the thing that tripped me. My fingers closed about it and I brought it up, a four foot length of two-by-four, old and beginning to rot along its edges, but still sound in the core.

A club, I thought, and this was the end of it. But one of them would die – perhaps two of them – while they were killing me.

'Run!' I screamed at Nancy, knowing she was out there somewhere, although I could not see her.

There was just one thing left, I told myself, one thing more that I must do. And that was to get Hiram Martin with the club before the mob closed over me.

They had reached the bottom of the slope and were charging across the flat ground of the garden, with Hiram in the lead. I stood and waited for them, with the club half raised, watching Hiram run toward me, with the white gash of his teeth shining in the darkness of his face.

Right between the eyes, I told myself, and split his skull wide open. And after that get another of them if there were time to do it.

The fire was roaring now, racing through the dryness of the house, and even where I stood the heat reached out to touch me.

The men were closing in and I raised the club a little higher, working my fingers to get a better grip upon it.

But in that last instant before they came within my reach, they skidded to a milling halt, some of them half turning to run back up the slope, the others simply staring, with their mouths wide open in astonishment and horror. Staring, not at me, but at something that was beyond me.

Then they broke and ran, back toward the slope, and above the roaring of the burning house, I could hear their bellowing – like stampeded cattle racing before a prairie fire, bawling out their terror as they ran.

I swung around to look behind me and there stood those other things from that other world, their ebon hides gleaming in the flicker of the firelight, their silver plumes stirring gently in the breeze. And as they moved toward me, they twittered in their weird bird-song.

My God, I thought, they couldn't wait! They came a little early so they wouldn't miss a single tremor of this terror-stricken place.

And not only on this night, but on other nights to come, rolling back the time to this present instant. A new place for them to stand and wait for it to commence, a new ghost house with gaping windows through which they'd glimpse the awfulness of another earth.

They were moving toward me and I was standing there with the club gripped in my hands and there was the smell of purpleness again and a soundless voice I recognized.

Go back, the voice said. Go back. You've come too soon. This world isn't open.

Someone was calling from far away, the call lost in the thundering and the crackling of the fire and the high, excited, liquid trilling of these ghouls from the purple world of Tupper Tyler.

Go back, said the elm tree, and its voiceless words cracked like a snapped whiplash.

And they were going back – or, at least, they were disappearing, melting into some strange darkness that was blacker than the night.

One elm tree that talked, I thought, and how many other trees? How much of this place still was Millville and how much purple world? I lifted my head so that I could see the treetops that rimmed the garden and they were there, ghosts against the sky, fluttering in some strange wind that blew from an unknown quarter. Fluttering – or were they talking, too? The old, dumb, stupid trees of earth, or a different kind of tree from a different earth?

We'd never know, I told myself, and perhaps it did not matter, for from the very start we'd never had a chance. We were licked before we started. We had been lost on that long-gone day when my father brought home the purple flowers.

From far off someone was calling and the name was mine.

I dropped the two-by-four and started across the garden, wondering who it was. Not Nancy, but someone that I knew.

Nancy came running down the hill. 'Hurry, Brad,' she called.

'Where were you?' I asked. 'What's going on?'

'It's Stiffy. I told you it was Stiffy. He's waiting at the barrier. He sneaked through the guards. He says he has to see you.'

'But Stiffy . . .'

'He's here, I tell you. And he wants to talk with you. No one else will do.'

She turned and trotted up the hill and I lumbered after her. We went through Doc's yard and across the street and through another yard and there, just ahead of us, I knew, was the barrier.

A gnome-like figure rose from the ground.

'That you, lad?' he asked.

I hunkered down at the edge of the barrier and stared across at him.

'Yes, it's me,' I said, 'but you . . .'

'Later. We haven't got much time. The guards know I got through the lines. They're hunting for me.'

'What do you want?' I asked.

'Not what I want,' he said. 'What everybody wants. Something that you need. You're in a jam.'

'Everyone's in a jam,' I said.

'That's what I mean,' said Stiffy. 'Some damn fool in the Pentagon is set to drop a bomb. I heard some of the ruckus on a car radio when I was sneaking through. Just a snatch of it.'

'So, all right,' I said. 'The human race is sunk.'

'Not sunk,' insisted Stiffy. 'I tell you there's a way. If Washington just understood, if . . .'

'If you know a way,' I asked, 'why waste time in reaching me? You could have told . . .'

'Who would I tell?' asked Stiffy. 'Who would believe me, even if I told? I'm just a lousy bum and I ran off from that hospital and . . .'

'All right,' I said. 'All right.'

'You were the man to tell,' said Stiffy. 'You're accredited, it seems like. Someone will listen to you. You can get in touch with someone and they'll listen to you.'

'If it was good enough,' I said.

'This is good enough,' said Stiffy. 'We have something that the aliens want. We're the only people who can give it to them.'

'Give to them!' I shouted. 'Anything they want, they can take away from us.'

'Not this, they can't,' said Stiffy.

I shook my head. 'You make it sound too easy. They already have us hooked. The people want them in, although they'd come in anyhow, even if the people didn't. They hit us in our weak spot . . .'

'The Flowers have a weak spot, too,' said Stiffy.

'Don't make me laugh,' I said.

'You're just upset,' said Stiffy.

'You're damned right I am.'

And I had a right to be. The world had gone to pot. Nuclear annihilation was poised above our heads and the village, wild before, would be running frantic when Hiram told what he'd seen down in the garden. Hiram and his hoodlum pals had burned down my house and I didn't have a home – no one had a home, for the earth was home no longer. It was just another in a long, long chain of worlds that was being taken over by another kind of life that mankind had no chance of fighting.

'The Flowers are an ancient race,' said Stiffy. 'How ancient, I don't know. A billion years, two billion – it's anybody's guess. They've gone into a lot of worlds and they've known a lot of races – intelligent races, that is. And they've worked with these races and gone hand in hand with them. But no other race has ever loved them. No other race has ever grown them in their gardens and tended them for the beauty that they gave and no . . .'

'You're crazy!' I yelled. 'You're stark, raving mad.'

'Brad,' said Nancy, breathlessly, 'he could be right, you know. Realization of natural beauty is something the human race developed in the last two thousand years or so. No caveman ever thought a flower was beautiful or . . .'

'You're right,' said Stiffy. 'No other race, none of the other races, ever developed the concept of beauty. Only a man of Earth would have dug up a clump of flowers growing in the woods and brought them home and tended them for the beauty that the Flowers had never known they had until that very moment. No one had ever loved them before, for any reason, or cared for them before. Like a lovely woman who had never known she was beautiful until someone told her that she was. Like an orphan that never had a home and finally found a home.'

It was simple, I told myself. It couldn't be that simple. There was nothing ever simple. Yet, when one thought of it, it seemed to make some sense. And it was the only thing that made any sense.

'The Flowers made one condition,' Stiffy said. 'Let us make another. Let us insist that a certain percentage of them, when we invite them, must remain as flowers.'

'So that the people of the earth,' said Nancy, 'can cultivate them and lavish care on them and admire them for themselves.'

Stiffy chuckled softly. 'I've thought on it a lot,' he said. 'I could write that clause myself.'

Would it work, I wondered. Would it really work?

And, of course, it would.

The business of being flowers loved by another race, cared for by another race, would bind these aliens to us as closely as we would be bound to them by the banishment of war.

A different kind of bond, but as strong a bond as that which bound man and dog together. And that bond was all we needed; one that would give us time to learn to work together.

We would never need to fear the Flowers, for we were someone they had been looking for, not knowing they were looking for us, not once suspecting that the sort of thing existed that we could offer them.

'Something new,' I said.

'Yeah, something new,' said Stiffy.

Something new and strange, I told myself. As new and

strange to the Flowers as their time manipulation was new and strange to us.

'Well,' asked Stiffy, 'do you buy it? There's a bunch of soldier boys out here looking for me. They know I slipped through the lines and in a little while they'll nose me out.'

The State Department man and the senator, I recalled, had talked this very morning of long negotiation if, in fact, there could be negotiation. And the general had talked in terms of force. But all the time the answer had lain in a soft and very human trait, mankind's love of beauty. It had remained for an undistinguished man, no senator or no general, but a crummy bum, to come up with the answer.

'Call in your soldier boys,' I said, 'and ask them for a phone. I'd just as soon not go hunting one.'

First I'd have to reach the senator and he'd talk to the President. Then I'd get hold of Higgy and tell him what had happened so he could tame down the village.

But for a little moment I'd have it as I wanted to remember it, here with Nancy at my side and that old reprobate friend of mine across the barrier, savouring the greatness of this tiny slice of time in which the strength of true humanity (not of position or of power) rose to the vision of a future in which many different races marched side by side toward a glory we could not guess as yet.